“Trust me, Skyl
who I am, an
be together.

“It’s not that easy.”

“It could be,” Mark countered.

“You say that as if you’ve said it many times before, to many other women,” Skylar said.

Mark flinched. “I haven’t,” he said. “I guess you’ve heard about my reputation…but believe me, it’s not all true. I don’t encourage my students, but student-teacher crushes are an occupational hazard.”

“Then I guess I’m no different from one of your students,” Skylar murmured, a flicker of a smile touching her lips. “Because I think I may have a crush on you, too.”

Mark stroked her cheek with the tip of his thumb. “I’m glad. Perhaps then you’ll stick around long enough for me to find out if this crush is one that’s gonna last?”

“Maybe,” she murmured, taking time to assess his features, as if seeking reassurance that she was making the right move.

“Just maybe…?”

Skylar felt his breath as Mark leaned over and eased his lips over hers.

ANITA BUNKLEY

is the author of seven successful mainstream novels and three novellas. A member of the Texas Institute of Letters and an NAACP image award nominee, she lives in Houston, Texas, with her husband, Crawford.

An avid reader all of her life, she was inspired to begin her writing career while researching the lives of interesting African-American women whose stories had not been told. A strong romantic theme has always been at the center of her novels, and now she is enjoying writing true romance for her many fans.

ANITA BUNKLEY

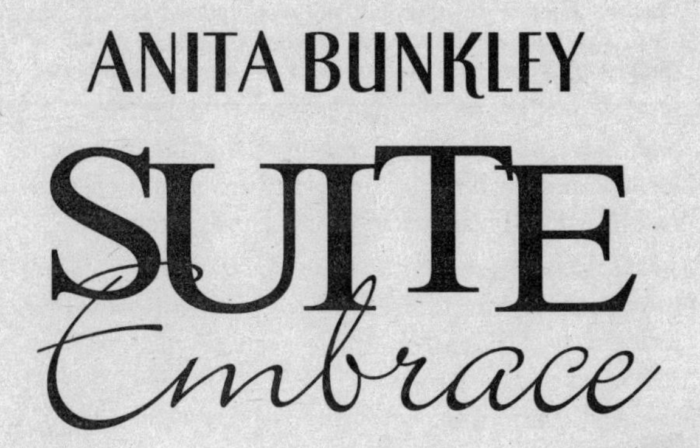

KIMANI PRESS™

ISBN-13: 978-0-373-86048-7
ISBN-10: 0-373-86048-X

SUITE EMBRACE

www.kimanipress.com

Printed in U.S.A.

Dear Reader,

I am very happy and excited to offer you *Suite Embrace,* my first Kimani Romance. Since I live in Houston, Texas, where temperatures rarely dip below freezing, I decided to go for a real change of setting and move my story to the snow-covered slopes of Aspen, Colorado. Though the weather outside may be cool, the romance between Skylar Webster, a concierge with a secret life, and Mark Jorgen, a hunk of a ski instructor with an international bad-boy reputation, heats up the pages. Join them on a thrill of a run as they test, tease, tempt and finally trust each other enough to surrender to the ultimate embrace.

Nothing pleases me more than to hear from my readers, so don't hesitate to e-mail me at arbun@sbcglobal.net or send a note to P.O. Box 821248 Houston, TX 77282-1248.

Read with love!

Anita Bunkley

To my husband, Crawford, my hero.

Chapter 1

Skylar Webster counted the zeros on the pale blue check for the tenth time, reluctant to hand the valuable piece of paper over to the man sitting across from her at the conference table. She had never seen a check for four million dollars before, and certainly never one with *her* name on it!

On her way to Tampa Commerce Bank this morning, to finalize her investment portfolio and deposit the money into her bank account, she had stopped at a nearby copy center to make a copy of the check for her records, and to prove to anyone who might not believe her story, that she *had* once possessed such a sum.

Now, the numbers shifted and blurred before her eyes, making her feel slightly dizzy and she wasn't sure if this sudden sense of euphoria was from the two aspirin she had taken earlier or the four cups of coffee she had drunk. Or maybe she was just overly excited that at last, her claim against Dorchester Elevators was settled and she could get on with her life.

It had been nearly a year since the accident, although it seemed like yesterday to Skylar, a paralegal who had been in and out of the Hillsborough County Courthouse thousands of times without ever thinking twice about stepping into its aging, temperamental elevators. For eight years, she had worked with many of the court-appointed lawyers and knew the building and its staff very well. In fact the courthouse had been like a second home to her, where she sometimes spent ten to twelve hours a day.

But her comfort level changed drastically on a cool December morning when she delivered a routine envelope of documents to Judge Flores on the tenth floor. After dropping off the package, she had chatted briefly with the judge's secretary and then entered the tenth floor elevator, expecting to head back into the courtroom. But she never made it back to work that day. As soon as the double doors slid closed, the car had rattled and jerked a few times and then spiraled downward, crashing to the basement floor, taking Skylar and six other terrified passengers to the bottom of the shaft.

One man had been killed, a teenage girl's legs had been so badly broken that she would never walk again, and the other passengers had suffered serious cuts and bruises, emerging shaken, but alive. Skylar, who had escaped with a shattered elbow and a fractured pelvis, knew she should feel relieved that both of her injuries had healed without complications—unless being unable to carry a child to term could be called a complication.

Now, after eleven months of sheer hell, the accident remained a nagging blur that she struggled to keep out of her mind, one that caused migraine headaches that her doctor insisted were a result of stress, and not from any of her injuries.

"Okay, Mr. Ray, where do I sign?" Skylar asked, coming back to the moment as she accepted a pen from her financial consultant.

"At the top. On the back, Skylar," Mr. Ray replied, watching as she turned the check over and wrote her name in a flowing script across the top part of the check.

Sitting back, Skylar let her body go limp, sighing aloud, as if expelling a tiresome burden from her soul. "So, I'm all set?"

"You sure are," Mr. Ray replied in a satisfied tone. "Your after-tax settlement of three and a half million dollars is now safely invested in a diversified portfolio that will keep you financially healthy for a long time to come. Your condo is paid for, as is your car. You have no outstanding credit card debt, and you have seventy-five thousand dollars in your personal checking account."

Leaning forward over the table, Skylar pressed out her lower lip, narrowed her smoky black eyes at Mr. Ray and propped a fist under her softly rounded chin. "So, I can hit the mall and shop till I drop when I leave here, huh?" she joked, eager to shake off the unsettling seriousness of the meeting. Ever since the accident it seemed as if she had had nothing but one serious, angst-filled discussion after another with a stream of doctors, therapists, lawyers, insurance representatives and bankers. Finally, the negotiations were over. She could believe that the money was hers. She had actually received a mind-blowing settlement from Dorchester for all of her pain and suffering.

"Well," Mr. Ray stated, studying Skylar over the top of

his small rectangular glasses. "Yes…you can go shopping, but you do need to be prudent in your long-term spending. You're only thirty-five years old, Skylar, and you're going to be around for a lot of years. A settlement of several million dollars doesn't last as long as most people think. The money will grow if you let it, but not if you spend as if there's no limit…or make risky investments. I know you're a practical young lady, but even sensible people can lose sight of what's important when they come into the kind of money you now have."

"I know. I was just joking, really," Skylar tossed back, giving the too-somber banker a hint of a smile as he paper clipped the check to the top of a manila folder and pocketed his Mont Blanc pen.

"I'll be right back with your deposit slip," he said, before stepping out of the room.

Skylar sat back in her chair, thinking about the banker's comment. *Risky investments? Nothing to worry about there. That's not my style at all. Unless I count Lewis Monroe.*

With a silent groan, she let her thoughts slip to Lewis, the man in whom she had invested three years of her life, an investment that had brought her absolutely no return. In fact, she'd been left with a hole in her heart so large she was certain it would never heal. Just thinking about him brought on a surge of pain. Their final argument still made her wince whenever she let it into her head. How long had he been sleeping with that flashy, weave-wearing model before she found out? The entire time that Skylar had been in the hospital? Even before? He had never had the guts to tell her.

Memories of Lewis's devastating betrayal pushed stinging, hot tears into Skylar's eyes. How could he have treated their relationship in such an off-handed manner after making her believe that they had been in a committed, exclusive relationship? She had *known* they were headed to the altar and had begun to mentally prepare the wedding. But he had trashed all of that with his cheating, low-life self. And he'd even had the nerve to act insulted when she refused to forgive him *and* give him fifty-thousand dollars to expand *Thredz*, his urban menswear shop.

What a jerk, she thought. *Lewis Monroe will never get his hands on a dime of my money no matter how many times he apologizes or begs for my forgiveness*. He was history, and she was damn glad to be rid of him. From now on she planned to focus on one thing, herself, and not the pain and humiliation of the past.

When Mr. Ray returned and handed Skylar her deposit slip, he extended his hand and wished her luck, clearly ready to move on to his next client.

"Thanks, Mr. Ray," Skylar told him, shouldering her new Coach purse as she prepared to leave. "I'm really glad my mother recommended you. I don't know what I'd have done without your help."

Mr. Ray leveled a fatherly expression on Skylar, causing the age lines in his dark brown face to soften. He raised his bushy eyebrows, which were heavily sprinkled with gray and focused on Skylar for a long moment. "You're level-headed, just like your father was. I'm sure you're going to make the right choices and have a long, happy, love-filled life." He shook her hand and added, before leaving, "Next time you speak to your mother, give her my regards."

"I will," Skylar promised, thinking that her father, who had been cautious about everything he did, and especially how he spent his money, would have been proud of the way she was handling things.

Herbert Webster had worked as an accountant for a chain of convenience stores for twenty years before dropping dead of a heart attack at his desk at the age of forty-two. He'd preached his belief to Skylar and her sister, Deena, many times: avoiding risky situations would keep them grounded, safe and in control of their lives. Taking unnecessary chances was foolish. Stick with what you know—that had been his motto, and Skylar had taken it to heart at a very early age.

After Mr. Ray walked away, Skylar stared down at the packet of papers in her hands, relieved that her money was safe. She hoped Mr. Ray's prediction about her having a long, love-filled life would come true, but somehow doubted it would. Her messy break-up with Lewis had undermined her confidence in the romance department—and the realization unnerved Skylar. She had never before felt so unsure about her future as far as men were concerned.

Knowing she had to get going, Skylar left the conference room, exiting through the glass doors that led to the elevator, and walked right into an open car. Taking a deep breath, she pushed Lobby and told herself that nothing was going to happen. After all, what were the odds of experiencing two elevator crashes in a lifetime? she wondered, glancing at the mirrored wall, pleased with her reflection.

Clear tea-colored skin. Shiny black hair that was twisted into springy locks that cupped her face. Prominent cheek bones and a softly defined jaw. Smoky black eyes that stared back at her, though she felt as if she were looking at a stranger who was fifteen pounds thinner than this time last year. And she was wearing a muted aqua pants suit trimmed in black leather that had cost three hundred-fifty-five dollars…more than she had ever spent on a piece of clothing in her life. It felt weird to realize that from now on, she could buy anything she wanted.

A happy love-filled life? So far, things sure don't seem to be going that way. I suffer from migraines. I can't have children. The man I thought I would marry one day cheated on me and then had the nerve to ask me for a loan. And now that I'm rich, Tanya and Loretta, my two best girlfriends no longer call or invite me to hang out with them. What good is cash in the bank when my life feels so empty?

Chapter 2

"Deena, it's all so strange. Suddenly being rich," Skylar confessed to her sister over the phone. At one time she and Deena had been content to talk to each other on the phone a few times a year and send e-mails back and forth now and then, but since Skylar's hospitalization last year, the two had grown very close, chatting almost daily.

As soon as Deena learned about her sister's accident she had flown in from Colorado and stayed with Skylar until she had been out of danger and able to manage on her own. Now, she was back in Colorado and back to managing the ski school that she and her husband ran.

"Yesterday, I met with Mr. Ray and settled everything with the bank," Skylar went on. "My money is properly invested and my checking account is flush. And Mr. Ray was so nice. He really helped me figure out what I needed to do."

"And what *are* you going to do with yourself now that you don't have to worry about holding down a job?" Deena asked.

"I don't know, but I do know it feels damn good not to have to jump out of bed and hit the freeway in the morning."

"Nothing stopping you from going to law school then," Deena prompted. "You put it off after college because you had to get a job and support yourself, but why not do it now? Seems like the perfect time to go for it."

Skylar let the phone remain silent for a long pause. After graduating from the University of Tampa with a degree in business economics, she had wanted to go on to law school, but hadn't had the funds. After she was hired as a paralegal with the county court system, she became comfortable with her position and accustomed to a regular pay check. Even though she had the money and the time to study law full-time now, did she really want to take on such a demanding academic challenge?

Finally, she told Deena, "I do want to study law, but something like that takes time and planning. Maybe down the road, I'll go for it, but not right now. For the first time in my life I have no one to answer to, so I ought to be in heaven, but I'm feeling kind of at loose ends. Too…free?" She thought about her remark and then asked, "Does that sound strange?"

"No, I'm not surprised," Deena replied. "Who wouldn't feel lost after all you've been through? Weeks in the hospital. Then months at that rehab place. A crazy legal battle with Dorchester. And then all that mess with Lewis." When Skylar didn't say anything, Deena went on. "Please tell me it's over with him, Skylar. You can't even think about taking him back."

"I know, I know," Skylar murmured into the phone. "It's over. Don't worry."

"But I do. You hung on to him way too long to begin with. He never was right for you. I'm just sorry that it ended with you getting hurt."

"We had some good times," Skylar defended, while knowing her sister spoke the truth. Now that the relationship was over, Skylar could look back and see that she and Lewis had never been really compatible. In the beginning, he had been attentive, charming, great in bed. But as the months passed, they had settled in to a routine that was satisfying and safe. She had known what to expect from him, and it had been easier to hold on to the man she was with than strike out to find someone new. Stick with what you know, her father had always told her, and now she guessed that was what she had done for most of the important decisions in her life.

"Skylar, you got dumped by a man you loved and trusted. While you were in the hospital, too! No way can he ever justify that."

"You don't have to remind me," Skylar tossed back, imagining that Deena was leaning into the phone, eyes wide with anger as she lectured her baby sister.

Deena wasn't finished. "Lewis has a way of charming people to get what he wants. He's fine, he's intelligent and he's slick. I know how much you wanted the relationship to work out, but I'm glad you found out what kind of man he was before you said, 'I do.' So, don't even talk to him. Don't give him an opportunity to work your emotions."

"All right, Deena! I hear you. Give me some credit, okay?" Skylar suddenly snapped, now irritated as hell that her big sister dared lecture her on men. What does Deena know about the dating scene in 2005 and how hard it is to find a good man? Skylar silently fumed. Deena had married her high school sweetheart at nineteen and moved with him to Colorado. She had no earthly idea of what a single, black, thirty-five-year-old female faces every day while trying to find love, Skylar thought.

"No need to get snippy," Deena tossed back. "I worry about you, that's all. With Mom now living in Brooklyn with Aunt Clara, you don't have any family nearby."

"What's that got to do with anything?" Skylar wanted to know. It wasn't as if she had ever consulted her mom about her love life when she lived across town in Tampa.

"Well, for starters, you're a very rich woman now, and your settlement was publicized in the paper. Men prey on women like you, so it's important to stay close to people you can trust."

"I assure you, I have enough sense to stay away from financial predators, con artists and low-life types. Including Lewis Monroe."

"I'm sure you do, Skylar. Sorry for the lecture," Deena meekly offered. "Just feeling a bit overanxious."

Skylar paused before saying anything else, struck by the timbre of worry that had crept into her sister's usually perky voice. Something more than Skylar's love life was on Deena's mind.

Deena and her husband, Jerome Simpson, owned Scenic Ridge, a private lodge and ski school nestled in an unincorporated area of the Roaring Fork Valley, northwest of Aspen, Colorado. The nearest town was Woody Creek, and it was linked to Deena and Jerome's property by a narrow winding road that ran high into the mountains, which no one traveled unless they were going to Scenic Ridge. With ski season in full swing, it was no surprise that Deena sounded as if she were under pressure. She had a staff of twenty to manage while dealing with demanding guests whom she treated like royalty. "Overanxious?" Skylar repeated. "What's going on, Deena? Problems at the lodge?"

"Yeah, but more so with Jerome," Deena slowly volunteered. "It's his father."

"Mr. Simpson is kind of up in years by now, isn't he?"

"Eighty-two."

"And he still lives in Oregon?" Skylar clarified, recalling having met her brother-in-law's father only one time—at Deena and Jerome's wedding twenty-one years ago.

"Right, and he's set to undergo surgery for prostate cancer day after tomorrow. Jerome's an only child and he *has* to be with his dad. I want him to go, but the timing is awful. While Jerome is away, *everything* he usually takes care of will fall on me for God only knows how long."

"You'll have to run the ski school in Jerome's place?" Skylar asked, aware that Deena was only an average skier, but hell on the slopes when it came to snowboarding.

"Oh, no. We hired a guy last fall…Mark Jorgen, you ever heard of him?"

"No, should I recognize the name?"

"He's a former Olympic gold medalist. He's our new ski school director and head instructor. He's great. Especially with the younger skiers and he's really boosted our bookings, too. But the biggest problem is that Jean-Paul, our long-time, trustworthy guest relations manager…or concierge, as he preferred to call himself, quit yesterday. Lured away by a Hyatt Regency in Utah. I need a new concierge now."

"That's a bummer. Call an employment agency."

"Not so easy. I've tried. No one I approve of is remotely

interested. I've got to find someone I can absolutely trust. Not just some stranger to come in and play the role. You know?"

"So what are you going to do?"

"Well, I was thinking. Skylar…"

"What?" Skylar interrupted, suspicious of the ingratiating tone her sister was now using.

"I was hoping that you might consider coming up to Scenic Ridge to help me out. Just until I can hire someone else?"

"Me? A concierge? I don't think so, Deena. I'm a paralegal, remember? Guest relations are not remotely related to my chosen field of work, and I know zilch about the Aspen area. Thanks, but no thanks."

"Think about it, Skylar. Please. You've worked in hotels before."

"Front desk duties while I was in college."

"So? You can do it. I've got to have someone I can absolutely trust," Deena pressed the issue. "Information on local entertainment, attractions, restaurants and transportation is prepackaged and ready to hand out to anyone who wants it. Not being from this area won't be an issue. What I need is a personal link to the hotel. You know…a discreet person to take care of sticky issues and unusual requests."

Skylar flinched. "Do you get a lot of those?"

"Well, you never know what can come up when people are on vacation and out of their usual element. My motto is 'Give the guests whatever they want.' It'll be easy, trust me. You'll be out of Tampa and away from Lewis. He may have been fine as hell, but he was also a dog. Trust me, Skylar, you can do better."

"Girl, you know I hate cold weather and I don't even

ski," Skylar said. "It's January and it's seventy-nine degrees here in Tampa today. I'm very happy right here, thank you very much. I'd rather spend my days at the beach than freeze my ass off in a lodge in the mountains…even though I know your place is as gorgeous as any five star hotel. However, I don't think it's where I ought to be."

"Skylar. Help me out. We haven't spent any real time together in years. When I was there after your accident, you were too sick for us to do anything together. I'd like to have you here with me for a nice long visit."

"Visit? Sounds like work to me!"

"Okay, but you know what I mean," Deena pressed her case. "You always said you enjoyed working front desk duties while you were in college."

"It was a motel near the campus and I got to meet a lot of guys who came there to party."

"Well, for your information, Aspen is going to be the site for this year's Black Winter Sports Reunion. Starts at the end of the month. There'll be brothers…and sisters from ski clubs all over the country here for the fun—ice skaters, snowboarders and skiers. I'm already booked solid for the entire ten days."

"Really?"

"Yes, really."

Skylar's arched brows slowly began to settle lower above her smoky black eyes as she mulled Deena's comment. The Black Winter Sports Reunion was going to be in Aspen? While confined to her bed, she'd been flipping through cable channels one day and had come across last year's reunion, filmed at Steamboat Springs, on Black Entertainment Showcase. She had been impressed with the crowd and knew what kind of people were about to descend on the area. Fine, well-toned brothers who were about something. Fashion conscious sisters who looked good on and off the slopes. Solid professionals who enjoyed the finer things of life. The change might be exactly what she needed in order to move on.

I've played it safe for so long. Why not take a risk on this? Might be just what I need to take my mind off my troubles and get Lewis out of my system. Plus, I can help Deena out and maybe have a little fun, too, she told herself, looking forward to being around people who knew nothing about her past or her wealth. "Okay, Deena. Only for you and Jerome. I'll do it. On one condition."

"Just name it."

"Absolutely no one knows that I'm newly rich," Skylar requested.

"You know, I think that's a very good idea," Deena agreed. "Attractive, single women with money can be magnets for shady men looking for meal tickets and scam artists on the hunt. They've been known to hang around places like Aspen. And you'll fit in better with the staff if they think you're simply my sister, in need of a job. Your secret will be safe with me," Deena promised. "Now go pack your bags and get on a plane."

"Pack what? I don't exactly have the kind of clothes I'm gonna need up there."

"No problem. You can go shopping when you get here. The salespeople in town are friendly and will be very happy to help you pick out everything you need."

And I'm gonna need all the help I can get, Skylar thought, hoping this unexpected adventure would not turn into an absolute disaster.

Chapter 3

"Okay. Let's try this again. Find your balance. Stand still and concentrate," Mark Jorgen patiently instructed as he gently placed one gloved hand on Goldie Lamar's left shoulder.

"I'm trying, really I am," Goldie whined in exasperation. She sucked in a loud breath and lifted her chin. "This is a lot harder than I thought it would be."

"You're doing fine. Stand tall in your boots until the pressure from the tongue of the boot feels equally distributed from shin to calf. Most of your weight should be felt between the heel and the arch of the foot."

With a shrug, Goldie pulled back her shoulders, pressed her bright red lips together in a hard pucker and stared out across the snow-covered slope. "All right. All right. I think I feel it."

"Good, now gently slide your right ski ahead of your

left," Mark told his student before letting go. He stepped back to watch Goldie try, for the fifth time, to push off the hill and head down the beginners' slope, praying she would be successful. She was a terrible student with no sense of balance, but she was also the mega-wealthy daughter of one of Colorado's finest jewelers and had paid quite a premium for the deluxe ski package. He had to make sure she got her money's worth.

He had been working with Goldie for two days without much progress at all, and was beginning to wonder if she had signed up for lessons only to spend time alone with him. That was not unusual, especially among the women he recruited while hanging out at the Ridge Rover bar in Woody Creek, where he often went to mix and mingle with the locals and guests from nearby resorts. His "impromptu" appearances always generated lots of excitement, leading to talk about his Olympic career, his worldwide travels and his methods of training. By the end of the evening, if he was lucky, he might have five or six new students lined up for classes at Scenic Ridge.

Now, with a jerk, Goldie moved one leg forward, hesitated and then let out an ice-shattering scream. Swaying unsteadily, she toppled to the left, clutched Mark, and collapsed against him, pulling them both to the ground.

"I can't do this, Mark!" Goldie loudly complained. "I'll never learn to ski!" She snatched off her goggles and hurled them across the snow where they shattered against a shaggy pine tree. Next, she yanked off her red knit cap and pressed her head hard to Mark's chest, slumping dramatically against him. "I guess I'm not cut out to be a skier," she groaned.

"Don't give up so easily," Mark encouraged, starting to push her away.

Quickly, Goldie leaned back and smiled up at him, shaking out her hair to release a cascade of tangled platinum curls that framed a startling, beautiful face. Her alabaster skin was flushed pink from the cold and her eyes were a cool aquamarine, now narrowed to half-mast in mock-anger. "And I wanted so much to have a successful lesson today. Maybe this whole ski vacation idea was not so great, huh? Maybe I ought to go home before I break something."

Mark shrugged, and then sat in the snow to calmly listen while Goldie continued to whine about her clumsiness, her disappointment in herself and the cold weather. He knew she was putting on an act, and that she was picking up the tab for three deluxe ski packages for herself, her sister and her mother-in-law, dropping a bundle of cash for their one-week stay at Scenic Ridge. There was no way he was going to encourage her to cancel her plans and leave. After all, he was more than a ski instructor at Scenic Ridge: he was part of the team, and as such, he had to make sure that each guest was a satisfied customer, which sometimes took some doing.

"Don't be so hard on yourself. We'll get there. It takes time," he reassured Goldie, taking in the scent of her perfume, which he recognized right away—Electric Orchid—two-hundred-fifty dollars an ounce. He also recognized a bored, rich, spoiled young woman eager for an affair with her ski instructor when he saw one. How many women like her had he dealt with over the years? Too damn many to count.

"Come on. Let's try again," Mark urged as he began to untangle himself from Goldie's clutch, convinced that she was much more interested in holding on to him than her two ski poles, which lay scattered in the snow a few feet away.

"No. Not now," Goldie decided, snuggling deeper into her instructor's arms, as if settling in for a chat. She zeroed in on Mark, adopting an expression that told him she was not going anywhere, anytime soon. She grabbed hold of the front of his jacket and pushed her face even closer to his. "Can't we just sit here and talk?"

Holding his breath, and desperate to mask his growing irritation, Mark eased her fingers off the zipper of his jacket. "No, I don't think so. It's getting late and I'm already way behind schedule." Somehow, he managed to stand and then help Goldie to her feet. Luckily her skis were still intact. "Okay. Assume the same position as before. Take your time."

Goldie started to do as Mark asked, but then suddenly stopped and whirled around. "My goggles!" she shouted, pointing to the broken glasses at the base of the pine tree in the distance. "I can't see a thing without them. I won't do this without my wrap goggles. I'll ruin my eyes."

Mark shot Goldie a dagger of exasperation, fully aware that her designer goggles had cost at least three hundred dollars and he knew she would not settle for a generic pair that he could pull from his equipment bag. "You're right," he acquiesced, scanning the bright, white blanket of snow spread across the gentle slopes and glazing the tall mountainsides. "You need to protect your eyes. Let's quit for today. We'll start again tomorrow. Ten o'clock."

"Thank God," Goldie agreed. "But what will I do about goggles? Mine cost…"

"I know," Mark interrupted. He certainly didn't need her to tell him what high end ski accessories cost. He'd bought and worn only the best goggles, jackets, boots and sports clothing—purchased from the most fashion conscious retailers in the world—throughout his entire career. If there was one thing Mark Jorgen knew, besides how to ski, it was how to dress to impress on the slopes. "I'm going into Aspen in the morning to pick up a package at the post office," he went on. "I'll be happy to get you another pair while I'm in town. I know *Gorsuch* carries them and they'll be compliments of Scenic Ridge. How's that? We'll try again tomorrow afternoon."

"Fine with me," Goldie decided, her annoyance quickly fading. "And if you're going into town anyway, I'd love to tag along. There's this gorgeous set of hand-carved...."

Mark tuned Goldie Lamar out as she rattled on and on about some trinket she had seen in a quaint shop on Cooper Avenue, knowing he would probably have to take her with him tomorrow. Anything to satisfy a big-spending guest.

After escorting Goldie back to the lift, Mark waved her off and finished his classes for the day. As pale shadows began to form on the snow-covered slopes, he shouldered his skis and hopped a lift to head back to his private lodgings at the foot of the mountain, jumping off as soon as the car swung close to the ground. The crunch of hard-packed snow crackled under his fur-lined boots.

Mark lived in the Snow King Suite, the largest of four cabins, situated far from the main lodge, among the tall Aspen trees. Though referred to as suites, the cabins were especially designed for special guests who required privacy, luxury and who were willing to pay a handsome sum for it. Each cabin/suite featured handcrafted furnishings, carefully selected accessories, peaked pine ceilings, wood-burning fireplaces, full kitchen facilities and an outdoor hot tub.

As the head of the ski school at Scenic Ridge, he knew he was being treated more like a guest than an employee, and understood why: his competitive days might be over, but his name still had drawing power among serious ski aficionados. Why shouldn't Scenic Ridge benefit from their association with him if it could bring in more money for the resort and keep him on the slopes?

Drawing in a deep breath, Mark slowed his pace and filled his lungs with crisp mountain air, in no real hurry to get home. He loved to walk home when he had finished working for the day, when the silence of winter calmed him down and muted the lingering echoes of all the shouting, complaining and chatter that he had to endure on the mountaintop.

Coming to work at Scenic Ridge was one of the best decisions he had ever made and he was very appreciative of Deena's efforts to make him feel at home. She had insisted he move into private quarters at the lodge, which she could have rented for a thousand dollars a week. All of his meals were covered in his contract, and though his finances were not nearly as flush as they used to be, he was able to live in comfort while maintaining the illusion of success that befitted an Olympian.

Mark looked around. In the fading light; Scenic Ridge resembled a perfect luminous pearl nestled in the most beautiful section of the Roaring Fork River Valley. It was quaint, yet luxurious. Far enough away from the glitz and shine of Aspen to maintain its rustic ambiance, yet near enough to get to Buttermilk, Snowmass and the fancy shops and restaurants within an hour's drive. The resort was small, but not cramped. Isolated, yet accessible. Exactly where he wanted to be.

He shrugged, a cynical smile touching his lips as he realized how content he actually was. It had not always been like this. Only a few years ago, he would have balked at living so far from the celebrity-filled world he had moved in. Then, he would have been staying in the most lavish suite in the most expensive hotel in Aspen, eating personally prepared meals in the most posh of restaurants and being entertained by the most beautiful girls within a five mile radius.

For most of Mark's adult life he had lived the high-life as a celebrated Olympian, as the most famous black skier in the world—a title that had both plagued him and made him proud. As a world class competitive skier throughout Europe and the U.S., he had spent much of life either training under the keen eye of his manager-mother, Virina, or partying with a *nouveau riche* crowd. Oh, the times he had had while traveling the world and making love to any woman who turned his head: black, brown or white. European, African, Asian or Hispanic. Tall or short. At the height of his career it had not mattered to him what country a woman came from as long as she was gorgeous, belonged to the exclusive world of money and social standing that he moved in, enjoyed partying and loved lots of good sex.

But now, things were very different. He moved more slowly, was less concerned with money and social status, and was aware of how little it took to make him happy. He viewed the future as a clear sheet of ice on which he hoped to carve a beautiful future with the right woman, and until he found her, he was going to steer clear of women like Goldie Lamar, who in his opinion were shallow, self-absorbed snobs.

He was thirty-eight years old and knew he wanted children, stability, a wife and a home—preferably a rustic pine-log cabin high on a hill with a ski slope at his back door. Yes, it was time to find the right woman to settle down with, one with values, charm, a real work ethic and one who would not flaunt money in his face. He'd had enough of those bored, rich types to last him a lifetime. He might have to put up with them on the slopes, but he didn't have to share his private time with them. In his opinion, having too much money could do more harm than good.

Chapter 4

Gorsuch, Ltd. was crowded and buzzing with conversation as men, women and a scattering of children oohed and aahed over the glamorous items on display in the upscale resort shop. Nestled beneath the towering Aspen Mountains, the store was an explosion of exquisite leather, fur and suede outerwear; fashion forward clothing in a fantasy of designs by world famous designers; unique home décor items for the ultrabeautiful homes of discriminating shoppers; and of course, skiwear of the highest order.

Skylar felt overwhelmed by the choices and the prices of the items surrounding her. Cautiously, she checked out the price tag on a pair of alligator boots—$4,250, and the matching handbag was only a few hundred dollars less.

"Ouch," she murmured, setting aside the unusual footwear. Even though she could have afforded them, she had no intention of spending that kind of money on a pair of boots. She had always been a conservative shopper, and her approach to shopping wasn't about to catch up with her bank account. Going crazy now would certainly undermine her desire to keep her wealth a secret while she was in Aspen.

Moving on, she picked out two fluffy blue sweatshirts off a clearance rack, and even though they were on sale, they still cost four times what she would have paid for similar items in Tampa. Next, she selected matching sweatpants, a red sweater and two fleece vests from another rack, and with a flip of her wrist, added two pairs of thick socks and a flannel nightgown to the pile. Unsure about what else she might need, she glanced around, spotted a salesclerk and signaled for help.

"Shoes," Skylar managed, jostling the bundle of clothing that filled her arms.

"What kind?" the young woman asked, eyes wide in interest.

"Boots. But not four-thousand dollar alligators," Skylar laughed. "That's a bit out of my league."

"I hear you," the clerk commented. "You need indoor or outdoor? Ski boots or dress boots? Fur lined or suede lined? Waterproof or stain resistant? We've got 'em all."

"Maybe indoor and outdoor. Not too fancy," Skylar started, not sure what else to say. "Guess I need *everything*. Or whatever you think a person moving here from Florida needs. I have no idea what I'm getting into…and I'm on a tight budget," she decided to add. "I just want to be comfortable, okay?"

A huge grin spread over the salesgirl's face. "Sure, I get it." She extended a hand. "I'm Cindy. Let me take those things from you so we can get busy, Miss…"

"Skylar. Skylar Webster."

"Okay, Skylar. Leave it all to me. I think I know exactly what you need. Plus, you came at the right time, too. We're having our annual 'Freeze-Out Sale,' and quite a few items are reduced. I'll be right back." The clerk hurried away, placed the bundle of clothing inside a dressing room and returned within seconds, a pamphlet in her hand. "Here's a list of the essentials, things you must have if you want to be both stylish and comfortable while vacationing in Aspen."

Skylar glanced over the colorful pamphlet and sighed. "I'm not really vacationing, and I don't ski. You see, I'm going to be working at Scenic Ridge."

"Oh, yeah, the ski school, right? Great. What are you going to be doing?"

"I'm the new concierge."

"All right. You go, girl. Beautiful place. I went up there once with a friend of mine a few years ago. The road is tricky, though. Real narrow in places. Be careful on your way up."

"Really? Thanks for warning me."

"So, you're from Florida, huh?" Cindy went on as she walked Skylar across the store. "What made you come up here?"

Skylar paused, knowing she ought to be careful. Aspen was not a very big place. It wouldn't take long for information about her to spread if she started telling too much, and she didn't want to take any chances. All this clerk really needed was her dress size, her shoe size and her credit card. Why bother to get into why she left Tampa or how long she planned to stay? "I have relatives in the area, and just wanted to be near them," she said, satisfied with her half-truth.

"You've come to the right place to get outfitted, then," Cindy said, stopping near a section of the store that was brimming with turtlenecks, blouses, slacks and jackets in every color and style imaginable.

"Okay. I'm lost, Cindy. Tell me what I need," Skylar commented, fingering a silky top as she set off to create her new wardrobe.

For the next hour, Skylar tried on a variety of slacks, tops, parkas, boots, sweaters, socks, gloves and hats. By the time she was completely outfitted she was exhausted, and her checking account was about to be a little thinner, though, with Cindy's guidance, she had found some very good bargains. Among them were a hooded parka with a fluffy raccoon collar, several thermo-stretch ski pants with matching tops, over-the-boot pants with coordinated wool cardigans, suede gloves and a Daniel Boone-style coyote hat.

"Fabulous choices," Cindy remarked as she finished ringing up Skylar's purchases. "And you saved a bit, too. But...oh my gosh, we forgot one very important item. Sunglasses and goggles. Up here, they're absolutely necessary. Gotta cover those eyes and keep those wrinkles away. And if you do decide to get out on the slopes, you don't want to go snow-blind, do you?" Cindy giggled and inclined her head toward a wall at the back of the shop. "Why don't you go pick out a pair of sunglasses while I package your purchases and finish up here? And if you give me your car keys, I'll have one of the stock boys put everything in your car."

Trusting Cindy's advice once again, Skylar handed over the keys to the Jeep she had rented at the airport and told Cindy where she was parked. Doing as she was told, she walked toward the back of the store where a number of display stands with a variety of sunglasses and goggles filled a corner.

Skylar stopped at the first display and selected a pair of shades with brown, tortoiseshell frames, slipped them on and then shook her head. Not for her. They didn't flatter her face at all. After several more try-ons, she moved over to the next rack to stand opposite a man and a woman who were discussing a pair of black wrap-around goggles.

The man was wearing a red down jacket with the hood thrown back, exposing a mass of tawny-brown hair that almost touched his shoulders. Skylar found the sight intriguing, yet a bit unnerving. How could a man have such gorgeous hair? Skylar thought, curious to see more of him. She edged forward a few inches and cut her eyes in his direction, visually following him as he walked over to a full-length mirror and tried on the goggles. She observed that his hair had a definite wave to it and his skin was golden tan. Skylar was pretty sure he was African-American, or at least of African descent.

After adjusting his goggles a few times, the man turned around and looked over at Skylar, catching her watching him.

With a start, she gasped and glanced away, unsure of why she had reacted so strongly, but keenly aware that she had been struck by something magnetic and powerful radiating from the guy, who quickly returned to studying his image in the mirror.

Curious, she chanced another peek. He looked mature. Maybe late thirties, she thought. She was stunned that she was actually calculating this stranger's age and checking out his left hand. Umm…no ring there. However, he did have a flashy sparkler on his little finger.

Either this brother is filthy rich or seriously into high-profile bling, she decided, certain that the stone flashing back at her was much too large to be real.

Moving to another rack of glasses, she acted as if she was trying to pick out another to try on as she fingered a wire-rimmed pair, trying to ignore the guy. But she couldn't resist peering over at him once more, and this time she really scrutinized features not hidden by his wraparound goggles. He had a prickly stubble of light brown hair shading his jaw and a tiny gold earring in his left ear. His nose, softly sculpted and wide at the base settled nicely above a set of perfectly shaped, white teeth that peeked out from behind lips that were generously full and wickedly sensuous.

Very kissable lips, she thought, sighing inwardly while admonishing herself for even thinking such crazy thoughts. She had come to Aspen to clear her mind, help her sister out and get over Lewis's betrayal, not check out the available brothers or get romantically involved with a new man. *But what harm was there in looking?* she asked herself, liking what she saw.

She guessed that the eyes hidden behind those dark glasses were probably hazel, or maybe golden-brown like tiger's eyes, and wondered if the broad stretch of his shoulder line was natural or the result of the padding in his parka. His skin, a beautiful tannish golden brown that perfectly matched his hair, stood in definite contrast to the woman with him, who was pale, blonde and ski-pole thin.

The blonde looked over and squinted, not happy to catch Skylar watching her man. The two locked eyes for a moment before Skylar broke off and focused on the sunglasses, putting the oddly matched couple and her curiosity about the guy out of her thoughts.

After a few quick try-ons, Skylar decided on a pair of silver framed aviators with bronze lenses reduced from $199 to $59.99. Turning, she prepared to leave.

"I wouldn't get those if I were you," the man in the red jacket told Skylar.

"Excuse me?" Skylar said, startled by the stranger's remark.

"Those won't do the job on the slopes. You need something with better protection," he admonished, as if talking to a child. "Inside the store, they look a lot darker than they are. Outside, they won't cut much light."

"Thanks, but I think they'll do just fine," Skylar replied, trying to sound pleasant, even though his remark had struck her as rather presumptuous. He might be good looking but he wasn't cute enough to take orders from. What did he know about sunglasses that made him such an expert anyway? She liked the aviators and they were exactly what she wanted.

"Try on the black wraps. You'll love them," the man suggested nonchalantly.

With a drop of her shoulders, Skylar simply stared at him as if he were crazy. She was tired, hungry and more than ready to get out of the store. The glasses in her hand would do just fine. It was getting late and she still had to stop at the drugstore to pick up a few toiletries and then hit the gas station to top off the tank of her rented Jeep before setting off to Scenic Ridge. She shook her head, "No thanks. I've got to get going." She started to walk away.

"Trust me. They won't be what you want," the man in the red parka called out after Skylar.

His bossy tone set her teeth on edge. She stopped in

mid-stride and whirled around. *Who the hell are you to tell me what to buy?* But, blinking her eyes and sucking back a smart remark, she decided it might not be a good idea to go off on the guy in public. This was a classy place and she didn't want to make a scene, but it was hard to keep from flaring up at him.

"I'm fine with these," she managed in a tight voice, thinking that the guy had some kind of an accent that she couldn't place. Not African. Not Hispanic. And not French. He must be from the islands...overly friendly. Or he didn't know any better, she decided, willing to forgive his rude behavior. "I appreciate your interest," she told him. "However, I prefer the ones I picked out."

"You'll be sorry," he insisted as he reached for a pair of Manu wraps similar to those that both he and the blonde woman were wearing. He held them up and swung them back and forth in Skylar's face. "These *are* a bit more expensive than the aviators, but if you can afford them, I'd go with these. Think of it as an investment in your eyes."

His condescending tone hit a nerve in Skylar that sent a hot flash into her chest. "If I can afford them?" she tossed back, trying to keep her voice within some kind of a normal range. "That's a rude thing to say. How dare you insinuate that I have to worry about money? Do I look like a sister who has money problems?" she asked, biting down hard on her bottom lip to keep from blurting out the secret she was determined to keep as long as she was in Aspen.

"No, no," the man stuttered helplessly, obviously embarrassed. "I didn't mean that at all."

Skylar glared at him, unable to respond. She was wearing dark rinse jeans, a white cable knit sweater, a brown leather bomber jacket and brown ankle boots. Her jewelry was understated, but real gold, and she knew her hairstylist back in Tampa had hooked up her locks just fine before she left town. *I might not look like a fashion diva, but I know I don't look ghetto, either,* she told herself. In her most flippant, sister-girl voice, she told the guy, "Look. You don't *even* know me, so don't get too personal, okay? I don't need your help, and I surely don't need your investment advice."

The man threw up both hands and stepped back, smiling. "Hey. Sorry if I offended you. I was only trying to help you save money in the long run. I was just offering a tip from experience."

"Leave her alone," the blond woman now interjected, moving close and slipping her arm possessively through her companion's. She graced Skylar with a smug, too-sweet smile, and clutched her apparent boyfriend's jacket sleeve even harder. "If the lady wants to waste her money, let her. We have other things to do than worry about *her.* I told you I wanted to go over to Duval's. Come on," she said and gave the guy's arm a hard tug.

Infuriated by the man's intrusion, the woman's catty remark and her fake smile, Skylar was tempted to snatch a handful of curly blonde hair from the woman's head. But instead, she rolled her eyes at the nosy couple and spun around. *If they're the kind of people I'll have to deal with up here, then this temporary gig is going to be hell. Deena owes me big-time.*

Mark watched the woman with the aviators push through the glass door and disappear, wondering who she was and where she was staying. Though his face appeared calm, his heart was pounding a steady drum beat inside his chest and he couldn't understand why. The woman was attractive in a refreshingly wholesome way that he rarely saw among the stressed-out, wealthy, high-strung types that usually frequented *Gorsuch*'s. Beautiful, flawless brown skin. Not too tall, but not too short, either. Well dressed, but not flamboyantly attired in trendy, overpriced clothing. She was a fresh vision in this spend-crazy, out-to-impress kind of town.

A real natural beauty!

While waiting for the clerk to ring up the sale, he glanced out the front window and saw the woman in the bronze aviators drive off in a bright red Jeep. Mark smiled. She'd be easy to find. All he had to do was pass out a bunch of twenty dollar bills to the doormen at every hotel in town and sooner or later he'd get a call informing him who she was and where she was staying. The thought of tracking down the beautiful stranger created a warm glow of anticipation that spread throughout Mark's body and made him want to thank Goldie for smashing her goggles against a pine tree yesterday and forcing him into town.

Chapter 5

Deena Simpson walked out onto the balcony of her five-room apartment on the fourth floor of the main lodge at Scenic Ridge, her cell phone pressed to her ear. Shading her eyes with one hand, she focused on the narrow winding road that led up from Woody Creek, watching for Skylar's Jeep. The only drivers who would be on the road that curved and twisted as it rose into the mountains were those bound for Scenic Ridge, as it dead-ended at the two stone posts that flanked the front gates of the resort.

"Where are you now?" she spoke into the phone, getting a bit anxious. Skylar had called her from the airport when she arrived in Aspen to tell Deena that she was going to stop in town to pick up a few things, but would be right along. That had been three hours ago. Deena guessed that her suddenly rich sister had decided to do some major retail damage in town. And she deserves to, Deena thought, elated that the Dorchester settlement had been so generous, freeing Skylar from any financial worries for the rest of her life—if she managed her money well.

It was amazing to think that Skylar was a rich woman now, and could buy whatever she wanted. When she and Deena were children, their hard-working parents had earned just enough money to cover life's necessities, with little left over to indulge their children. They had been ultraconservative in their spending and cautious about everything they did, refusing to take risks or try anything new that might upset their carefully balanced lives. Deena often thought that her parents' approach to life was what had made her run off to Colorado and marry Jerome. His plan to build a ski school in Aspen country was bold, risky and exciting. Now, her life in the mountains was very far removed from her childhood upbringing, and Deena never regretted setting off on this grand adventure with her husband.

"Have you passed the covered bridge yet?" she asked. "You have? Good, then you're on the right road. Just stay on it and keep driving uphill, even when it narrows down to a single lane and you think you're going to drive off the edge. Trust me, you won't. See you in a bit."

Deena snapped off the phone and leaned against the rough pine railing that surrounded the spacious wraparound balcony.

As she waited for Skylar, she surveyed the spectacular wintry landscape spread out across the two hundred acres that she and Jerome had turned into a working ski school and vacation resort over the past twenty years. As newlyweds and avid skiers, they had purchased the remote parcel of land at the upper end of the Roaring Fork Valley from Jerome's father for a fraction of its market value. The land, part of a land grant settlement originally deeded to Jerome's great-great-grandfather, had remained wild and undeveloped for over fifty years.

Jerome and Deena threw themselves into the project with a great deal of enthusiasm, risking everything they owned to create the small, intimate teaching resort. It had been a struggle to turn a profit, but now it was beginning to draw ski enthusiasts and students from across the country as well as from some of the more popular resorts in the Aspen area.

The main lodge of Scenic Ridge was a four-story replica of a classic Swiss mountain chalet, but with all the conveniences of a modern hotel. Years ago, when she and Jerome were designing the main lodge they decided to turn the east-facing end of the fourth floor into their private five-room apartment, decorated in a sleek modern style, while the guest suite at the other end of the hall had a definite Western flair.

Each of the other fifty-two guest rooms was exquisitely decorated in an Old World European manner with touches of the silver mining days of the Victorian West tossed in.

In addition to the main lodge, five private cabins that represented the ultimate in modern convenience and rustic charm were strategically placed around the property, booked by those who were willing to pay a premium price for the privacy and independence such accommodations provided.

As African-Americans living in an area of the country where less than two percent of the population was nonwhite, Deena and Jerome had quickly realized that the only way to attract more folks like themselves to the slopes was to build a resort that was affordable, comfortable and focused on teaching people how to ski. Deena and Jerome decided to take on the task of teaching beginners what they needed to know to take up skiing as a recreational sport and send a message to everyone of any class or race that all were welcome and would feel at home while learning how to safely hit the powder and have a good time.

By optimizing the available terrain on their property, Deena and Jerome served the needs of beginning skiers, ice-skaters and snowboarders, creating a niche resort that differed from the larger ski areas.

It did not take long for news about Scenic Ridge to spread as visitors told others about the program and returned year after year. For African-American skiers, it soon became known as one of the most unique novice programs in the country. Jerome had further enhanced the resort's reputation and expanded its customer base among minorities by hiring Mark Jorgen as their ski instructor. Mark was a great draw and he guaranteed that he could teach students to ski confidently on green circle trails within three days or they would get their money back. So far, no refunds had been made.

Today, there was absolutely no breeze stirring the cool January air, and the warmth of the sunlight on Deena's pecan-brown face felt calming and most reassuring. She pushed back a few strands of black hair that had sprung from the loosely gathered ponytail she had managed to pull together this morning and sighed. She had hit the ground running as soon as the buzz of her alarm clock sounded at 5:00 a.m., and though it was just a little past noon, she felt as if she had already put in a full day's work.

Yesterday, she had stood in the same spot where she was now waiting for Skylar and watched Jerome drive away, her heart filled with dread. By now he was in Oregon and probably at the hospital waiting for his father to go into surgery. Deena missed him terribly and was worried about how she was going to manage the place in his absence, especially since Jean-Paul was no longer on staff.

Losing Jean-Paul to a Hyatt Regency had been disappointing. She and Jerome had always depended on their long-time concierge to handle the messy, unexpected situations that came with running a ski resort. Now, they'd only have Skylar.

Today was starting off rocky. The grocery delivery had come up short—missing twenty-five pounds of baby back ribs and the case of a hard-to-locate Norwegian liquor Deena had counted on having tonight. And with all of that to deal with, she'd had to pacify Goldie Lamar's very demanding party, and she was sick to death of all of them.

The road suddenly narrowed down to less than a full lane, making Skylar very nervous. Though the road's surface was covered with a mixture of gravel and hard-packed snow, it provided good traction. Still she worried that the Jeep was going to spin out of control and crash down the mountainside at any moment. The sun was directly overhead, bathing the snow-covered hills with blinding light that made it nearly impossible to see.

"Dammit!" Skylar cursed aloud, ripping off her sunglasses, which she tossed out the window. The guy in the store had been right! The bronze aviators were useless. They didn't block the glare and even made things worse by casting an amber sheen over everything. Squinting bare-eyed into the windshield and praying that Deena's instructions were right, Skylar pressed on, clutching the steering wheel as she inched her way up the mountainside.

When Deena's cell phone rang again, she answered quickly, certain it was Skylar asking for more directions. However, it wasn't her sister. It was Burt from the liquor store in town.

"What do you mean, you can't find it?" she groaned.

"There's not a case of *Linie Aquavit* in the entire valley. At least not that I can get my hands on right away. The St. Regis has four cases, but they're not willing to part with them."

"But you said getting *Linie Aquavit* wouldn't be a problem," Deena reminded her beverage vendor.

"Yes, I know," Burt admitted. "Guess I was a bit overconfident. However, I do have Vikingfjord Vodka in stock and I can send up a case right away."

"No. That won't do," Deena shot back. "This is a very special client and he specifically requested *Linie Aquavit*. So, please keep trying to locate it, okay? Even if you can only find one bottle."

"Will do," Burt agreed. "I'll get back to you later today."

Clicking off, Deena sagged against the railing, feeling deflated, while praying that Burt would be able to come through with the specialty drink as he'd promised. However, in case he couldn't, she had better let her client know that his request might not be fulfilled today.

Just as she was about to place the call, she saw Skylar's red Jeep turn into the entry and start up the road leading to the main lodge. Shoving her phone into the pocket of her jeans, Deena hurried to the outside staircase and headed down to greet her new concierge. "Let Skylar deal with the missing Norwegian liquor," she muttered to herself, sending up a prayer of thanks that help had finally arrived.

After Skylar dropped her bags in the efficient studio apartment where she would live during her stay at the lodge, she and Deena set off on a tour of the resort, during which she met all of the staff. Everyone greeted her with an enthusiastic welcome, making Skylar feel less nervous about her decision to set off on this spontaneous adventure. However, when Deena suggested that they ride out in a snowmobile to explore the rest of the property, Skylar had to decline.

"All of a sudden, I feel so tired, Deena. Lightheaded and dizzy," Skylar complained, drawing in a deep breath as she and Deena crossed the attractive lounge area. A fire blazed in the massive stone fireplace where some of the guests had gathered to chat and sip drinks, while others sat on high bar stools facing windows that showcased the picture perfect peaks surrounding the resort.

"Think I'll go lie down for a while," Skylar said.

"Good idea. It's the altitude," Deena offered, pausing at the foot of the winding staircase that led to the mezzanine on the second floor where someone was playing the piano. She placed one hand on the banister and scrutinized Skylar with concern. "It might take a few days for you to get fully acclimated to the thin air up here, but it'll pass."

Skylar shook her head and blew air through her lips. "Whew! This is not good. My head aches, my stomach is doing flips and I feel as if my skull is stuffed with cotton balls."

Deena nodded sympathetically. "Yeah, mountain sickness. Strikes quite a few of our guests. It's caused by a sudden lack of oxygen after moving too quickly into a higher elevation. Your body hasn't adjusted to having less oxygen."

"Right…and my body's sure tellin' me I'm not in Tampa anymore! What's it gonna take to pull out of this?"

"Drink lots of water and stay away from alcohol. Go ahead and lie down for a while. I'll give you a buzz at dinnertime."

"You don't have to tell me twice," Skylar replied, moving swiftly toward the elevator, desperate to lie down.

Chapter 6

A soft tapping sound at her door awakened Skylar from a restless, semiconscious half-sleep. Tossing off the soft, wool throw she had wrapped around her body when she fell across her rustic, four-poster bed, she struggled to sit up. The room was light, so she knew it was still daytime. Unable to sleep, she had gotten enough rest to feel a lot better. Her head no longer ached, but her stomach lurched with each step she took, and after pausing to run a hand over her tangled hair, she pulled open the door.

It was not Deena standing there holding the tray with a tea caddy on it, as she had hoped, but a woman dressed in black pants and a crisp white shirt.

"Ah, hello. Miss Webster...hope I didn't wake you," she started. "I'm..."

Skylar nodded in recognition, her mind beginning to clear. How could she forget the tall, big-boned girl with light brown skin, frizzy dyed-red hair and a heavy dose of brown freckles scattered across her nose and cheeks. "You're Kathy. Food and Beverage supervisor, right?"

Kathy beamed. "Yes. You remembered! My husband, John, is the assistant director of the ski school and I'm your backup concierge, don't forget."

"Right. Kathy, you'll have to excuse me. I know I look a mess. I had to lie down for a few, my system is really jacked up."

Kathy nodded sympathetically. "Altitude sickness?"

"Yep."

"Too bad, honey. But it'll be gone by tomorrow."

"I sure hope so," Skylar commented, rubbing her stomach. "So, Kathy. What can I do for you?"

"I need your help. I wish I didn't have to bother you, but I have a big party to tend to and there's no one else to go and…"

"No, no. Come in," Skylar invited, stepping back to let the nervous girl inside. "And I hope that's a pot of hot tea you've got there."

"It is. Thought you might need something to help calm your stomach."

"Thanks. Just needed a little downtime to adjust. What can I do to help?"

"You have a car right?"

"Yes, a rental."

"Good. I need you to pick up an important delivery in Crested Village. It's a small town about fifteen miles from here. It's not a bad drive and if you leave now, you ought to get back before dark. I hate to ask you to do this on your first day here, but the delivery is a custom order for the head of our ski school and he's been waiting for it for a week."

"For Mark Jorgen?" Skylar asked.

"Right. We've had a heck of a time tracking down this particular kind of liquor. Called *Linie Aquavit*—a type of schnapps that comes from Norway. According to Mark it's placed in oak barrels and sent on Norwegian vessels back and forth across the equator to enhance the flavor," she finished with a grimace. "Terribly expensive stuff."

"Sounds like it must be very special stuff, too, huh?" Skylar remarked, surprised that Deena would go to so much trouble for the resort's ski instructor. After all, it wasn't as if Mark Jorgen was a major player on the sports scene anymore or even a movie star! He was an employee, just like she was. "Is he that particular about everything?" she wanted to know, thinking ahead about her involvement with him.

Tilting her head to the side, Kathy considered Skylar's question, obviously not about to answer too quickly. "Let's just say that he, and his mother, are accustomed to having the best of everything."

"His mother works here, too?"

"Oh no, but she's arriving later this month for an extended visit. Deena has already filled me in on her tastes, and *Linie Aquavit* is her favorite drink, so Mark wants to have it on hand."

"How nice of him," Skylar murmured, curious to meet this Olympic gold medalist who was so devoted to his mom.

"Anyway," Kathy went on, "the *Lainpour* shop in Crested Village will only hold the liquor for us until seven o'clock tonight. So, you've got to hurry. And after you pick it up, can you deliver it directly to Mark in the Snow King Suite?"

"And where's the Snow King Suite?" Skylar wanted to

know. Deena had mentioned that there were several private cabins on the grounds for special guests, but Skylar never would have guessed that the ski school director would be living in one.

Kathy went to the window, pulled back the sheer curtains and pointed to what looked like a mini-lodge set high on a knoll in the distance. "Over there. When you return, use the service road that runs behind the main lodge to get to the Snow King Suite. Think you can manage that?"

Blinking away the last vestiges of sleep, Skylar nodded. "Sure. Now all I need are really good directions and a cup of hot tea before I leave."

"Oh, that's no problem! I brought you both," Kathy told Skylar, making a rapid exit.

Within half an hour, Skylar was in her Jeep and driving higher into the mountains, headed east with the late afternoon sunlight at her back. Kathy's map was easy to read and Skylar had no trouble finding *Lainpour,* a tiny shop on the main street of Crested Village. However, when she told the shopkeeper that she was there to pick up the case of *Linie Aquavit*, he told her that she had to go to his warehouse, ten miles down another winding road to get it.

By the time she got there, it had started to snow and the sun was rapidly disappearing. The slow-moving, too-chatty warehouse manager was in no hurry to stow the case of Norwegian liquor in the back of Skylar's Jeep, and when he finally finished, heavy snow was falling and dark shadows that resembled silhouette cut-outs of the forest were hovering over the snow-crusted road.

Questioning her eagerness to take on this crazy mission,

Skylar waved a grim good-bye to the man in the warehouse and settled behind the steering wheel, praying she would be able to get back to Scenic Ridge without getting lost.

She could see that more and more snowflakes were dotting the air. Her headache was back with a vengeance, her stomach churned, and she feared she was going to either throw up or pass out at any moment. Reaching into her purse, she grabbed a bottle of aspirin, shook out three pills, popped them into her mouth and washed them down with the bottled water she had wisely brought along. The bitter aftertaste of the medicine stuck in her throat, making her feel even more uncomfortable and nauseous. However, she forced the sensation out of her mind, unfolded her map and studied it, mentally reversing Kathy's directions as she pulled onto the road.

The drive back was frightening and tense. The snowfall steadily intensified until Skylar found herself staring into a sheet of blurry white, her vision reduced to a strip of light illuminated by the beams of her headlights. Slowing her pace, Skylar crawled along the single lane, praying she would not encounter another vehicle coming from the opposite direction.

"I'll just take my time," she murmured, forcing her shoulders back as she tried to relax. She turned on the radio and settled for a John Denver retrospective as she clutched the steering wheel and inched her way down the rocky path.

It took Skylar an hour and a half to get back to Scenic Ridge, where snow was rapidly piling up on the pitch-black service road. But, the moment she turned her Jeep toward the Snow King Suite, a wave of relief swept over her. She had successfully returned with her precious cargo and fulfilled her first assignment as the new concierge. In spite of her pounding headache, she felt pretty proud of herself.

Lights burned in every window of the cabin. Smoke curled from the chimney and drifted off into the snow-filled sky, filling the air with its pungent smell. Several pairs of skis were propped on the front porch alongside a shiny, red, old-fashioned bobsled and three pairs of boots. Skylar reached into the back of the Jeep and pulled out one of the bottles of schnapps to personally deliver to Mr. Jorgen, and then, on wobbly legs, stepped out of the car and gulped down a mouthful of cold air, fighting the urge to get totally sick right where she stood. Clutching the bottle with one hand and her stomach with the other, she cautiously mounted the three steps that led to the front door.

Before she had a chance to knock, the door swung open and Skylar locked eyes with a man standing in the entry.

"Oh. It's you!" she gasped, stepping back in surprise. It was the intrusive, but handsome, guy from *Gorsuch* who had so annoyingly butted in on her shopping spree that morning. "You're Mark Jorgen?"

"Yes, that's me," he said, in his accented voice. "And you are?" he prompted.

"I'm..." Skylar stammered, fighting back a violent wave of nausea. All of the blood in her body suddenly rushed to her feet, making her feel as if she were falling from the top of a high mountain peak. Dizzy and off-balance, she stared blankly at Mark, dropped the bottle of *Linie Aquavit* and sank to the floor with a crash.

Chapter 7

Skylar could feel herself being lifted and carried by strong arms, her head pressed against a muscular chest. Then everything went black again. However, within a few seconds, she recovered and opened her eyes.

Inside the cabin, the cold, crisp air had been replaced with a blanket of warmth that enveloped Skylar and calmed her down. A woodsy scent, like fresh cut pine mixed with earthy soil, filled her head and roused her from her near-faint, awakening her to the realization that Mark Jorgen's right hand was cupping her buttocks much too tightly and she was not resisting. She thought about protesting this stranger's brazen hold on her, but instead of mouthing off, decided to hold her tongue for now, thinking she was far too weak to put up much of a fight, anyway, and not all that eager to be released.

"There you go," Mark said as he gently placed Skylar on

a distressed leather sofa facing a hearty fire. He covered her with a plaid wool blanket and then sat down beside her, his hard thigh pressed into the side of her leg. "Are you okay?" he asked, leaning over her, his face very close to hers.

Skylar held her breath and held his eyes with hers, savoring the sudden rush of heat that shot through her chest and settled between her legs. This guy was too fine to be real! And his eyes were dark green, nearly black, and not hazel as she had predicted!

For a moment, she simply stared at him, as if she were still suffering from a dizzy spell when in fact her mind was as clear as the spring water that pooled at the base of the mountains. She recognized the same trace of a foreign accent that she had heard earlier, and her immediate impression was that he resembled an exotically wild and powerful mountain lion. His hair, tawny brown and streaked with gold, was thick and shiny, nearly falling to his shoulders. Of medium height, he had a strong, stocky build, and his skin-tight ski apparel accented the impressive muscles that swept across his chest, down his arms, over his thighs. His skin was tawny golden brown like his hair, and just looking at him caused a tremor of excitement, mixed with a ripple of fear, to shoot through her body and banish her mountain sickness.

"Are you okay?" he asked again.

Finally, Skylar breathed her reply, "I think so," and then struggled to sit up. "Sorry about the bottle of schnapps, Mr. Jorgen."

He smiled and gently eased her back. "Don't worry about that, and don't try to sit up just yet." He re-tucked the blanket around her shoulders. "I spoke to you in *Gorsuch* earlier today, didn't I?"

"Oh, yes…" She grimaced. "You were trying on sunglasses with your girlfriend…the blonde."

"Goldie? She isn't my girlfriend. She's one of my students," Mark promptly corrected.

She sure looked like she wanted to be a lot more than your student, Skylar wanted to say, but didn't. "I'm Skylar Webster," she went on. "The new concierge here at Scenic Ridge."

"Yes, I heard you'd arrived today. Funny meeting you in town like that. But Aspen is a very small place."

"So, I'm beginning to see."

"So, Miss Webster, altitude sickness got to you, huh?"

"Looks that way," Skylar agreed. "Mr. Jorgen, I apologize for…"

"Please call me, Mark."

"Okay, Mark. I'm terribly sorry I broke that bottle of liquor. I'll pay for it. Just let me know how much it cost."

Mark shrugged off her offer with a lift of his broad shoulders. "Hey. Don't worry about that. What's important is that you're not hurt. Or are you?" Keeping one eye on Skylar, Mark slowly pulled back the blanket and began to sweep both of his firm hands the length of Skylar's wet jeans, squeezing her thighs and legs at intervals. When finished with his examination, he rested his hands against her ankles. "I don't feel any pieces of glass. Any cuts, or pain?"

"No," Skylar whispered hoarsely, her legs burning at each point where he had touched her. "But I know I must smell like I bathed in schnapps."

"You do, and it's driving me crazy," he laughingly teased, in a put-on kind of voice that was low, deep and full of humor.

They both broke into laughter, amused by their unexpected encounter.

However, I wouldn't mind if you licked every drop of it off my body, she mused, unable to stop her mind from drifting ahead of the moment. With a jerk, she shook off that image and sat up. "Thanks for your help, but I'm feeling a lot better," Skylar went on. "I gotta get back to…" She paused and broke eye-contact with him, suddenly flustered. He was much too attractive, in a dangerous way, and his piercing gaze was very unnerving. She gave herself over to imagining what it would be like to kiss those smooth, full lips of his, to touch that hair…

No, no. I've got to get a hold of myself and focus on my job. Skylar bit down on her bottom lip, in an attempt to crush the anxiety building inside her. "I need a shower, a good night's sleep…I…have to go," she told him, quickly swinging her feet to the floor. Before standing, she cautiously looked over at Mark, unable to say another word.

"Yeah. You'd better go and get out of those wet clothes," he commented, sounding a bit distracted. "After a good night's sleep you'll feel better. So, did you bring the full case of schnapps with you or just the one bottle?"

"Oh! The case. Yes. From *Lainpour*."

"Good. Please thank Kathy for going to get it this afternoon, and thank you for bringing it over."

Skylar stiffened. His offhand comment hit her like an icicle stabbed into her heart. *Thank Kathy? I don't think so!* she thought, recalling her frightening trip back from Crested Village. "For your information, Kathy didn't pick it up," she started. "She was too busy and couldn't get away, so you can thank *me.* In spite of a bad case of altitude sickness, I got out of bed and drove all the way over to Crested Village, then to *Lainpour*'s warehouse in some backwoods part of the town. On the way back, I got caught in a blinding snowstorm, but

I gladly put myself through all of that in order to deliver your precious liquor…which remains in the back of my Jeep," Skylar finished in a huff, not feeling particularly charitable.

"That took some doing," Mark commented, a slight smirk tugging at the corner of his mouth.

"Damn straight it did! But I managed just fine."

"Good for you. So, why all the fuss? After all, you are the concierge," he stated, his too-smug smile growing wider. "Aren't you just doing your job?"

Skylar's jaw dropped. *What a jerk*, she thought, realizing she had pegged him right the first time. He was a know-it-all snob, just as she'd thought he was when they met in *Gorsuch* earlier. Before she could form an appropriate comeback, Mark reached over and opened a carved wooden box that was sitting on the coffee table and pulled out a twenty dollar bill.

"Here. For all your trouble," he said, extending a fold of cash.

A tip? He's actually offering me a tip! Her temper flared to the point of screaming. Feeling totally offended, she was tempted to decline the money. However, a good concierge deserved generous tips, and refusing to take his cash might seem out of character.

I want this self-centered jackass to believe, as the staff does, that I am simply the underemployed sister of the owner, who desperately needs this job. "Thank you very much," she told him, palming the bills with a flick of her wrist before stuffing them into the pocket of her wet jeans. Rising, she went outside and opened the hatch of her car.

Mark came up behind her and reached into the back of her vehicle to remove the heavy box of bottles.

Glad to be finished with this crazy assignment, Skylar

walked to the driver's side of the Jeep and was about to step in when Mark leaned around the side of the car and said, "You call this a blinding snowstorm?" Chuckling, he shook his head. "This isn't even a flurry, Miss Webster. You've got a lot to learn about life in the mountains."

"And you've got a lot to learn about me," she fumed under her breath, climbing inside. She glanced into the rearview mirror and saw him standing in the middle of the road, holding the box, a huge grin on his face. Furious, Skylar started the engine, jammed her foot down hard on the accelerator and sped off down the service road.

"Wow!" was all Mark could say as he watched Skylar's red Jeep disappear around a curve. Hefting the heavy box, he went back inside and set the liquor on the black granite bar in his small, but well-appointed kitchen. Still rattled from the unexpected encounter, he pulled a glass from the cabinet and a bottle of schnapps from the box.

"May as well sample this," he murmured, adding ice to the crystal tumbler. After opening the liquor, he poured himself a generous amount, added a thin slice of lemon and then wandered back into the great room to sit down.

The first thing he noticed was the blanket that he had used to cover Skylar. It was still on the floor where she had tossed it. He bent over and picked it up, then sank back against the pillows on the sofa, inhaling her scent.

"Too gorgeous to be a concierge," he mused, staring into the fire. "And what a woman." He could still see her warm, tea-colored skin, silky, black twists that bounced against her cheeks, intriguing, black eyes that had clearly assessed him in a gently provocative manner. She was petite, but well-toned. And she had great legs, he had felt every curve himself. She was small, but definitely not fragile. This was a woman with grit and guts, no trace of a diva attitude. He had to get closer to her!

Concentrating on this brief, but stimulating encounter, Mark tried to analyze his reaction to Skylar, certain he had never felt this way before. His body hummed with a kind of anticipation that made his palms wet, his throat tight and brought a strange sensation to the pit of his stomach. What was going on?

Mark let his head fall back against the sofa as he savored the *Linie Aquavit,* his thoughts riveted on Skylar. At one time in his life, a working woman like Skylar Webster would never have turned his head. With one foot planted in the African-American world of his father and the other in the Euro-rich world of his mother, Mark had always felt uncertain about where he belonged.

When Mark was eleven, his parents divorced, and his mother took him to Norway to live. His mother's motivation, other than to remain far away from his father, had been to push her son into a career as a professional skier. She became his agent, his trainer and manager and his best friend, setting the direction for the rest of his life. Mark had always regretted that she had deliberately kept him isolated from links to his paternal heritage, but there had been little he could do about it, and his mother always got what she wanted.

For years, Mark's world had revolved around a stream of globe-trotting, glitzy, super-rich people—and women who had begged to occupy his time and his bed. He'd never loved any of them, but they had been fun to party with. He had had his choice of gorgeous women around the world, and he had wasted a great deal of money and time on them.

However, now that his fast-paced professional career was over and he had severed professional ties with his mother, things were different. He was back in the United States, where he planned to live permanently, and he knew exactly what he wanted to do. He wanted to settle down with a grounded African-American woman who was not afraid to work hard and whose world did not revolve around money, society events and outrageous status symbols. He wanted to start a family with an intelligent, beautiful woman who would appreciate him for who he was now, not for who he used to be. He wondered if Skylar Webster might be the woman he was looking for. There was only one way to find out—put her to the test.

Chapter 8

The best features of Skylar's new office, a cozy space only a few steps from the registration desk, were the two tall windows that faced an inner courtyard where a huge fire pit, a hot tub with an outdoor movie projector and a deck provided the guests an unparalleled view of Aspen Mountain.

Cupping her mug of hot chocolate with both hands, Skylar leaned over her desk and rounded her shoulders, stretching out her back. She had made it through her first full day of work without any major incidents, mishaps or encounters with dissatisfied guests, and her mountain sickness had eased. Between fielding calls for general information and making spa and massage reservations, she had provided directions to the various activity areas of the resort and chartered a limousine to take Goldie Lamar and her companions to the Silver Hills Theater.

At least her job kept her busy and kept her mind off of Lewis, except when she saw couples in love sitting by the fire or having fun on the ice or the slopes. The sight made her feel empty and sad, and she sometimes wondered if perhaps she'd broken off too quickly with Lewis. Should she have tried harder to work things out? Would it have been possible? The turmoil of that failed relationship still simmered in her heart.

Did Lewis cheat on me before the accident? Did he leave me for another woman because I can't have children? Had he really expected to benefit from my financial windfall? Did he ever really love me? The unanswered questions went round and round in her mind whenever she allowed herself to drift back in time.

The good thing was that she was definitely feeling much better than when she arrived back at her room last night, nauseous, half-frozen and irritated as hell at Mark Jorgen. Thank God she had not seen or spoken to him all day.

"I'm getting rave reviews from my guests," Deena remarked as she entered her sister's office and settled into the chair across from Skylar. "I think you passed the first hurdle when you managed to get Goldie Lamar's mother-in-law those tickets to Silver Hills Theater for tonight."

"If all of my requests should be so easy," Skylar replied, grinning over at her sister. "Your decision to buy a full page ad in the theater's next promotional booklet sealed the deal. Thanks."

"Glad we could work it out and it'll be good publicity for us, too," Deena replied.

"Hey, have you heard from Jerome? How's his dad doing?" Skylar wanted to know, hoping things were not too rough for her brother-in-law, whom she liked very much, even though they were not particularly close. With Skylar living in Tampa and Jerome and Deena in Colorado, the three simply hadn't made the effort to visit over the years, and now it was too bad that Jerome had to be away during Skylar's first extended stay in the mountains.

The cheerful expression that had been on Deena's face when she entered shifted into one of concern. The worry in her eyes told Skylar that things were not going well. "I just spoke to Jerome," Deena said. "His dad is not bouncing back as he and the doctors had hoped. Seems the cancer was much more advanced than the doctors had thought and the surgery took its toll. He'll be in the hospital quite a while longer than the two days he had been told he'd have to spend there, and he'll need at least a month at home recuperating while undergoing chemotherapy."

"Gee, I'm really sorry to hear that. Think you need to be with Jerome?"

"No, not right now…maybe later…after the reunion is over. Not much I can do now but wait, and I can do that right here. Jerome seems to be holding up okay."

"Well, you know best."

Deena nodded, and then said, changing the subject, "Kathy told me you drove all the way over to Crested Village last night by yourself to get the liquor for Mark. I would have gone with you, Skylar. Why didn't you ask?"

Skylar shrugged. "Guess I wanted to prove to myself that I really can do this job. However, I have to admit it was a pretty scary trip. Started snowing. Got dark on me. And when I finally got to Mark's cabin, he acted all smug, as if what I'd done was no biggie. What's up with him anyway? Where is he from? He has some kind of a funny accent."

"Mark is biracial," Deena replied. "His father is black

and his mother, Virina Dagrun, is a well-known Norwegian model."

"Was Mark born in Norway?"

"No, California, but when his parents divorced, his mother took him back to Norway to live."

"So, that's the reason for his accent," Skylar murmured. "Well, he's probably upset with me."

"Why?"

"After I arrived with his delivery, I kind of fainted... passed out for a few seconds on his doorstep. Overwhelmed by the altitude, I guess. Anyway, I broke a bottle of schnapps and soaked my jeans. He took me inside and then had the nerve to try to tell me what my job was...and that was after he had flirted like crazy with me."

Struggling to suppress a chuckle, Deena pressed her lips together, one hand to her mouth. "He flirted with you, and you're upset?"

"Yeah, put me on his couch and was leaning over me, putting his lips real close to mine. Even felt my legs. Got all in my face and everything. It was really rude."

Now, Deena laughed aloud. "Please! He was probably just making sure you were all right."

"Hump. Working his Afro-European charm on me, you mean, as I'm sure he loves to do with all of your female guests."

"He does generate a lot of attention," Deena admitted.

"Well, I'm not one of his starstruck students like Goldie Lamar. I swear that woman has a major crush on Mark. When I called her to tell her I had the theater tickets for her party, all she wanted to do was rattle on and on about her fabulous ski lesson with Mark this morning and how gentle he had been with her."

"Mark's quite the star around here," Deena said.

"He's an employee, just like me, and he ought to remember that."

"Lighten up, Skylar. You have to admit, he's a hunk. Real easy to look at and a nice guy, too."

"Rather exotic, I'd say," Skylar said grudgingly.

"So what if he creates a stir among the guests. Nothing wrong with that. You may not know it but he has an international reputation as a very eligible bachelor, so you shouldn't complain that he flirted with you. Wouldn't it have been much worse if he had paid you no attention at all? Really, Skylar. You're smart, attractive, single. Stop being so damn sensitive. Mark Jorgen could be quite a catch."

"A catch? What makes you think I'm in the market for a man?"

"Oh? You're not?"

"No!"

"Maybe you should be, 'cause I hope like hell you're not holding out for a second chance with Lewis Monroe," Deena said.

"Hell would freeze over before I'd give Lewis a second chance. But I'm not gonna lie. I loved Lewis and I know he hurt me, but it's not that easy to forget and move on. I trusted him," Skylar said in a small voice.

"He cheated on you."

"I know…but you think I can just forget about our good times together and take up with a new man, like buying a new pair of shoes or a dress? I need time to get over Lewis, and an affair with a playboy ski instructor is not the way I plan to do it," Skylar said.

"Okay, okay. I hear you," Deena replied, backing off. "I was simply suggesting that you not judge Mark too harshly."

"Fine. Anyway, back to Mark Jorgen, what's with this special liquor…and his mom?" Skylar continued, asking the question in a way that she hoped sounded very innocent. Truth be told, she had lain awake for a long time last night thinking about Mark Jorgen and wanted all the details Deena could provide. Her intense desire to know more about this man, both angered and intrigued Skylar: she had never met a man quite like him and definitely didn't want anyone, especially her sister, to suspect how strongly he had affected her.

"Oh, yeah. Virina Dagrun. Mark's mother. As I said, she still lives in Europe. She was also a very good amateur skier when she was younger. Now, I believe she's the spokesperson for some high-priced line of cosmetics."

"Does she still ski?"

"No. She gave up her dream of turning professional when she left Norway and got into modeling. After her divorce, she returned to Norway, focused on Mark's talent and became his trainer and agent," Deena explained. "She got him to the Olympics, but somewhere along the way, their relationship turned rocky. I don't know the details, but Mark did say that she didn't want him to leave Europe to settle in the States, and she was not too happy that he decided to teach here at Scenic Ridge instead of a better-known, European ski resort."

"Sounds like quite a mom," Skylar coyly commented, hoping Deena would give up more. A man's mother could be a powerful influence and a key to understanding him. It might be good to know just how important a role Mother Virina played in Mark's life.

"Yeah, Virina is something else. She's coming for her first visit soon—right in the middle of the Black Winter Sports Reunion—which is just around the corner," Deena reminded Skylar. "It's going to be a crazy, hectic time with a full hotel and the slopes as crowded as they've ever been. I hope you can handle it."

"I'll have to," Skylar noted, flipping through the pages on her desk calendar. She stopped when she saw that Jean-Paul had not only penciled Virina's name in on his calendar as arriving on January 29th, but had drawn four stars above it. "I assume Mrs. Dagrun..."

With a shake of her head, Deena stopped Skylar. "I spoke with her when she made her reservation—she prefers to be called Miss Dagrun. Her maiden name, so make a note of that."

"Got it. And I assume she wants one of the corner rooms," Skylar went on, making notes on her calendar. "Maybe on the second floor, facing east so she can watch the sunrise in the mornings?"

"No. The Vista View cabin. Already reserved. She made it clear that she didn't want to stay in the main lodge. I know what she was thinking, after all, if Mark can have a private cabin, why shouldn't she?"

With a laugh, Skylar nodded. "Right. I don't know the woman, but I can imagine her saying something like that. But if she's so picky, I'm surprised she isn't staying in town at the Little Nell or the St. Regis," Skylar noted. "I'm sure she could arrange for a car to bring her out here to visit her son whenever she wanted to see him."

Hunching closer to the edge of Skylar's desk, Deena crinkled her soft, brown eyes until they were half shut. "That would never do. She wants to be close to Mark. She told me so. I think she's lonely. He must have been the center of her life."

"But he's a grown man!" Skylar commented.

"Thirty-eight to be exact."

"And never been married, I assume?" Skylar prompted thinking that if Mark felt comfortable enough with Deena to discuss his relationship with his mother, maybe he'd shared information about his love life with her, too.

"Not as far as I know, but I've never asked him about his romantic past. Maybe you can get that out of him…if it's important for you to know."

With a scowl, Skylar shrugged, "I'm afraid I'm not that interested."

"Doesn't sound that way to me."

"Oh, drop it, Deena, please."

"Okay. But I wouldn't be surprised if Miss Dagrun gives you a real workout when she gets here. But don't let her rattle you, okay?"

"Afraid I might run off and join Jean-Paul at the Hyatt Regency in Utah?" Skylar joked.

"No, but you might be tempted. She sounds like the kind of guest who can be a real pain in the butt. Demanding, picky and insistent on having things done a certain way. It wouldn't surprise me if she's coming to Scenic Ridge to convince Mark to leave."

"Leave? But you said he was happy here."

"He is, and I plan to keep him happy and keep him here."

Skylar sipped from her mug, intrigued by Deena's remark. "You talk about Mark Jorgen as if he's a guest, not an employee."

"In a way he is a guest," Deena agreed. "And I expect you and the staff to treat him as such. As an Olympic gold medal winner he has clout…a following of devotees that attracts high profile clients. Whatever he asks for, you get it, or do it. Okay?"

With a jerk of her shoulder, Skylar puckered her lips and nodded her understanding, pleased with herself for already having shown him exactly what *she* was all about. Fulfilling Mark Jorgen's requests would be easy, as long as he didn't overstep the boundaries she planned to put in place right away.

Chapter 9

The sculpted candle in the center of the table gave off the delicious scent of white gardenias and cast a golden glow over Virina Dagrun's model-sharp features. Her silver blonde hair, cut into a short-boyish style, softly cupped below her ears, shimmered in the candlelight as she reached for her balloon-shaped wine glass. She leaned closer to the flame, appreciative of the muted lighting in the intimate restaurant, hoping it helped disguise the newest wrinkle she had discovered beneath her left eye that morning. What a drag! If she'd had more time she would have made an appointment for a Botox injection before dinner, but she'd been too rushed, having flown in from Oslo only five hours earlier.

"Do you like my choice of restaurants, Richard?" she asked her dinner guest, lifting a hand layered with jewels as she glanced around the New York City establishment.

Each table was nestled inside a private semicircle booth and was covered with a crisp white lace cloth, sparkling crystal and silver so shiny that it created tiny bursts of light throughout the room. Virina found so many of New York's better restaurants too boldly lit and open for her tastes, but the atmosphere at *Jannike*'s was perfect. It was dim, decorated in old European style and expensive enough to keep the riffraff out.

"A very elegant place," Richard replied, nodding his approval. "Quiet, and as private as you said it would be. The kind of place where people can actually talk to each other without screaming in their faces or worrying that the people next to them can overhear every word."

"Precisely, and we have a lot to discuss, Richard. I'll be leaving New York in a week, so we don't have a lot of time to get everything settled," Virina began, taking a quick sip from her glass. She placed her goblet on the table and a bright red fingernail to the side of her mouth, as if struggling with a thought, when in fact, she was sizing Richard Nobel up while formulating her strategy.

She knew how to play the negotiating game with the best and knew she was going to get what she wanted from this good-looking journalist who was sitting across from her, drinking the two-hundred-dollar-a-bottle wine she was paying for. He was thin, almost gaunt, but carried himself with an aristocratic air that she found very appealing. His earthy brown skin, black eyes and bright white teeth reminded her of Nat King Cole, the most gorgeous black man ever, in her opinion. A man as good looking as Richard was probably used to women coming on to him, so why not take a chance? If flirting with him didn't work, she had other ways to get what she wanted.

"Are you married?" Virina impulsively asked, with a flick of her tongue over her glossy red lips. She squinted at Richard, as if trying to read his mind as she waited for his answer.

"For ten wonderful years," Richard replied, smiling and giving her an even better view of his flawless teeth. "Three kids, too."

"A pity," Virina murmured, sitting back in her chair. Infusing a new man into her life had been in the back of her mind for months, but finding the right candidate was not going to be easy. Bored with the men she socialized with in Europe, Virina was hoping that this trip to America might be just what she needed to cross paths with the perfect replacement for her last husband—a generous, but deathly boring count who had been fifteen years older than she. Though a film producer like Richard Nobel certainly wouldn't have the financial means to indulge her tastes, it might be a kick to get involved with a man for purely sexual reasons. But not a married man. That was where she drew the line. With a drop of her shoulders, she dismissed that fantasy and moved on to a new approach to the business at hand. "If you had the financing, could you complete the filming in two weeks?"

Richard Nobel, award-winning documentary filmmaker, paused and blew air through his lips, clearly confused by Virina's request. "Whoa! Let's slow things down. As I told you on the phone, Mrs. Dagrun..."

"It's *Miss* Dagrun, but please, call me Virina."

"Fine. As I was saying, Virina, I've got the ear of a distributor connected to Black Entertainment Showcase who is interested in my next project. It's going to be..."

"A series of documentary profiles on unusual African-

American sports heroes," Virina smugly finished. "And as I've already told you, I think it's an absolutely fabulous idea."

"Right. Skiing is fast becoming a very popular sport for African-Americans and ski resorts have finally awakened to the fact that their future is tied to luring a more diverse crowd onto their powdery slopes. Black ski clubs are popping up everywhere and the members are usually sophisticated folk with quite a lot of disposable income. I want to do a short film, an entertaining and educational piece that would inspire more minority athletes to take up the sport professionally, as well as to entice more families to head to the snow-covered mountains for vacations."

"How do you plan to finance it? That's the bottom line, isn't it?" Virina pressed, knowing she had his ear.

"Exactly. I'm looking for private investors. All of the details of my proposal are outlined in the Acquisition Distribution Agreement I brought along for you to read." He reached into the open briefcase on the seat beside him, pulled out a multipage document with a blue cover, and handed it to Virina.

She flipped through the sheets of paper, glancing quickly at the headings before she spoke. "And this means, if you can get the film in the can, BES will make sure it airs?" Virina clarified.

"And make sure it makes money," Richard added. "I had been thinking of profiling either your son, Mark, or Sonja Bendry, a black female national ski champion from Lansing, Michigan. She overcame an amputation of her left leg to go on to win all of the national titles last year."

"Sounds impressive, but of course, you must feature Mark," Virina injected in a haughty voice.

"Haven't actually decided, yet. I haven't spoken to

Mark and I need to fly out to Michigan to speak with Sonja. I'll decide on which one would be the best to profile after I visit with both candidates."

Leaning over the table, Virina twirled her glass between her slender fingers and stared into the deep red wine, a solemn stillness on her face. "Richard, let's get real. Didn't you just say that you're looking for investors?" Virina reminded him.

"Yep, and that's the hardest part of any deal. I've gotta raise all the money, produce the product, and take all of the financial risk. But once the film is finished, I'm home free since BES will take care of distribution, publicity and promotion."

"That's what I thought." Virina paused. "This girl in Michigan…what kind of a family does she come from?"

"Modest, I would guess. I think her parents are both college professors. Why?"

Cradling her chin in one hand, Virina focused on Richard and shifted even closer. "I have a proposition. If you agree to make my son, Mark, the subject of your documentary, I will get you the money that you need," she tossed out, as easily as if she were agreeing to pick up the check for a meal.

Once the deal was set, she could pitch it to her wealthy friends, who would jump at the chance to own a piece of the project. If done correctly, the film would serve as the catalyst for spin-off deals that could make everyone a lot of money.

"Sure you can raise the kind of money I'll need?" Richard asked, taking the project folder from Virina. He flipped to the page that outlined production costs and tapped the columns of numbers with his index finger. "Look this over."

Now Virina slid a pair of slim reading glasses onto her nose and quickly reviewed the numbers.

"So you can see, it's not going to be cheap," Richard commented. "Plus, I'll need to talk to Mark before I agree to anything with you. He has to be on board."

"Don't worry about him. He'll agree. In fact, I'd prefer that you don't tell Mark about it before I have a chance to talk to him first. He's become so touchy lately about my interest in his affairs, though I will always look out for him." With a toss of her head she pulled off her reading glasses and finished the last of her wine. "How much would you need right away? To get the project rolling?"

"Depends on a lot of things—the length of time needed to shoot it, how big my film crew is, travel and living expenses. Equipment rental, studio fees, talent fees. Musicians to score it. It can add up pretty fast."

Virina frowned, hating the man's rambling, I-know-what-I'm-talking-about attitude—one that always set her perfect teeth on edge.

"Don't worry about the money, and forget about going to visit the woman in Michigan, Richard. You will make your film about my son. His life, his career, his wonderful achievements in a sport where he was always the only man of color on the slopes. And I will get the investors. When can you start?" Virina pressed on in an insistent tone. She hated dickering with people over useless details. Obviously, the man needed to be told what he was going to do and she had no problem telling him.

"The first stage is to create a rough cut of the project to show to the distributors…a short piece that will give them an overview of what I envision. If they like it, we'll sign contracts and I'll move ahead to complete the film. You know, now that I've had a chance to talk to you, I do think a documentary on Mark Jorgen would be best. It'll sell...and I know I could get him a book deal and a DVD that ought to sell like crazy on the Internet."

"You're right," Virina commented with self-important assurance. "My son remains one of the most highly rated skiers in the world. Of any race. His story is inspiring, his talent is tremendous. All because I managed his career and kept him in Europe where he was able to train with the best, compete at an intense level and move in the right social circles. That's extremely important, Richard."

With a lift of his brows, Richard Nobel went on, "I understand he's working in the States now...running a ski school near Aspen."

"Just a temporary thing," Virina managed, sniffing back her displeasure. "For some reason he got it into his head that he wanted to slow down...and teach. Why he wants to bury himself in that nondescript place, I don't understand. However, that's all well and good for now, but things are going to change. He'll soon realize that he must remain in the spotlight if he wants to profit from his accomplishments."

"If I profile Mark, I'd want to bring his story right up to today...to include what he's doing now. I'd like to cover him teaching at the ski school, working with his staff, interacting with young people. You know what I mean?"

"Of course," Virina agreed. "He's an excellent instructor and any student who is fortunate enough to train with him is very lucky."

Richard nodded his agreement. "You know, I plan to cover the Black Winter Sports Reunion in Aspen for *Sports Challenge* magazine, anyway, so I'll be hitching a ride with a group of journalists who are going out there at the end of the month. I can talk with Mark then."

"No, no. I'll talk to him first, and if you want, you can fly out with me on my plane," Virina told him, calculating that her last husband, Count Wilhelm Willard, owed her six more trips on his private plane—part of her divorce settlement.

She pulled a slender, silver Tiffany pen and miniscule notepad with a green leather cover from her Mary Francis bag and began to write. "Give me your contact information so my pilot can call you after he arranges the flight to Aspen."

"Thanks. That'd be fantastic," Richard gushed, going on to give Virina three different phone numbers that she could use to reach him.

"Umm. Is your wife...your family going, too?" she ventured.

"No. Just me," Richard replied.

"Fine. So it will be just you and me. I plan to leave New York around January 29. And don't talk to Mark before we get there. I will arrange everything. Agreed?"

Lifting his hands, Richard shrugged. "Don't you think I ought to give Mark a call and run the preliminary details of the project past him before I show up? What if he doesn't want to be profiled?"

"He will," Virina snapped. "Let me handle him. Richard, my son can be very impulsive and shortsighted. He doesn't realize that a documentary like the one you are proposing could make him a hot property once more. Commercial endorsements will follow. Sales of the video, the DVD. Book deals. Media appearances. He, and my investors, could make a great deal of money."

"Yes, they could," Richard agreed. "If this is what Mark wants to do."

"He doesn't know what he wants," Virina shot back, screwing up her red-hot lips. "That's why he still needs me to manage his business affairs, and his life for that matter, though he refuses to admit that I know what's best for him. Trust me, Richard. I've never been wrong."

Chapter 10

The Internet had become Skylar's best friend since assuming her role as concierge at Scenic Ridge one week ago, and she had become quite adept at using the most popular search engines to quickly fulfill the more unusual requests that came her way. She could get just about anything delivered overnight and into her guests' hands in record time, and prided herself on being extremely organized and timely in her work.

Thank God for Google, she thought, glancing at her to-do list on the yellow legal pad that she kept beside her keyboard. A Snow Bunny cuddle suit for the McLeary's baby daughter, Mountain Mist Triple Protector sunscreen for Mrs. Romero and another request from Mark Jorgen.

Skylar frowned at the yellow paper. Mark Jorgen. Did the guy really need all the stuff he'd been asking her to get for him? The Swiss chocolates with pink cream centers?

The wool argyle socks from Australia? Or the German made, handheld de-icing machine that he had asked her to track down this morning? She knew he was deliberately testing her to see if she'd come through, while trying to get her back inside his cabin. So far, she hadn't taken the bait. Whenever his latest order showed up, she promptly delivered it to Mark, but waited outside on the porch while he went to get her a tip, which she always accepted with a great show of appreciation.

After that incident with the case of schnapps on the day of her arrival, she'd decided to treat Mark like any other staff member whenever their paths crossed, keeping everything professional, nodding in friendly greeting and going on her way.

Now, settling down at her computer, Skylar launched her search and easily located the Snow Bunny cuddle suit and the pricey sunscreen, both of which she ordered and set up for overnight shipping.

"Now, for Mark Jorgen's fancy-thinga-ma-gig," she said aloud, both annoyed and challenged by his most recent request. As she waited for the page she was searching for to pop in, her thoughts wandered against her will, back to her encounter with Mark. Though she had told Deena that he was the last thing on her mind, she had lied: she couldn't get him out of her head. As hard as she tried to force him away, his touch, his smell, his tiger eyes; the way he had looked at her—every second of her time in his presence remained branded into her memory.

She groaned aloud, wishing this obsession with him would ease. Skylar knew if she were not careful, Mark Jorgen could become a real distraction and she refused to set herself up for another dose of man-trouble so soon after getting untangled from her disappointing relationship with Lewis.

Impulsively, Skylar opened the middle drawer of her desk and took out the twenty dollar bill that Mark had given her. Holding it in her hand, she recalled how his fingers brushed over hers when he'd handed the money to her, how he'd kept his mesmerizing gaze riveted on her face and how inflamed her body had felt as she made her way back to the lodge.

If only he knew that I can match him dollar for dollar, Skylar thought as she thrust the money inside and slammed the drawer shut. She had no intention of ever spending any of his, or any guest's, tips for that matter. Her plan was to let the money accumulate until she had enough to make a donation to the local children's fund. She certainly didn't need Mark Jorgen's cash, or his intrusion into the peaceful life she had found at Scenic Ridge.

Late the next afternoon, the familiar brown UPS truck pulled up to the lodge at its regular time and delivered the items that Skylar had ordered the day before. She handed the baby's bunny suit and the expensive sunscreen to Victor, the easygoing, Brazilian desk clerk, and asked him to deliver the packages to the appropriate guests' rooms. Then she took Mark's package into her office, placed it on the corner of her desk and went over to the window.

Looking out, she saw that Mark was returning from the slopes after his last class for the day, walking with a group of young students who were crowded around him, all talking at the same time. When he threw back his head and laughed at something one of them must have said, the late afternoon sunlight touched his face lighting his smooth tan skin. Skylar drew in a soft breath, not surprised to see that one of the girls was gazing at Mark with adoration in her eyes as she trudged along beside him, holding tightly on to her skis.

Skylar could tell that Mark was enjoying the attention, and his self-satisfied expression suddenly infuriated her.

Mark Jorgen is a demanding, picky and impossible man who thrives on the attention of his female students. It's a wonder he can keep his balance on the slopes, with an ego as large as his, she mused, faking a gag as she turned away from the window and went back to her desk.

After sorting through the rest of the day's mail and taking care of a near-crisis with a guest who had lost her ski lift tickets, Skylar shut down her computer, prepared to leave her office.

She glanced nervously at the box on her desk—Mark Jorgen, Snow King Suite, Scenic Ridge. She stared at it as if it were a bomb about to explode. Why hadn't she simply asked Victor to drop it off while he was making his other deliveries? Why was Mark's fancy de-icing gadget still in her office when she knew he'd said that he needed it right away? Why not ask Kathy, her backup, to take it to Mark?

But no, she couldn't do that. *I'll take care of this request personally. After all, I'm just doing my job.*

The phone was ringing and Mark was outside taking off his heavy boots. "Leave a message," he commented to himself as he struggled with the snaps on one of his boots. He'd had a rough day and hoped he'd never have another class of twelve year-old girls from Harlem again. He'd take the enamored matrons any day over pubescent adoration.

Finally free of his boots, he entered his cabin and went to his phone, engaged the voice mail, and listened.

"Hello, Mark. Skylar Webster here. Your ice-melting machine arrived today. I'll bring it up when I get off work."

A jolt of satisfaction, tinged with anticipation, shot through Mark. She was coming to his cabin again, even though they both knew there was no need for her to drive all the way to the Snow King suite, which she had done with each of his deliveries. He grinned, a mischievous smile that lit his eyes and warmed him inside. He might not be able to get Skylar Webster out of his mind, but he was going to get her into his suite tonight.

"And if I ask her why she decided to personally deliver my de-icing machine, I'll bet she'll tell me that she's just doing her job," he laughed, turning off the answering machine, more than ready to see her again.

He had been watching Skylar for the past week as she moved around the resort, but had been uneasy about engaging her in a conversation. She seemed so aloof and content to be alone that he knew he had to respect her desire for space until, hopefully, he could make a move.

He had seen her walking alone near the ice skating rink, and then wandering the foothills at the western edge of the property. She always appeared to be in deep thought, as if trying to settle some problem. He had even asked Kathy if Skylar was happy with her job, or upset about something, and Kathy had told him that, as far as she knew, Skylar was very content to be at Scenic Ridge and grateful to her sister for giving her the job.

Mark was fascinated with Skylar, yet he didn't want to seem pushy or overly friendly by making his interest known too quickly. During their first encounter in the store, he had recognized an inner strength that told him she was a woman in control. She held her ground, spoke her mind, and was serious about her work. He admired her for her strong work ethic as well as the fact that she treated him in a professional manner, but with luck, that would change very soon.

Mark knew he had pushed her buttons yesterday, demanding that she find the German de-icer immediately. And she hadn't balked, he realized, impressed with her ability to locate the exclusive gadget. She wasn't a quitter or a whiner—traits that Mark detested. She was natural. Not spoiled. Appreciative and honest. He would love nothing more than to wait on Skylar Webster hand and foot and show her what life with Mark Jorgen could be like. If only she would trust him.

Chapter 11

Mark's enthusiastic "thank you" made Skylar blush. With a demure nod of her head, she accepted his praise, pleased with herself for passing another one of his childish, and obvious, tests. *Who did he think he was fooling?* she mused, feeling a ripple of amusement.

"This is miraculous! In one day? I can't believe you found it," he gushed as he took the package from her and lifted the small box high.

"I have my sources," Skylar teased in a pride-filled voice, mentally scoring another point in their unspoken competition.

"Do you have time to come in for a cup of coffee? Hot chocolate? Wine?" Mark offered, cradling the package under one arm.

She shrugged, noncommittal.

"Please?" He stepped aside to let her in, as if she had already accepted his invitation.

Masking a smile, Skylar pressed her lips together and pretended to consider Mark's offer while her heart thudded under her parka. She looked him up and down, her gaze flitting quickly over his figure. He was dressed in a gorgeous gray and white snowflake sweater, gray corduroy slacks and soft black suede loafers. His longish hair was pulled back and tucked behind his ears and he was wearing a thin silver chain around his neck. In Skylar's opinion, he looked like one of those male models in *GQ* magazine—manly, yet stylish, powerful, but not overbearing and fully aware of how handsome he was.

"Uh…I don't know," she hesitated, deliberately taking her time in responding, enjoying the look of disappointment that flashed over Mark's features. "Deena said she might need me to help out on the front desk later."

"You have your pager, don't you?" Mark rushed to ask.

Skylar nodded, not trusting her voice.

"Fine. Then she can page you if she needs you."

"Right. I guess so," Skylar managed, now stepping inside. She pulled off her gloves and began to unzip her parka. "Coffee, then. And I can only stay for a minute. Just to warm up a bit before I head back," she added, thinking, *What harm can there be in a friendly cup of coffee with a coworker?*

She settled down on the same sofa where she had lain semiconscious only a week before while Mark went into the kitchen and returned with two cups of piping hot espresso. He sat on a low ottoman to the right of the sofa, angled so he could focus on her.

With his back to the glittering fire, he seemed to blend into the glowing, intimate setting and everything took on a surreal effect. Skylar forced her shoulders down a notch and tried to relax.

"So, how are you liking Scenic Ridge?" Mark began. He shifted closer, as if to let Skylar know that he planned to be fully engaged in their conversation.

Edging back slightly, Skylar put a little more space between them and offered Mark an awkward smile, trying to appear at ease. However, she was definitely nervous and unsure of what to say now that she was finally alone with Mark again. She had rehearsed this moment many times, and now, here she was. He was close enough to touch, to smell, and his deep green eyes were just as amazing as she recalled. Tightening her jaw, she reminded herself that she had to hold it all together and keep him from knowing just how rattled she was.

"Fine," she managed, forcing strength into her voice. "Just super. It's a beautiful place and everyone has been so helpful and nice."

"Yeah, your sister, Deena, and her husband run a first-class place. The staff is great, and rumor has it that you're the perfect replacement for Jean-Paul."

"I hope so," she replied, in a more confident tone, settling in for a real conversation. Obviously he was interested in talking to her, and she sure wanted to know more about him, so his invitation to come in for coffee had provided the perfect opportunity for her to get all the information she could. "From what I understand, no one really misses Jean-Paul," Skylar added with a short laugh. "I've heard a lot of wild stories about his very eccentric ways. I'm surprised Deena and Jerome put up with him so long."

"Apparently, he took extra-special care of the guests and they loved him, even though he gave the rest of the staff a hard time," Mark said. "He and I got along okay, but I have to admit that I didn't call on him to help me out with anything…not once."

"Is that so?" Skylar coyly commented. *And this is my fourth request for a special delivery to your suite in little more than a week.*

"Yeah," Mark commented, missing her reaction. "I'm pretty self-sufficient." He raised his chin, as if thinking back. "Jean-Paul did have a certain flair that added charm and drama to everything he did; however, at times I think he took himself, and his job, much too seriously. He was beginning to come off as pretentious."

"Well, I take my job as concierge seriously, too," Skylar quickly interjected, narrowing her eyes. "Do you consider me pretentious?"

"No, of course not," Mark hurried to say. He studied Skylar, a half-smile tilting his lips. "If anything, you're the most unpretentious woman I've met in a long time, and I find it very…attractive."

With a quick nod, Skylar accepted his compliment. "Thank you, Mark. I consider myself a working girl who wants to do a good job. After all, my sister is my boss. She's placed her trust in me and I can't let her down."

"Very commendable," Mark said, and then went on to ask, "What other resorts did you work at before you came here?"

His question hit Skylar like an unexpected snowball to the back of the head, and she momentarily froze. "Oh," she uttered, looking up, her mind spinning with possible answers. Should she fabricate some stuff, avoid the question with a rambling answer, or tell the truth? After a beat, she decided to give him as little information as possible without really lying. "I've worked in a few hotels, mainly in Florida, but this is my first job at a ski resort."

"So you don't ski?"

"No," Skylar confessed rather sheepishly. "But, let me clarify that. I'm damn good at skiing on water, but not on snow." She laughed, shrugging her shoulders.

Pressing a finger to his lips, Mark assessed her with a nod. "Well, we'll have to do something about that. I'd love to give you a few lessons. No way can you work at a place like this and not get out on the slopes. The thrill of gliding downhill, the beautiful scenery. You'll love it."

"I dunno," Skylar began, thinking of how much she wanted to reveal. "You see, I was in an elevator accident some time ago and I'm not real keen about gliding downward on anything."

"An elevator accident? Really? Were you hurt?"

"A few broken bones and some very bad bruises," Skylar replied, downplaying the extent of her injuries and not ready to get into a conversation about all of the pain, both physically and emotionally, that she suffered as a result of the disaster.

"That must have been terrible," Mark said, his words laced with genuine sympathy.

"It was. Believe me, it took months of therapy and a lot of mental determination to get inside an elevator again. So, skiing? I don't think so."

"Well, I wish you'd try. But I understand why you'd be afraid," Mark replied. "I promise to go slow, on the baby hill. Let me give you just one lesson. After that, I guarantee, you'll be hooked."

While considering Mark's request, Skylar's mind slipped back to that awful sensation of falling that had been with her since the elevator accident. The thudding crash. The darkness. The pain. No way could she face sliding down an icy, snow-covered hill with two narrow pieces of fiberglass strapped to her feet no matter how competent an instructor Mark might be. However, the expression of anticipation on his face tugged at her, so she told him, "I'll think about it, okay?"

"It's a deal. I'm going to hold you to that," he vowed, and then asked, "So, was it because of your accident, that you decided to leave Florida?"

"In a way, yes. After I recovered from my injuries, I was out of a job. So, when Deena called and told me about her opening here at Scenic Ridge, I grabbed it. Needed a change."

"You sure got it. Aspen isn't like Florida, is it?" Mark commented with a grin that showcased a single dimple in his right cheek.

God, he has the nerve to have dimples, too? Skylar realized, her stomach lurching in a too-pleasurable way. How had she missed that delicious feature? She sat up straighter and pulled back her shoulders before speaking. "Really a huge difference, you're right. It's so cold up here, but not that unpleasant. Very strange to be outside when the sun is shining and there's a ton of snow on the ground. When I'm in the sun, I'm not cold at all. Something to get used to," she finished, pressing the rim of her cup to her lips as she averted her eyes to the red-gold fire, desperate to avoid Mark's intense green gaze. It seemed to cut into her soul and thread its way to every part of her body, creating a tingling sensation that was making her far too warm.

"You grew up in Tampa and lived in Florida all of your life?" Mark continued.

"Um, hum," she murmured, regaining her composure, going on to tell him about her work as a paralegal and that when her widowed mother left Tampa to live with an aunt in New York, Skylar was the only member of her family still residing there.

"Did you ever think about moving to New York, too? To be close to your mom?"

"Oh, no. I'd lived in Tampa all my life. I never dreamed I'd ever leave…but here I am in Colorado. The first time I've lived any place other than Florida. Can't believe I'm actually here. But this is only temporary. Deena is still looking for a permanent replacement for Jean-Paul," she said, deciding to change the subject. "I understand that you lived in Europe for a long time," she began, inching cautiously into his background.

"Right," Mark replied. "I was born in California, where my father lived, but I don't have any contact with his family. My mother's from Norway, so I have relatives in Oslo. But I've spent most of my life on mountainsides in Switzerland, Germany, Spain and Italy."

"Sounds like you've led a glamorous life," Skylar commented, not certain she envied such a nomadic way of living. She preferred things to be stable, familiar and predictable. To her, change was unnerving. "Skiing professionally must have been demanding. Did you train all the time?"

"No, not all the time. I got to meet a lot of interesting people and the competitions were the best."

"Right. What is it like being famous?" Skylar asked, and was surprised to see a frown come over Mark's face, as if she'd touched on a topic he found distasteful.

"Famous? Yeah, I guess I was, at one time." His voice was flat and without much spirit. He set down his coffee cup and pulled the ottoman so close to Skylar that one of his knees pressed lightly against hers. "But, you know something?" he asked, eyes wide.

"What?" she breathed, fully aware that their legs were touching, but not about to move.

"I haven't said this to too many people…but at the height of my career, when I guess you could have called me famous, I wasn't that happy. There was so much pressure to please so many people. Training all the time. Traveling from city to city, never making real friends, just hanging out with people who drifted in and out of my life. It seemed as if I was always taking orders from my mother, or a sponsor or someone who controlled my every move. I'm happy it's behind me. I'm thirty-eight years old now and perfectly content to be out of the spotlight and out from under the pressure of skiing to win medals and money…and my mother's approval."

Skylar blinked at him, taken aback by this candid confession. "Gee…really? I'm surprised to hear you say that."

"You know what would make me happy?"

"What?"

"To simply ski for pleasure and share the sport with those who thought they'd never be able to enjoy it. For too many years, I dealt with power-hungry types who were more concerned with making money or flaunting their wealth, than what I wanted."

"That's why you decided to teach?" Skylar asked.

"Partly. I like deciding what I want to do without running it past agents and managers and handlers and sponsors. I like living far away from my mother, too."

Skylar simply stared at Mark and did not respond, thinking that she wished her mother still lived nearby.

"Don't get me wrong," Mark hurried to say. "I love my mother, but I need my space. Sometimes she makes it hard for me to be around her. Likes to smother me, if you know what I mean." He was breathing hard when he finished, as if he had not been able to stop the torrent of words that spilled out so quickly.

His passionate outburst took Skylar by surprise, and she was embarrassed that he would say such things to her, yet at the same time, pleased that he felt comfortable enough to speak his mind. "Well, it sounds as if Scenic Ridge is the perfect place for you," she lamely added, trying to fill the uneasy lull in the conversation.

"Yeah. I look forward to working with the kids. Most of them have never seen snow or even seen a person ski, except on television. We get young people from all over the U.S., Mexico, South America and the Caribbean who are thrilled to strap on a pair of skis. A lot of the black ski clubs give scholarships for underprivileged kids to have access to lessons and experience the powder. Makes for very gratifying work. I feel as if I'm finally doing something worthwhile with my life. Up to now, I sometimes think I've been selfish with my talent…too focused on winning another competition, another golden trophy, another dose of my mother's approval. It was never enough. Now I know what's been missing."

When Mark remained silent for a long moment, Skylar couldn't help asking, "Why are you telling me all of this?"

Mark shook his head slowly back and forth. "You know…I'm not sure," his voice had fallen to a whisper. "All I know is that I feel comfortable with you. I trust you. It's as if you're someone I've been waiting for, and for some strange reason, here you are, just when I need to talk to…to…" He hesitated.

"To a sister?" she helped him out, thinking she knew what was on his mind.

"Yeah, I think that's it," Mark softly acknowledged. "I've gotta be honest, Skylar. I haven't had much experience with black women. My world simply didn't collide with too many women like you...and that's just a fact. But now that I'm living in the States, I know what I want and I want to know you, Skylar." He paused, allowing Skylar to absorb his confession.

"That's very flattering," she told him, suddenly feeling a little sorry for Mark, who had bravely exposed a vulnerable side of himself to her.

"Can I give you a little test?" Mark went on.

"Shoot."

"If someone asked you who I am, what would you say?"

A warning hammered in Skylar's ears: *Be careful...this is another one of his ploys to pull me closer, to test me again.* "Well..." Skylar started. "I'd say that you're an unusual man, being a black Olympic gold medal winner and all...that you were a famous skier who broke records..." Her voice trailed off, unsure of where he was headed and not wanting to say the wrong thing.

"Exactly what I mean!" Mark reacted, lifting a finger to emphasize his point. "You focused on my career, as most people do. But what I want everyone, and especially you, to do is appreciate *me*...for who I am now...not who I *used* to be. Does that sound crazy?"

"No, not at all," she managed through a tightly constricted throat. She could see how frustrated he was, as well as embarrassed, for having revealed so much about himself to her. But still, he went on.

"Skylar, the first time I saw you in the store in town, I was struck by your beauty, of course, but also your spirit.

You really held your ground about those glasses, which was exactly what you should have done."

"Another one of your tests?" she teased.

"Oh, hell no," he laughed. "But I was impressed with your sense of confidence. There was something about you that got to me that day, and it's still stuck in my head. If you'll let me, I'd like to find out what it is about you that is driving me crazy."

Disturbed by his candid admission, Skylar pulled in a quick breath and blinked, knowing she ought to get up and leave, prevent him for going any further. After all, she had come to Scenic Ridge on a temporary gig to get over Lewis and decide what direction her future should take, not get tangled up in a rebound-romance with a guy who had a reputation as an international playboy.

While her fears increased by the second, her eyes remained locked with Mark's, boldly assessing the virile, vulnerable, gorgeous man who was making it clear that he wanted more than friendly conversation from her.

When he reached out and covered her fingers with his, she stared down in awe at their clasped hands; his, strong and browned by the sun; hers, a shade lighter and small. She was unable to resist when he gently tugged her toward him.

Skylar's nostrils flared when his woodsy pine-scent drifted up and filled her head, making her tremble with a sudden urge to toss aside all apprehension and fully embrace the moment. An oddly primitive urge swept through her and all she wanted to do was savor the taste of Mark Jorgen's lips.

When he brushed his mouth softly over hers, she froze, desperate to control her reaction to his touch, but knowing she was already lost. The past year had been a journey of painful surgeries, excruciating therapy and a long difficult recovery, all without the support of the man she had loved, Lewis Monroe.

Lewis had abandoned her both physically and emotionally when she'd needed him the most, had disappointed her while she had been at the lowest point in her life. Now, Skylar could not deny that she longed to be held, yearned to be touched, and hoped to be loved again one day. The full weight of her pent-up need to be with a man flooded back with a frightening rush.

Shifting forward, a weak moan slid from her throat as she felt herself slipping under Mark's entrancing gaze, unable—or unwilling—to stop his mouth from claiming hers. His lips smothered hers in a warm, insistent caress that set every nerve in her body afire, and when his tongue began to tease hers in a series of delicate, tender strokes, she responded by opening her mouth fully to the sweetness of his kiss and clasping both hands behind his neck to draw him even closer.

Inflamed by his presence, his scent and her own selfish need to be caressed and loved, Skylar relaxed and tilted back her head, inviting Mark to move his lips to her neck, to the delicate skin along her throat and over the exposed flesh at the neckline of her fluffy, white sweater.

He eased one hand down her back, searing her skin through her clothing, making his way to the base of her spine.

Skylar shuddered when a current of electrifying need shot through her chest and plunged into that pulsing spot between her thighs that had been dormant far too long. She couldn't suppress a cry of pleasure that sprang from her lips and hung in the air, echoing back to her.

Mark eased his fingers beneath her sweater and touched

the bare skin of her back. Again, a muted cry slipped out, her mind clouded with a mixture of joy, fear and anticipated relief. She wanted to feel his hands on her, hoped the wave of desire he'd initiated in her would strengthen and pulse and stay with her until it burst in a flash of heat. Silently, she urged his fingers ever deeper into her flesh, knowing it would be up to her to interrupt this journey—or live with the consequences of plunging recklessly ahead.

When Mark moved one hand to the front of her chest and placed it very close to her breast, Skylar came back to her senses and pulled away, clearing her head with a shake.

"Sorry," Mark apologized, immediately releasing his hold as he sank back and shyly assessed Skylar. "That was wrong of me, I know."

Tugging at her sweater, Skylar untangled herself from Mark's embrace and stood, her chin lifted high, knowing she had let him go too far. How had she been so stupid, courting disaster like that? "Yes, it was wrong, but I shouldn't have let you..."

"It wasn't your fault," he interrupted. "It won't happen again."

With a vigorous nod, Skylar agreed. "No, it won't." She exhaled loudly, breaking the tension that strung them together like prickly barbed wire. "Mark, I came to Scenic Ridge to work. I didn't come here to fulfill some fantasy of yours about being with a sister. And I'm not looking for a romantic interlude in the mountains. This little scene was a huge mistake, and you're right. It definitely can't happen again."

She picked up her car keys, went to the door and pulled it open. Turning back, she let her gaze linger on him for a moment, knowing she was doing the right thing by cutting off any romantic thoughts he might have. "I'm sure there are many, many women here at Scenic Ridge…in Aspen, for that matter, who would love for you to hold *their* hands and let you make love to them, but I'm not one of them. Sorry."

Mark rose, but did not approach her, as if afraid of making her run away. "I understand what you're saying, Skylar. And I respect where you're coming from." He dug his hands deep into his pants pockets and looked up at Skylar from beneath lowered lashes. "But I'd still like to teach you to ski. How about it?"

"Maybe," was all she could manage before breaking her gaze and leaving.

During her drive back to the main lodge, Skylar struggled to calm her heartbeat and get her breath.

Chapter 12

At ten o'clock the next morning, Skylar looked up from her computer monitor to see Mark standing in her doorway, dressed for the slopes and assessing her in a serious manner. He glanced away when their eyes met, but then looked back and held her gaze.

"I have a two-hour break until my next student," he hesitantly began, head tilted to the side, an expression of uncertainty on his face. "How about that lesson you promised you'd take?"

A giggle burst from Skylar's lips. From the distress on his face she had thought he had come to deliver some very bad news, not ask her out on a ski date. She pressed her hand to her mouth to regain her composure, not wanting to embarrass him. "You've got to be kidding!" she finally blurted. "Going skiing is the last thing on my mind." She picked up her yellow legal pad and waved it at him. "I've got tons of work to do, so please. Go! Leave me alone." She shooed him away with her pad of paper. "I'll let you know when I'm ready to strap on a pair of skis and hurl myself down a hill. Okay?"

"Okay," Mark replied, shrugging. "I'll check back. Soon." Without another word, he was gone.

Three days later, while standing outside watching the ice-skaters twirl and glide across the slick surface, Skylar realized that Mark was sitting beneath the sheltered stands on the opposite side of the rink. Feeling a bit rattled by his unexpected presence, she sucked in a short breath, wondering how long he had been sitting there, watching her.

On most mornings, when she took a break from her work, she strolled along the foot paths at the base of the mountains, with only the crunch of snow beneath her boots to break the serene silence. She was getting used to life in the mountains, and now better understood why her sister, a tropical girl like herself, had been drawn to this beautiful place to start married life with Jerome.

Had Mark been watching her like this for the past three days? she wondered, trying not to feel impressed with his determination to get to her.

Mark tensed his jaw when he realized that Skylar had seen him. Things were working out just fine. He had hoped to catch Skylar outside today, after noticing that she usually took a short break outside in midmorning and was always alone. She didn't hang out with other staff members very much, or socialize with the male guests who made no effort to hide their interest in her. He wondered why she preferred to keep to herself so much. She always seemed preoccupied. What was on her mind? Why did she seem unhappy some days, and very upbeat on others? And why wouldn't she let him teach her to ski? Women rarely turned down an opportunity to ski with Mark Jorgen. What would he have to do to make Skylar want to be with him?

Skylar turned her face fully toward Mark and boldly held his attention. When he lifted a gloved hand and waved, she was unable to keep from smiling and waving back. Immediately, he started around the ice skating rink toward her and she exhaled, unaware that she had been holding her breath.

"Hey," he said, stopping to prop one arm on the metal rail that enclosed the circle of ice. "I hoped I'd see you out here today."

"You've been waiting for me?"

"Sure have."

"Why?"

"Because I know you sometimes take a break and come out here alone and I wanted to see you…talk to you."

"About what? Not about that ski lesson I stupidly agreed to take, I hope?"

Mark lifted both hands and stepped backward a few feet. "No pressure. I promise."

Skylar nodded. "Good. Because I'm not in the mood for a hassle. I get enough of that from the guests."

"I'll bet you do," he agreed with a light laugh. "I hope you know that I'd never deliberately hassle you; however…" he started.

"Oh, no. Here it comes," Skylar groaned.

"Since tomorrow is Tuesday, and I know it's your day off, why not spend it with me?" A beat. "What else do you have to do? Kathy will be covering the concierge desk, and Deena agreed with me, you've been working here almost three weeks and haven't strapped on a pair of skis yet. Not a good thing, Skylar. Tomorrow, we ski."

Skylar shot Mark a glint of a scowl, her lips parted in surprise. "You sure are into my business. Monitoring my breaks, scheduling my free time, consulting with my sister, who is also my boss. I'm not sure I like that." Her tone was sharp, but secretly she was enjoying this pursuit and not surprised that Mark wasn't letting her off the hook. "Remember, I said *maybe* I'd let you teach me to ski. I didn't agree to anything. But, if I have time tomorrow, then *maybe* we can," Skylar finished, trying to sound noncommittal.

"Then, I'll take that for a 'yes,'" Mark said, sounding very satisfied. "But I don't want to wait until tomorrow to spend some time with you. What are you doing tonight?"

"I'm driving into town to see a play at the Morning Star Theater."

"Alone?" Mark asked, scowling.

Skylar nodded. "Sure. Why not? I know my way into town from here."

"That may be true, but the road's gonna be very dark and icy. Could be tricky. I wouldn't chance it if I were you."

"Well, you're not me, are you?" Skylar tossed back. "Don't worry, I won't have any trouble."

At 6:00 p.m. it was already dark, but Skylar set off toward town anyway, feeling fully in control and looking forward to an evening at the theater, away from the resort and all of its pressure. Since her arrival, it seemed as if she had done nothing but take care of other people's needs ten to twelve hours a day, and now she was going to do something nice for herself.

The road was narrow, but clear of snow and her Jeep was the only vehicle buzzing along the isolated road. With her CD player blasting Mary J. Blige, she relaxed, and let her thoughts slip back to Mark, as they seemed to do far too often.

"I just might give in and go skiing with him tomorrow," she whispered into the empty car. "What else do I really have to do? If I'm gonna work at a ski lodge, I'd better learn to ski and why not learn from the best?" Having made that decision, she relaxed and settled back in her seat to concentrate on the road.

Mark, who had pulled up to the main lodge seconds after Skylar left Scenic Ridge, was uneasy. He watched her Jeep disappear down the road, fearful about her decision to take off alone like that. She was new to the mountains and didn't understand how quickly the weather could turn nasty or how easily a complication could arise. Chunks of ice and snow often tumbled down the mountainsides, blocking the highway, smashing into cars and even killing small animals that got in the way.

He couldn't let Skylar go off like that. He'd never forgive himself if something happened to her. Impulsively, Mark turned his Range Rover toward the road and took off after her, trying to stay far enough behind her so that she would not know that he was following. "She'd hate me for that," he told himself, keenly aware of just how independent and stubborn Skylar could be.

Though the road was dark, the sky was lit with stars, creating an atmosphere that was almost festive. Skylar glanced up at the thick blanket of shiny, bright lights strung across the sky and marveled at the sight. The heavens had certainly blessed Colorado with a show of light that she'd never seen over Florida, causing a surge of joy to shoot through her, making her thankful to experience it.

Leaving Tampa to work as a concierge had been a risky move, but also the best decision Skylar had ever made, after dumping Lewis Monroe, of course. Change had always been difficult for Skylar, but this was one change that she did not regret. She felt liberated, stronger, more competent and useful than ever, an indication that something must have been missing before now. She was enjoying the close ties she and Deena were rediscovering. She liked her job, even though it could be quite demanding. And she was getting over her obsession for the cheating man who had stripped away her happiness and left her reeling in regret. The clean slate that spread out before her now was both challenging and tempting. It would be up to her to fill it, any way she wanted.

"And my happiness has nothing to do with a fat bank account," she murmured, realizing that money was not the reason she was filled with such happiness. However, it sure brought peace of mind.

Mark suddenly pressed down harder on the gas pedal, feeling that he ought to catch up with Skylar, whose red taillights glimmered up the road. He could see that there was one car between himself and Skylar's Jeep, and the driver was tailgating her. Mark watched the scene in fear. The driver behind Skylar was determined to pass her, inching closer and closer to her bumper at a high rate of speed. Mark held his breath as the two cars approached the narrowest section of the road where it shrank down to one lane.

Skylar cut her eyes to her left side mirror and frowned. The vehicle behind her seemed to be closing in on her very fast. She checked the right shoulder and calculated that there was just enough room to pull over and let him pass.

She switched off the music, which had suddenly become a distraction, and concentrated on getting out of the way of the fast-approaching headlights. Cautiously, she swung her Jeep off the road and onto the rocky shoulder, gripping the steering wheel hard with both hands. It was pitch-black outside and her only guide was the strip of yellow light that beamed from her headlights into the black unknown that lay ahead. She prayed she had made the right move. Immediately she heard the crunch of hard packed snow and ice grinding under her wheels and began to relax. She'd made it.

Feeling safely out of the way of the approaching car, she lifted her foot from the accelerator, preparing to brake, but her boot buckle caught on the gas pedal and kept it in place.

The rear end of the Jeep spun sharply to the right. Quickly, she whipped the steering wheel to the left, praying she'd be able to pull out of the spin as she yanked her foot loose from the gas pedal. However, instead of correcting her course, she forced the Jeep into a severe left turn that sent it into a full circle spin and off the shoulder, hurling her down an embankment and into a wall of snow.

Skylar screamed, lowered her head, and braced herself for the impact, which turned out to be a lot less forceful than she had anticipated. When the car settled, she raised her head just in time to see the car that had been behind her speed past and continue down the road as if nothing had happened.

Panic set in. What in the world was she going to do now? She might freeze to death before anyone found her, or be eaten by mountain lions. A swell of fear crowded her mind, threatening to bring tears to her eyes, but she inhaled slowly and pulled herself together. No time for tears, she mentally reprimanded. She had a cell phone with her and a bundle of flares in the back. She was going to be fine.

Just as she reached for her phone, planning to call Scenic Ridge and get Victor or John to come and help her, there was a loud pounding sound on the driver's side window and someone was shouting her name. She jerked back in surprise and glared at the glass. It was Mark and he was screaming like crazy at her.

"Impossible," Mark informed her after trying several times to rock her Jeep out of the frozen ditch. "You're stuck until a tow truck can come get you out tomorrow."

"What a mess," Skylar commented, going on to rant some more about the driver who had done this to her.

"Yeah, I saw it coming," Mark said. "Good thing I followed you. I told you not to go out alone. Look what happened. It could have been a lot worse."

"Well, it wasn't," Skylar muttered, not in the mood to hear an I-told-you-so lecture from him! "So, without a car, I guess I'm forced to ride back with you."

"Yeah, unless you want to walk," Mark commented in a level tone. "And since you won't be going to the theater tonight, you're coming back to my place to warm up."

"I guess I can't object, can I, since you're in control?"

"No, you can't." he agreed in a take charge tone.

Once they got to Mark's cabin, he made hot chocolate and insisted that Skylar sit by the fire to thaw out. Though she didn't want to show it, she was pleased to be there with him, and very grateful that he had come along. Maybe she had been too harsh with him. He had taken it upon himself to watch out for her. He cared, and he was neither pushy nor obnoxious. He was simply Mark: easy-going, but focused. Confident, but not prideful. Handsome, but not vain. She had never met anyone like him.

In the calm, warm atmosphere, Skylar began to relax and when he asked her again about hitting the slopes, she finally acquiesced.

"Okay, okay. I'll do it. But you know I'm still afraid of sliding downhill. Probably will always be like this."

"I understand. And I'm sorry. But I hope you sued that elevator company. Surely they were liable?"

Tensing, Skylar pressed her lips together, knowing she had to proceed very carefully. "I didn't have to sue. The company covered all of my medical bills, and I received enough money to pay off my car, clear up my credit cards, and put a little away." She laughed nervously, hating to lie to Mark, but not wanting to get into her multi-million-dollar status right then. "It was a frightening experience and I don't think I'll ever get over the pain it caused, both physically and emotionally. You see, the accident cost me a relationship that I had hoped would work out."

"A boyfriend?"

Skylar nodded.

"Do you want to talk about it?"

Now, she shrugged. "Sure. Why not?" She moved to sit on the floor, closer to the fire as she told him about Lewis and his infidelity while she was in the hospital. When she finished, she realized she was crying and didn't know why. She had thought everything was under control, that Lewis's betrayal was behind her, but apparently it wasn't.

Mark sank down beside Skylar and wrapped his arms around her from behind, holding her until she settled down.

Could he fulfill the needs of such a vibrant, lovely woman and heal her pain? Could he erase her obsessive attachment to a man who had not deserved her in the first place? All Mark could be certain of was that he planned to try, and spending as much time as possible with Skylar was the key.

"If you'll trust me, I'll help erase your fear of falling. I know I can do that in a day, but as for your broken heart…that may take some time."

"I know it will. That's why I don't want things to move too fast. Between us. You know?"

Mark nodded his understanding. "Sure. I feel the same way. So, you'll take a ski lesson with me tomorrow?"

Skylar turned in his arms and smiled.

Mark wiped a tear from beneath her eye with the pad of his index finger.

"Yes," she whispered. "I want to get over that fear, and then maybe I can move on to tackle other things."

"Perfect," Mark said, giving her a firm hug. "Ten o'clock tomorrow morning. I'll be waiting for you at Bunny Hill. Don't be late!" he said, indicating that everything was settled.

"Bunny Hill!" Skylar groaned, watching Mark closely.

She knew what that meant: she'd been relegated to the status of the children, the athletically challenged—like Goldie Lamar—and seniors who probably had no business on skis. And she had to be prepared to take more orders from Mark.

Chapter 13

The four-layer seaweed and mineral massage treatment at Michele-La Que's Day Spa was the most luxurious that Virina had ever experienced. The hour and a half session in the exclusive Manhattan salon was re-hydrating, rejuvenating and nourishing every cell in her jet-lagged, fifty-eight-year-old body and she was in no hurry to leave. When Thurgo, her Hungarian masseur, began to slather the musky, black mud into her upper back, Virina let out a delicious sigh and closed her eyes.

Lying facedown on the table, she let her body go limp and surrendered herself to the expert attention she knew she deserved. She wanted to be in tip-top shape and looking and feeling her best when she met Mark, after a year of long-distance, less-than-positive communication with him via e-mail and brief telephone calls. She was furious that he was acting so indifferent to her offers to help him establish himself as an instructor, since that was what he seemed determined to do. She had contacts all over the world, and knew her son could be the head of a ski school in St. Moritz or Innsbruck or Lillehammer, and not settle for a second-rate resort in a remote part of the Roaring Fork Valley that catered to God knew who! She had never met anyone who had skied Scenic Ridge and doubted she ever would.

Tapping her nails along the side of the massage table, Virina faced her dilemma head on: Mark's stunning career had kept her connected to people with wealth, social status and class, allowing her to move among them as if she, herself, were rich and famous. Over the years, she had been fortunate enough to marry both old money and new, and had luxuriated in the sense of privilege that came with each union. However, since her last divorce—from Wilhelm Willard, who claimed to be a count and a distant cousin of a Dutch prince—her funds had begun to thin out.

Soon, her contract as the face of Deleur Cosmetics would end. She'd be out of the spotlight, unattached, and facing a financial struggle that she didn't want to deal with. Her future just might depend on how well Mark married, and it looked as if she was going to have to help him choose the right woman to make sure that they both lived in the style they deserved.

But what were her son's chances of finding a rich wife at Scenic Ridge? Virina shuddered to think of how much time he had already wasted. She had to get Mark out of that place, back to Europe, or at the very least into circulation in the States among women with healthy bank accounts.

Virina's mind clicked over a list of things she needed

to discuss with Mark, uppermost being Richard Nobel's documentary: pulling that project off was going to require finesse, energy and all the stamina she could muster. But it had to be done, and done correctly.

While Thurgo's fingers drummed on her skin, she let her thoughts linger on Mark a while longer. Her only son. Her only child. When she returned to Norway, she had ditched her modeling career to dedicate her life to making him a star in the sports world. Now, it would be up to her to make his star shine just as brightly in the world of entertainment. He was all she lived for. He was so handsome and talented, he deserved to be in the spotlight forever and she knew how to make such things happen.

And why shouldn't he be famous again? His father, James Jorgen, had been the most gorgeous, witty and talented man Virina had ever met, and the qualities that had drawn her to him were present in her son.

James Jorgen, a rising designer in the California fashion industry had literally pulled Virina from the unemployment line, shoved her into one of his dresses, and pushed her onto a Beverly Hills hotel runway within hours of discovering her. His impulsive decision to use an unknown model to showcase his dresses had catapulted eighteen-year-old Virina Dagrun into the world of haute couture and saved her from the dead-end life of a struggling model working odd jobs while dreaming for a break.

She married James thirteen months after meeting him, despite objections from his parents, his sister and his two brothers, who were disappointed that James not only planned to marry a white girl, but the whitest of white girls, a pastel Norwegian blond.

Snubbing his family, the couple got married in an oceanside cabana and flew to the East coast to settle in New York, quickly joining the fashion scene where they made a stunning entrance wherever they went.

James had been powerfully built, brown-skinned and imposing, while Virina was delicately pale and icicle thin. Adored by the snobby fashionistas and embraced by the *nouveau riche* set they ran with, life had been one big party for the striking couple…until James fell in love with an Ethiopian princess, and moved back to Africa with her, leaving Virina to raise their son, Mark, alone.

After her divorce she never saw James Jorgen again until his funeral ten years later.

Over the ensuing years, Virina married four more times, always for money, never able to recapture the kind of love she had felt for James. Mark was her gift from James, and she planned to spend her life making sure he was happy, and a big part of that meant seeing to it that he married well. The fact that he had isolated himself in an obscure resort in the Colorado Mountains didn't change a thing as far as she was concerned. As a mother, it was her responsibility to watch over her son, ensure his future, and that was exactly what she planned to do.

Today was Skylar's day off and Deena had invited her sister to have breakfast with her in her apartment. She was looking forward to some uninterrupted girl talk, as well as an opportunity to discuss a few hot issues related to the fast-approaching Black Winter Sports Reunion.

Scenic Ridge was hosting a kick-off party called Slide and Glide, and it was turning into *the* event to attend on the opening night of the international gathering. Five hundred tickets had been sold, with the proceeds going to a scholarship fund to support training of talented underprivileged young skiers, while the food and drink had been donated by local sponsors. A huge section of the property would be tented, with heaters, and available for the overflow crowd they expected.

Since Skylar's arrival a month ago, the two sisters had barely had time to do more than chat briefly about the special needs of specific guests or problems requiring the concierge's immediate attention. Deena was pleased by the way Skylar had jumped right in and taken over Jean-Paul's duties in such an efficient, professional manner.

"I knew she'd be perfect," Deena murmured, hurrying to answer the knock on her door. "Right on time," she said to Skylar, who was standing with the room service attendant who had arrived with his cart filled with condiments and covered plates.

Turning to the attendant, she told him to take the cart into the small dining area off the kitchen and to set out the food. Once he had left, she and Skylar settled across from each other and launched into a breakfast of bacon, sausage, eggs benedict, hash browns and homemade biscuits, as they discussed the activity schedule for the ski club reunion.

"I'll have four additional vans available for transportation into Aspen proper," Deena said, crunching on a piece of toast. "We're totally full. Not even an extra fold-out bed is available. So, unless we get a cancellation, tell anyone who asks about staying here that they'll have to find a room in Snowmass, Aspen or Carbondale. However, we'll provide transportation between the towns if they have family staying here."

"What about those who want to come up from other hotels just for the Glide and Slide party?" Skylar asked.

"Can't handle that. They're on their own. We're only responsible for those staying here."

Skylar made a quick notation on the pad she had brought along. "Is the music set? The menu?"

"The DJ, Red Boys III, is on board, Kathy's got the food under control, and Mark will oversee the valet service. Just about everything else is in place."

"Sounds good," Skylar said, sipping her coffee.

"I'm excited. This event is going to showcase Scenic Ridge as *the* place for minorities and young people to come to learn to ski. A good number of reporters from across the country will be here to cover the reunion, even a producer from BES called to inquire about our party."

"That'll be great publicity for you!"

"Sure will," Deena agreed, folding her linen napkin and sitting back. She placed a hand to her waistline. "I'm stuffed."

"Me too, but I guess I'm gonna need a meal like this to get me through the day."

"Why? What's on your agenda today?" Deena asked, toying with her teacup.

"My first ski lesson," Skylar replied, rolling her eyes. "As if you didn't know! Mark told me that he consulted you *and* Kathy, before he *informed* me that I was having a ski lesson today. He's practically forcing me to do this."

"Forcing you?" Deena mocked, wide-eyed. "Oh, calm down, Skylar. Sure, I told him I thought you oughta get away. Enjoy yourself today. You've been working nonstop since you got here. Go on, get out there and have a good time."

"He's been bugging me for days, so I gave in. Why, I don't know. Ever since my elevator accident, the thought of sliding downhill on skis has not seemed like something I'd like to do. Plus, I don't have the right clothes."

"Don't worry about that! Mark will arrange for your gear. You can borrow my red and white Helly Hansen ski pants and jacket, which will work great with that black turtleneck of yours. You have heavy socks, a warm hat and gloves, don't you?"

Skylar nodded.

"Okay. Long underwear?"

Skylar shook her head, "Nope. Just regular bras and panties."

"Won't do," Deena said. "I'll give you a pair of my Cuddly Duds."

"Gee, thanks. I'm beginning to feel overwhelmed," Skylar complained. "I have no idea of what I'm getting myself into."

"You can trust Mark to keep you safe. He's a pro. Just do whatever he says, and you'll be sailing down the mountainside in no time."

"Right," Skylar groaned. "Seems like that's all I ever do…whatever he says. He can be very demanding, you know? Over the past week, I've located more items and delivered more packages to his cabin than for any other guest. For example, yesterday, I arranged limos for a group of his students who wanted to go on a shopping trip in town, then I had two hundred copies of his Ski Tips pamphlet printed and shipped overnight to some ski club in Pennsylvania and found a repair man to service his snowmobile."

"Clearly, he wants both your assistance and your attention," Deena said. "So, play along with him. Lighten up! Mark is really a very nice guy. Polite, easy to work with, never complains and gorgeous! Since he's been here, I've never received a complaint from a guest or the staff. I think he's just challenging you. His competitive nature, I suppose."

"He's a challenge all right," Skylar replied in a voice that carried her frustration. "He thinks he's gonna break me with his constant demands, but I've got some ideas of my own about how to show him who he's dealing with."

With a thump, Deena plunked down her teacup, both puzzled and amused. "Sounds like you two might wind up doing a lot more together than just ski. Or am I imagining things?"

"You're imagining things," Skylar shot back. "Besides, I didn't know you were listening so closely."

Chapter 14

Bunny Hill was crowded with what looked like a boy scout troop in snowsuits, accompanied by a scattering of middle-aged chaperones who were having no luck getting the boys to stop throwing snowballs and pay attention to Mark, who was standing with his back to them while demonstrating the correct way to hold their ski poles.

With her rented skis balanced on her shoulder, Skylar trudged up the slope feeling bulky and off balance. She was wearing Deena's microstretch long johns, three layers of clothing under her parka, heavy boots, insulated goggles, double-thick, waterproof gloves and a bright red knit cap. She felt like the abominable snowwoman and feared the sheer weight of her clothing was going to bury her beneath the freshly packed snow.

"I'd better not make a fool of myself," she muttered crossly, feeling her earlier surge of confidence begin to wane.

After reaching the top of the hill, she stood to one side and watched as Mark patiently lined the boys up, checked their posture, and then sent them off on a downward run over the gentle slope. Now that she was closer, she realized that he had been speaking French with them. Very impressive, she thought as she watched the way Mark was interacting with the boys.

"Find your balance," he called out after them, now in English. "Feel where your weight is centered and try to maintain it." When two of the boys fell down, he quickly encouraged them to return to the top of the hill and try again. Both made successful runs on the second try and beamed their joy back at Mark.

"Great job all around!" Mark congratulated the group. "Now that you know how to get going and how to stop, I want you to practice with John. He's even tougher on students than I am," Mark joked as the boys groaned and hooted playfully. "John will teach you how to control your speed, okay?" And then turning to Skylar, he waved her over. "Your turn. Are you ready?"

"As ready as I'll ever be, I guess," Skylar replied, moving with Mark to a less crowded section of the hill. "You were speaking French with those boys, I noticed."

"Yeah," he said. "They're immigrants from Haiti. A local resident, a big shot in the energy industry who lives in Woody Creek, is sponsoring them. The boys live in foster homes in Aurora and are spending the weekend here."

"That's wonderful. I see why you love your job so much. They're having a ball!"

"Yeah, it's great to watch them getting their snow legs. Now, for *your* lesson," Mark started, bending down in front of Skylar. "First, let's pull your ski trousers over the tops of your boots. Keeps snow from getting into your boots." He gripped her ankle with one hand, gave the bottom of her ski pants a hard tug and created a snug fit between her boots and her pant legs.

"Oh, I see what you mean," Skylar remarked, glancing down at him, steeling herself for his touch as he began to work on the other boot. Instantly, her mind went back to the night when she broke the bottle of schnapps and he had felt her legs for injuries and broken glass. His touch had stirred her then, in a curious mix of excitement and apprehension, as it did so now, hitting her with an intensity that made her heart beat race.

Finished, he stood up and took her skis from her, separated them and placed them across the top of the hill. "To keep you from skiing off before you're ready and landing in a heap at the bottom of the hill," he casually remarked as he helped her into one ski, then the other. "Take your poles, place your hands through the straps from the underneath and then hold the straps below your hand when you grip the pole."

Skylar did as he instructed.

"All set. I see you've got wraparound goggles, now," he observed, and then paused. "I have to ask. How did the bronze aviators work out?"

Gritting her teeth, Skylar was tempted to lie. Why give him another reason to feel so damn superior, as if he knew everything and she was a ditz? But against her will, the words flew out, "They didn't work at all. I tossed them out the window that day. You were right. I should have gone with the wraps the first time around."

"I tried to tell you..." he said, maneuvering into position beside Skylar.

Resisting the urge to snap back with a smart reply, she let his blunt remark pass, knowing he spoke the truth. If there was one trait about Mark that she could count on, it was his tendency to say exactly what was on his mind with little concern about how it sounded. *I wonder if that's because he grew up speaking a foreign language,* she calculated, groping for an explanation for his ability to simultaneously irritate and entrance her.

"First, we learn how to 'walk' by alternatively sliding one ski ahead of the other," he started, demonstrating the action. "Okay, you try it."

She did, and managed to keep her balance as she set out to cross the top of the hill.

"Good job," he called out, following along behind her. "Keep going until you feel comfortable, okay?"

She could feel his body close behind hers as she practiced her walking technique, and his nearness made her more nervous than her fear of falling down on the hard-packed snow.

After mastering the walk, she headed back to the spot where she'd started out, with Mark still close behind her.

"Doing fine," he called out. "Now, point your skis sideways and stand there for a minute to get focused."

This is hard work, she thought, clumsily shifting into position, feeling the strain in the calves of her legs. *Why am I punishing myself like this? I feel like hell and I've only been out here for fifteen minutes.* However, she knew she wasn't about to back out and let him call her a quitter. No, she was going to finish this lesson, and show him what she could do. Grateful for the short break, Skylar let her shoulders relax and sagged back on her heels for a moment.

"No, no! Stand up in your skis," Mark suddenly shouted

from behind, wrenching her back to the task at hand. "Put your weight forward slightly."

Again, she complied.

"Good. Now, face your shoulders down the hill, while your skis are still sideways. Take small steps now, point your skis downhill and put weight on your poles. Bend your knees, and when I give the word, just lift your poles and off you go!"

Right, Skylar thought with a dry swallow, not sure she could do it. The awful fear of falling that had been with her since crashing into the courthouse basement flooded back and crowded her mind. *This is different. I'm in control*, she kept telling herself, desperate to follow through. She wet her lips, crouched down and set her sights on the bottom of the hill.

"Oh...one more thing," Mark called up to Skylar. "Tuck in your lovely behind."

Skylar's head snapped around and she shot him a look that could have frozen water, but then burst out laughing. "You certainly have the best view to determine if it's lovely or not," she tossed over her shoulder as she lifted her ski poles and slid down the hill.

"That, I do," he yelled out, whizzing up beside her.

After an hour and forty-five minutes on Bunny Hill, Mark took Skylar to the loading area to teach her how to properly catch the ski lift, a feat much more complicated than Skylar had ever imagined. Once they were aboard and their skis safely stowed, she turned to Mark, breathless with excitement. "That was pretty tricky!"

Mark nodded. "Safely getting on and off a ski lift is crucial. It all comes down to timing and positioning. We probably have more accidents at the lift loading area than on the slopes."

"I see why," Skylar commented, settling in to enjoy the view.

After a few minutes of silence, Mark suddenly turned to her. "You did okay," he told her, grinning. "Well, more than okay. I wish all of my students were such fast learners. With practice, you could become a pretty good skier."

"Thank you," she smugly stated, assessing him from the corner of her eye. She was totally psyched about skiing, in awe of Mark's talent and having more fun than she'd dared to dream she would have on her first day of lessons. He had been patient, professional and encouraging during their time together and she was eager to continue. It was not as difficult or scary as she'd thought it would be, and now she understood that confidence and balance were keys to a successful run, and she had lots of both.

During their many practice runs, she'd seen the playful, humorous side of Mark and knew why so many of his female students wound up totally smitten with him. He had laughed at her many tumbles; tossed snowballs at her when she was down; and allowed her to grab onto his hands, clutch his legs, wrap her arms around his waist and press her body to his as she'd struggled to stay upright. The intimacy he'd brought to the experience was raw, sexy and real. He'd made her feel alive, energized and desirable: a lethal combination for Skylar, who could sense that Mark was slowly inching his way into her heart, edging her toward a slippery slope from which she might not want to return.

"Look over there! To the right," Mark shouted, interrupting her thoughts. He leaned across her and pointed toward an opening in a stand of pines at the bottom of a snow-covered knoll. "That's the old Brookman Mill.

There, beside the creek. It's the original sawmill that was built by homesteaders on this property. You know Deena and Jerome restored it? It actually works."

"So I heard," Skylar commented, zeroing in on the huge paddle wheel and the wood-shingle roof that was peeking out of the trees. "She told me all about it. I understand that it's a popular site for school field trips. A local historical landmark."

"Yeah…have you been inside?" Mark asked.

"No, I haven't had time to make the trip."

"Well, there's no time like the present. We'll hop off at the next stop and hike over. You'll love it. Authentic, but still working." He paused, and then swept his arm in an arc and drew in a deep breath. "Isn't everything beautiful from up here?"

Skylar leaned forward to get a better view of the old mill. Her cheek brushed against Mark's. He jerked up in surprise. Their eyes met and held, allowing her to read the message in the depth of his gaze. He wanted to kiss her as much as she wanted him to. Something strange and wonderful was happening to them both. "Yes, everything is beautiful," she answered in a whisper. "It's as beautiful up here as it is down there."

When he kissed her, she returned his bold move without hesitation. Leaning back, she snuggled into the corner of the chairlift and drew him closer, pushing back his hood to see his face more clearly. It was lit with a glow of desire.

"I've wanted to do that all morning," he told her, words thick with longing.

"I know," she whispered back.

"Then, trust me, Skylar. Let me show you who I am, and

how much fun we can have together. I want you to be with me. Always."

"It's not that easy."

"It can be," he countered.

"You say that as if you've said it many times before, to many other women."

Mark flinched. "I haven't," he said. "I expect you've heard that I have a reputation as a flirt, but believe me, it's not true. I don't encourage my students. I do try to get them to relax and forget about their fears, to have fun on the snow, and perhaps they take my interest in them too seriously. But student-teacher crushes are an occupational hazard that come along with being a ski instructor."

"Then, I guess I'm no different than your other students," Skylar murmured, a flicker of a smile touching her lips. "Because I think I may have a crush on you, too."

Mark stroked her cheek with the tip of his thumb, taking in her admission. "I'm glad," he said. "Then you'll stick around long enough for me to find out if this crush is one that's gonna last?"

"Maybe," Skylar murmured, taking time to assess Mark's features, as if seeking reassurance that she was making the right move.

"Just maybe?" he pressed.

"All right, yes. I do want to know you better, Mark. And for you to know me, too. But I don't want to go too fast."

"I'd never hurt you, if that's what you're worried about. Never," he breathed, easing his lips over hers again. His tongue pressed into the sweet hollow of her mouth, seeking, claiming, telling her without words how much he needed and wanted her, while every part of her body longed to feel him, taste him and hold him close until nothing separated them. While her fingers moved to the back of his neck, both of his hands caressed her cheeks, holding her captive, their lips locked together, an invisible cord binding them.

Their caress lasted until the lift lurched to a stop, forcing them to scramble to get their skis and jump off. They tumbled to the ground and lay there laughing in each other's arms as a gentle snow fell over them.

It wasn't until the lift had moved on that Skylar realized that Brookman Mill was quite a ways off and she was hardly prepared to ski her way to the bottom of the steep hill facing her. "Now what?" she asked Mark, glancing uneasily at the narrow trail that led to the mill.

"Just follow me," he told her shouldering both pairs of skis. "I've made this trek a few times. Stay behind me and walk in my tracks."

Once again, Skylar did as he ordered, content to study the play of muscles in his shoulders and the cocky, but adorable, way he held his head to one side as they trudged off through the snow.

Chapter 15

Deena stood at her bedroom window and stared into the white swirl that was raging outside, realizing that the weatherman's prediction of light snow flurries had been way off track. More than a foot of snow had fallen since midafternoon and a rainy sleet had begun to come down, coating everything in ice. It was only five o'clock in the evening, but it was already dark outside, and she knew that the road from town would soon be impassable and access to the outlying cabins on the property could be cut off. She turned on the television in time to hear the weatherman issue a severe winter storm warning. Things did not look good for the Roaring Fork Valley area.

A bus load of rowdy college students from Denver had arrived late in the afternoon, just as the storm descended with a fury, and they had been very unhappy to find the lifts closed and all guests confined to the lodge or their

THE EDITOR'S "THANK YOU" FREE GIFTS INCLUDE:

- Two NEW Kimani Romance™ Novels
- Two exciting surprise gifts

168 XDL ELWZ 368 XDL ELXZ

FIRST NAME	LAST NAME
ADDRESS	
APT.#	CITY
STATE/PROV.	ZIP/POSTAL CODE

Thank You!

Offer limited to one per household and not valid to current subscribers of Kimani Romance.

Your Privacy – Kimani Press is committed to protecting your privacy. Our Privacy Policy is available online at www.eHarlequin.com or upon request from the Reader Service. From time to time we make our lists of customers available to reputable firms who may have a product or service of interest to you. If you would prefer for us not to share your name and address, please check here. ☐

DETACH AND MAIL CARD TODAY!

Accepting your 2 free books and 2 free gifts places you under no obligation to buy anything. You may keep the books and gifts and return the shipping statement marked "cancel." If you do not cancel, about a month later we'll send you 4 additional books and bill you just $4.69 each in the U.S. or $5.24 each in Canada, plus 25¢ shipping & handling per book and applicable taxes if any.* That's the complete price and — compared to cover prices of $5.99 each in the U.S. and $6.99 each in Canada — it's quite a bargain! You may cancel at any time, but if you choose to continue, every month we'll send you 4 more books, which you may either purchase at the discount price or return to us and cancel your subscription.

*Terms and prices subject to change without notice. Sales tax applicable in N.Y. Canadian residents will be charged applicable provincial taxes and GST. All orders subject to approval. Books received may vary. Credit or debit balances in a customer's account(s) may be offset by any other outstanding balance owed by or to the customer. Please allow 4 to 6 weeks for delivery.

If offer card is missing write to: The Reader Service, 3010 Walden Ave., P.O. Box 1867, Buffalo, NY 14240-1867

POSTAGE WILL BE PAID BY ADDRESSEE

THE READER SERVICE
3010 WALDEN AVE
PO BOX 1867
BUFFALO NY 14240-9952

cabin suites until the extreme weather alert was lifted. The restless students had taken over the lounge and were still at the bar, drinking and singing and shouting and generally raising hell. Dealing with them, as well as an overly nervous couple who had been adamant about leaving for the airport, had exhausted Deena completely.

A heavy dump of powder might be great for skiers, but a total snow-in was never good for business. Arriving guests could be stranded at the airport for days, and those currently staying at the resort might have to cancel excursions and outdoor activities. She sighed, uneasy about going through the storm without Jerome. She longed for his patient reassurance and strength as she prepared for a long, tense night of watching and waiting to see how bad the storm would become. She knew how to start the backup generators if the power should go out, and the staff stood ready with flashlights, oil lamps and candles if required. But Mark, who was in charge of snow-removal had not yet returned from his outing with Skylar, and Deena prayed that they were okay.

Picking up the phone she dialed the number to the ski school office, anxious to know if anyone had heard from Mark. John, the assistant director, picked up.

"No, Deena. He's not here, but I do know he got off the lift with Skylar near Brookman Mill."

"Really? Well, that's pretty far out. They'd have to walk back to the lodge in this weather," Deena remarked, wondering why Mark hadn't used his handheld two-way to call into his office to tell John where he was.

"Don't worry," John said. "I'm sure they'll be along any minute."

"I hope so," Deena said. Then she added, "Ask Paul to go

ahead and start checking the snow removal equipment, as well as our supply of rock salt so he and Mark can get out early in the morning to get this icy situation under control."

"Will do," John agreed, clicking off.

The phone rang as soon as Deena replaced the receiver. She snatched it up, hoping it would be Mark or Skylar, but was equally relieved to hear Jerome's voice on the other end of the line.

"I've been watching the Weather Channel. How's it going out there?" he asked.

"Terrible," Deena replied. "Nearly a foot of new snow since two o'clock and it's sleeting now. There's a winter storm warning out. By morning, things could be real bad. We closed the lifts early and made sure everyone was off the mountainside, but Mark and Skylar are still out."

"Mark and Skylar?" Jerome repeated. "Uh…where are they?"

Deena went on to tell Jerome about Skylar's ski lesson, including the fact that it was obvious that Mark had more than a casual interest in her sister.

"They'd make a nice couple," Jerome casually commented. "After Skylar's disaster with that guy in Tampa, Mark Jorgen might just be the kind of man she needs. He's mature, stable and a good-looking guy. Skylar could do worse."

"That's exactly what I told her," Deena said. "However, she's being very stubborn. Swears she's through with men, but I know her. She's not as tough as she wants me to think she is. Nothing to do but let her handle things her way."

"I hear you," Jerome replied. "Well, don't worry. I'm sure they'll be in soon. Mark knows his way around the property. He'll take good care of his boss's sister."

"I hope you're right," Deena replied. "Now, if I can just keep the guests calm."

"Open a few bottles of champagne and give them complimentary drinks. That'll keep their minds off the weather," Jerome told Deena.

"Good idea," Deena agreed. "No one's complaining…yet." A short pause. "I miss you."

"I miss you, too."

"How's your dad?" The silence that followed told Deena that the situation was not good.

"He's alert. Talking," was all Jerome could offer.

"What do his doctors say?"

Another long pause. "That he has a few good weeks left," Jerome managed in a voice rough with pain. "They've done all they can. It's just a matter of time."

Deena swallowed back the sob that crowded her throat and inhaled sharply, feeling the distress in Jerome's voice. "You're staying, of course?"

"Yeah. Until the end. I can't do anything else."

"I know. I know," Deena said in a comforting tone. "As soon as things here become a bit more stable and the weather breaks, I'll be there."

"Deena…you don't have to…" he started.

"Yes, I do. This place can manage itself while I'm gone. The staff knows what needs to be done. And besides, I'll have Skylar here to watch over everything, and she's doing a heck of a job."

Exhausted, and nearly frozen, yet flushed with delight after her exciting day with Mark, Skylar literally collapsed when she returned to her room. After giving Deena a quick call to let her know that she was safely back at the lodge,

Skylar stripped off her wet clothing, pulled on her robe and stretched out on her bed to let the strain of the day drain away.

Following in Mark's footsteps, she had hiked to Brookman Mill and tromped around outside the rustic landmark with him while listening to the story of the original settlers, now thought to be a ghostly presence that watched over the mill. Taking shelter inside, they had found a cozy, sun-warmed spot beneath a huge paned window to sit and talk, learning more about each other.

Mark had told her about his childhood, his early years as a competitive skier and how close he had been with his mother. Though he was glad to be managing his own life now, Skylar sensed that he was infused with guilt over the professional and personal break he'd created with his mom, and remained conflicted about their relationship. He spoke openly and honestly about past romantic entanglements, of which there had been many, though none, he swore, had been serious enough to consider making a trip to the altar.

"When I look back," he had admitted, "that time in my life blends into one long blur of too much liquor, too little commitment and very little conversation. I never took the time to get to know any of the women I dated, and they really weren't interested in knowing me. Life was one big party."

"Then life at Scenic Ridge must be a bore," Skylar had commented.

"Not at all," he'd said, leaning over to give her a soft kiss. He'd held on to her chin with two fingers as he'd watched for her reaction. "This is exactly where I want to be, and with no one else but you."

She had removed his hand from her chin, slid it around her waist and turned around to settle her back against his chest. Sitting in his arms, she told him about her family; her childhood and what growing up in a seaside city like Tampa had been like; and how she'd thought her sister had lost her mind when she left Florida to live in the Colorado mountains. She had told him nearly everything about herself, except the fact that she was a multi-millionaire and that she was, most likely, unable to have children. However, she did admit that her career as a paralegal had begun to grow predictable and stifling and that working as a concierge was much more exciting.

"You said there had been a special man in your life back in Tampa," he had prompted.

"Yes, there was," Skylar had confessed, now ready to go on and tell Mark all about Lewis. "And as I told you, our relationship ended abruptly when I found out he was cheating on me. It hurt to know that the man I'd trusted with my heart could be unfaithful."

"I'm sorry you had to go through that," Mark had replied, massaging her back. "Is that why you wanted to leave Tampa? To forget about him?"

"One of the reasons," Skylar had replied.

"Do you still love him?"

She had shrugged off answering and slipped out of Mark's arms, then, standing as she told him, "I'd rather not talk about love. Who knows what it is, what it means? I just know that I never want to feel as disappointed in a man as I did about Lewis."

"Fine," Mark agreed, rising. "And as far as I'm concerned, you never will again." He'd kissed her on her neck and held her close, as if infusing his promise into her soul. "Do you believe me?" he'd asked.

Turning to face him, she'd told him, "I think I do."

"Good," Mark had replied, a touch of relief in his voice. "And now that that is settled, we'd really better start back."

"Yes, it's snowing pretty hard," Skylar agreed.

The wind had picked up and the snow flurries had turned into blinding sheets of white by the time they arrived at the trail leading back. Mark convinced her to follow him on skis down a hill that brought them to the service road, and setting off, she had been terrified. But she kept her focus on Mark and stayed with him, proudly congratulating herself when she reached the bottom of the hill, still upright. From there, they had plodded through intense snow, freezing wind and stinging sleet to make their way back to the lodge on foot.

Now, Skylar placed her fingertips to the side of her mouth where Mark had planted a quick kiss before hurrying off to see what needed to be done before the full impact of the snowstorm hit. She grinned, reveling in the sensation of pleasure that slid through her body like warm honey. All she wanted to do was lie on her back and relive every moment of her day with Mark, to taste his kisses again, feel his embraces, hear his voice whispering in her ear. And, as much as she hated to admit it, she was helplessly under his spell and hoped to stay there forever.

After a short rest, Skylar pushed herself off the bed and made it into the bathroom. Twenty minutes later, she emerged from the shower, feeling refreshed and renewed. After drying off, she pulled on her bright yellow terrycloth robe, put on her fluffy Big Bird slippers. She went to her closet and took out a pair of red wool slacks, a black sweater and her black flats, preparing to go downstairs to dinner. Being snowbound was really not so bad. With everyone crowded into the dining rooms and the lounges, it would be like one big family party.

Just as she was about to plug in her hair dryer, a clap of thunder split the air and everything went dark.

"Damn!" she blurted out, shocked at having been plunged into sudden darkness so quickly. "This sucks," she muttered, knotting the belt to her robe a bit tighter. In pitch-black darkness, Skylar groped her way from the bathroom into the kitchenette where she kept a flashlight next to the microwave oven. She flipped it on. Nothing happened.

"Dead batteries," she muttered, reaching into the cabinet over the stove to pull out the candles and matches she kept inside for just such an emergency. She quickly lit several candles. Moving through her suite she placed them in the bathroom, the bedroom and the sitting area, bathing the rooms in soft yellow light.

"So much for drying my hair," she remarked as she removed the towel and began to hand-dry her locks. With a touch of gel and a finger comb, she knew she could pull herself together enough to be presentable. She had to get dressed and downstairs right away, to be available for the guests, who were probably panicking about being in the dark. Deena was going to need all of her staff to be alert and on the job in order to deal with this situation.

Just as Skylar was about to tackle her hair, there was a tapping sound at her door. Taking a candle with her she went to look through the peephole.

"Mark!" she said aloud, blinking at the distorted image

in the small round hole. He was holding several flashlights and still wearing his red parka.

"Yes, it's me," he called back. "Thought I'd bring up an extra light, if you need it."

"Oh, right," Skylar blew the words out on the edge of a sigh. Damn. She was a mess. Her hair was tangled and wet, her face was scrubbed bare of makeup and she was naked underneath her robe. "Just a minute," she yelled back, adjusting her robe. No time to put on anything else. Cracking the door, she leaned into the narrow opening. "You didn't have to bother," she began.

"No problem," Mark replied, staring at her, taken by her natural beauty. She looked young, fresh and warm and he knew she was probably wearing very little under that robe. Their day together was still fresh in his mind, her kisses still lingering on his lips. Clamping down with his jaw, and determined not to show his reaction in a way that might prove embarrassing, he jammed his hands into the pockets of his parka and took a deep breath. "Paul said to check the window in your bathroom. He said the glass is loose and I need to tape it up. We're expecting some pretty fierce winds tonight."

"Uh, fine," Skylar said, pulling the door open wider. She touched her wet hair, suddenly embarrassed to be caught looking like a total wreck. "It has been rattling like crazy and I was getting worried about it cracking or falling out."

"Don't want that to happen," Mark assured her as he entered the room. He looked around. "Cozy, with the candles and all."

"It's light," Skylar replied matter of factly, watching as Mark unzipped his parka and hung it on the back of a chair. He had changed out of his wet ski clothing and was wearing faded jeans and a soft blue turtleneck. He reached down and removed a roll of duct tape from the inside pocket of his jacket. "This ought to do the job. No sense in taking a chance."

"Right," Skylar agreed, beginning to feel a coil of heat gather between her thighs. In the shadowy dimness he resembled a dark silhouette that was both powerful and tender. She liked the way he moved, in the easy manner of a professional athlete who had total control of his body. A sudden fantasy spun into her mind: he was a mountain man, come to rescue her from a devastating snowstorm, and not sent by Paul to fix a rattling window. Here she was in a secluded mountain resort with a handsome international Olympic skier, who according to Deena was one of the most eligible bachelors in the world. Suddenly, Skylar wasn't nearly as worried about Mark as she was about herself and the fact that she was wearing only a robe over her naked body.

"Go ahead and check it out," she told him, breaking out of her fantasy. "If the window might blow out, please fix it."

Skylar followed Mark into the bathroom, aware that every toiletry she owned was scattered across the counter and she hated for him to see her most private space in such a state, but there was nothing she could do.

He went to the window, flashed his light over it and then tapped the glass. "It's loose all right. Can't leave it like this." He turned around. "Uh…can you hold the flashlight on this while I tape it up?" Mark asked, extending the light to her. "I'm gonna need both hands."

"Sure, no problem. Give it to me." She stepped closer, took the light and aimed it over his shoulder, toward the foggy window.

"Good, this won't take long," Mark said, focusing on the job. He deftly unrolled one length of tape after another and secured them in a crisscross pattern over the glass, making sure he filled in all the gaps along the edges. "All finished," he declared, suddenly turning around at the same time that Skylar stepped forward to examine his handiwork.

Their bodies swung together.

With a gasp, Skylar stiffened, but stood very still. Not too long ago, she'd told Mark that he would never make love to her, that he ought to find some other woman to fulfill his fantasy. She'd told Deena that she was not in the market for a man. And she'd told herself that she needed time to get over Lewis, to heal her heart and her badly bruised ego before getting caught up in any kind of romance. But now here she stood with her eyes locked to Mark's, both confused and clear about what she wanted.

Unable to help himself, Mark lowered his gaze and fastened his eyes on the swell of Skylar's breasts, which were pressing prominently against the front of her robe. He wanted to reach out and trace a finger along the open edge of her collar, move his hand so close to her skin that he could feel the heat radiating from her body. But of course, he didn't dare. He was not going to press his luck and risk offending her, even though he sensed that she would not deny him if he tried.

All day, he had gone to great lengths to avoid pushing too hard, too fast. They had kissed, embraced and talked, but he had not let his hands stray to parts of her body that had not been exposed. He'd made that mistake when she'd come to his cabin and he wasn't about to ask for more trouble.

A delicate scent of apples came from her dark, damp

hair, sending a jolt of desire straight to his groin and making him hard. He wanted to grab her, bury his face between her soft brown breasts, press his lips to nipples that he knew would be hard, firm and sweet. The fire she was igniting inside him was one that Mark knew could only be extinguished by claiming Skylar completely. Would he ever be able to do that? he wondered, closely watching her for any sign that he had a chance.

From their very first encounter, she had let him know that she was a woman in total control of herself, and one not easily impressed. While other women had thrown themselves at him and made his conquests easy, this was a woman he would have to approach very carefully if he expected to earn her trust. He hadn't had much practice with this kind of a pursuit, and the restraint it required was driving him mad, as well as initiating a blaze of anticipation that burned hotly in his belly.

Skylar felt as if every nerve in her body had been lit with a match. Holding her breath, she let Mark run his gaze over her breasts, up to her lips, across her eyes and back down, without moving a muscle. She could easily pull back to avoid an encounter, but she didn't. Shifting to one side, she silently dared him to make a move, and when he shifted in tandem with her, she sank back against the marble countertop and rested on the edge, parting her legs as she raised her face toward him.

Mark didn't hesitate to accept her dare, embracing her with an urgency that made Skylar go weak. Quickly, he positioned his hips between her legs, his lips against her neck. He sagged against her, giving up a deep moan of pleasure, inhaling her scent while steadying himself.

Skylar wrapped both arms around Mark's shoulders, pulled him more deeply into the split of her robe, and locked her bare thighs around his legs. Raising her hips, she pressed the pulsing heat between her thighs to the rough fabric of his jeans, pressing harder and harder, holding her breath while firming her grip on his shoulders.

Lifting his face from her neck, Mark hooked his thumbs into the collar of her robe and slid it off her shoulders. The fabric settled in a soft pile at her back. Looking into the mirror behind Skylar he let his eyes travel the length of her spine, to the curve of her waist, down to the flare of her hips. Leaning back, he took in the full round shape of her breasts, standing erect with their dark brown nipples pointed lusciously at him. With a moan, he sought her lips and this time his kiss was solid and insistent, as if pushing her to admit that she wanted all that he could give.

With a slight push, Skylar moved upward to sit fully on the cool black granite countertop, her legs clamping even tighter around Mark's thighs.

Mark moved his hand low, swept it softly across her stomach, and then between the open folds of her robe to find the silky skin of her inner thighs. Ever so gently, he massaged one leg, then the other, inching closer and closer to the mound of curly hair that lay between his touch and her fulfillment. Its dampness caught him off guard, causing a catch in his throat that made him cry out, and he wondered briefly if he had been the cause of her wetness or if she was still moist from her shower. Either way, her rocking motion was driving him wild, pushing him deeper and deeper into his mission to satisfy her. He wasn't concerned about himself, though he could feel a rush of need vibrating deep in his stomach. Making Skylar happy was all that mattered now.

When she sucked in a breath and opened wider to him, he slipped a finger into her core and stroked her wetness with a feathery touch, rocking back and forth, his lips still sheltered hers, his soul aflame with the joy of bringing her to fulfillment. When she cried out and shuddered convulsively against him, he finally broke off their kiss and eased his hand to rest against her thigh, feeling as if he had been to heaven and back and hoping she felt the same.

I don't want this to ever end, Skylar silently admitted, clinging to Mark, wishing he did not possess such a mesmerizing, hypnotizing effect on her. Breathing hard, she pressed her face into his soft sweater, knowing their encounter had to end at this point. She could not give him more. Not now.

When he pulled back, she let him go with a kiss on his forehead and a sheepish, but grateful smile. He wasn't going to ask for more than what she'd offered and she knew he would not push her.

Chapter 16

On Sunday morning, when Count Wilhelm Willard's private airplane touched down at Aspen/Pitkin County airport, Virina settled her slim hips more firmly into the soft beige padding of the Italian leather seat and turned her profile to the window. Huge piles of snow lined the perimeter of the airport, rising high enough to create a frozen wall of packed ice between the busy landing strip and the area where small planes, like the one she was in, filled a parking lot.

She studied the lines of mini jets which, in her opinion, resembled colorful birds that had been temporarily grounded and were poised to take off once more. The sky was vividly blue, free of clouds and sunlight bathed the snow-covered mountains in the distance. The setting was picture-postcard perfect, with its quaint buildings and tall Aspen trees rising majestically as a backdrop—just as she remembered.

It had been five years since Virina had been to Aspen, and she was glad to be back, though she knew that the exclusive ski town was becoming alarmingly popular and much more accessible, luring all kinds of regular folk to the rustic enclave of the rich and famous. Hopefully, the better hotels, restaurants, shops and clubs were holding firmly to their rigid standards.

"So, you said this is your first time in Aspen?" she asked Richard, who was sitting across from her, finishing his third Bloody Mary and looking out the window.

"That's right," he confirmed, leaning forward in his seat. "And as I said, I'm really looking forward to enjoying myself even though I've got a lot of work to do. I've covered ski club reunions many times, and I know that things can get kind of crazy. The crowds, the social scene, the competitions. There'll be a bunch of parties and celebrities all over the place, so I hope to get some great candid shots and impromptu interviews for *Sports Challenge*."

"I'm sure you will," Virina concurred. "When celebrities come up here, they're so much more relaxed and willing to talk to the media. As long as you don't crowd them or make a pest of yourself, you'll probably get much more from them than you think." She reached for her heavy designer tote, slipped the copy of the magazine that she had been reading into the side pocket and then handed her empty champagne glass to Henri, the flight attendant. "Now, you told me that you ski," Virina reminded Richard. "Are you good?"

"Average."

"Only average?" Virina arched a brow and grinned. "Come on. Is that the truth? Usually when someone says that, they're afraid to admit that they can handle themselves on the slopes pretty well."

"You got me," Richard confessed. "I lied. I'm really a klutz. Not close to average."

"So, you're not going to enter any of the competitions during the reunion?"

"Naw," Richard said. "I'm what you might call a chronic beginner. I take lessons, ski for the weekend, then forget everything I learned. Each time I go out, I have to start all over. Can't seem to master anything." He chuckled. "Maybe one day it will stick."

Nodding, Virina wet her lips in a knowing way. "You've probably had poor instructors. A good instructor like myself or Mark could cure you."

"Think so?" Richard teased, grinning playfully at Virina.

"Definitely," she said, picking up on his relaxed mood, unsure if it was due to the Bloody Marys he'd been drinking or if he was actually flirting with her. Either way, it didn't matter. She found Richard Nobel to be terribly attractive, but he was married, and she had made up her mind that there was no possibility of getting him into her bed while they were at Scenic Ridge. That kind of complication, she didn't need. "I'm going to get you out on that powder and teach you the right way to do it," Virina promised. "Unwarranted fear of failing is the only thing standing between a good time gliding down the mountainside and a miserable time on your backside. I'll set aside a few hours tomorrow to show you what I mean."

"I'd be down with that," Richard quipped, twirling his drink on the gleaming cherry wood table between them. "Might be fun."

"Trust me, it will be an eye-opening adventure, and I'm going to hold you to it," Virina replied. *If only I could teach you a few other things when we're off the slopes and alone,* she wished, assessing Richard closely. A romantic affair—with a future to it, was exactly what she needed right now and she planned to keep her antennae up for suitable prospects while she was in Aspen.

When the plane had come to a complete stop, Henri opened the door and released the steps. Virina pulled her oversize Dior sunglasses over her eyes, slipped her short, blue frost fox coat over her shoulders, grabbed her Gucci tote and preceded Richard through the door, nodding her thanks to Henri.

As soon as her stylish boots touched the ground, she lifted her chin even higher, took off across the tarmac in her most dramatic catwalk stride and entered the terminal building with Richard hurrying along behind her, anxious to keep up.

At the passenger pick-up area, Virina paused in front of a knot of drivers who were holding up signs as they waited for their passengers to arrive. She scanned each sign, and after not finding her name, stepped outside and frowned. Hotel shuttles, town cars, Range Rovers, a few Hummers and a black limousine were parked in the passenger pick-up area.

"I thought Mark was arranging for my limo," she complained, her voice high-pitched and tight. "A white one, I told him, not black, and with a bar stocked with *Linie Aquavit*."

"Probably on its way," Richard offered as he walked a few paces farther down the sidewalk, scanned the line of cars and then returned.

"It should be here right now," Virina spat out. She whirled around and focused on Henri, the flight attendant, who was busy struggling to get Virina's skis and her five-piece set of Louis Vuitton luggage onto a rolling cart.

"Henri. Where's my limo? Find out what's going on and let's get out of here!" she demanded.

"Right away. I'll check on it," he called over to Virina, who had turned around and was walking back inside the busy terminal building.

With a grunt of annoyance, Virina sank down into an empty chair near the rental car area and glared at no one in particular while Richard hovered nervously nearby.

"I absolutely hate waiting around like this," she complained. "Wasting valuable time. There are so many things I could be doing other than sitting here." She pulled out her cell phone and began punching in numbers. "I don't understand how Mark could have mixed things up. I specifically told him to make sure the limo was on time. He knows how much I detest delays like this."

"I'm sure your car will be along," Richard lamely comforted, moving aside to let a woman pushing a stroller pass by. When the woman gasped and stopped abruptly, he stepped back, unsure of what she was going to do and thinking something must be wrong with her.

"Virina Dagrun!" the woman called out in a heavily accented voice that sounded like German to Richard. She quickly maneuvered the baby stroller closer to Virina and bent down. "You are the face of Deleur Cosmetics, aren't you?" She beamed at Virina while fumbling in her purse to pull out a mint-colored tube of cream, which she waved back and forth in the air. "I just love your night cream. Love it! Took years off my face. I can't live without it."

Smiling, Virina clicked off her cell phone and stuck it back into her tote, gracing the woman with a megawatt smile. "Why, thank you." She extended her hand and touched gloved fingers with the stranger's in a polite, but tepid greeting. "Everyone who tries it is hooked immediately. So glad it's doing the job for you."

"Oh, it is. My skin has never been so smooth!" the stranger gushed.

"And you're a very beautiful woman, so I can see that you'll need my cream for many years to come…it's so important to maintain, you know?" A throaty laugh slipped from Virina's lips and brought a beaming smile from the woman. Looking up, Virina scanned the lady from head to toe. "Gorgeous Prada puffer," she finally commented, giving her approval of her admirer's attire.

"Thanks. Isn't it delicious? Now, may I have your autograph?" the woman rambled breathlessly, digging once again into her oversize hand bag. She located a crumpled piece of paper and a pen, which she held out to Virina.

"But of course," Virina agreed with a wave of her hand, clearly not interested in using the materials the woman was offering. She reached into her tote and removed a peach-colored notepad and her silver Tiffany pen, wrote her name with a flourish on the paper and then handed it back to the woman, who gushed her thanks and moved on.

Richard, who had watched the exchange with interest, stepped over and studied Virina. "Seems you're about as well-known as your son, huh?"

Glancing over at him, Virina pointed her chin at Richard and blinked several times, as if trying to grasp his meaning. "Why, yes. Of course, I am," she bluntly replied. "More so in Europe, of course. As the face of Deleur Cosmctics, I owe everything to my clients, and I enjoy chatting with them when they take the time to stop and speak with me."

Before Richard could respond, Henri returned to tell Virina, "Your transportation has arrived."

"Thank God," she snapped, rising. She swept past Richard, through the glass double doors and emerged on the curb once more, where she scowled into the sunlight, clearly frustrated. "Where?" she demanded. "I don't see a white limo out here."

"Over there. That red Jeep," Henri replied. "The woman driving it said she was sent to pick you up and take you to Scenic Ridge."

"She looks exactly as I expected," Skylar remarked to herself as she shut off the engine and stared at the striking blonde woman draped in fur who was shouting at a small man pushing a luggage cart. Virina Dagrun was mature, yet youthful looking at the same time, and must have been wearing at least ten thousand dollars worth of clothing by Skylar's calculation. She was tall, slim, delicately pale and bore little resemblance to her powerfully built, muscular, tawny son, who seemed casually unaware of how handsome he was.

Everything about Virina screamed money, high style and class, and her striking figure was drawing curious stares from some of the people rushing past, who stopped to stare at her, obviously thinking that she must be some kind of a celebrity.

Skylar bit her lip, surprised by the sensation of envy that flooded through her and gave her pause. All around her, she saw gorgeously dressed people wearing outrageously flamboyant clothes as they hurried to get their luggage loaded into limos, luxury cars and fancy SUVs.

"So what?" Skylar murmured, resting her gaze on a

man wearing a chocolate-colored suede long coat and knee-high leather boots that were so heavily tooled with silver that they resembled works of art.

I could afford to drive a Hummer and wear thousands of dollars worth of fancy clothes, too, if I wanted to make sure everyone knew how rich I was, she thought, feeling a bit grumpy. *I could turn heads and stop traffic. I could glam myself up and walk around with a flunky tagging along behind me juggling a load of designer luggage.* However, Skylar knew that her self-imposed circumstances prevented her from flaunting her money, and it was just as well. She was getting along fine with the staff at the lodge, and they would probably either snub her, resent her or hit her up for a loan if they knew the truth.

Thank God, Mark didn't have a clue about her wealth, either. He seemed totally turned off by people with too much money and bored with the whole status symbol thing. He dressed simply, drove a Range Rover, not a Hummer, and lived in a cabin in the woods when he could afford to live in a luxury hotel. He was tired of people with too much cash and too little substance and was content to live a normal, unpretentious life. So far, he seemed to respect the fact that Skylar's needs were as simple as his and she didn't plan on upsetting what they had found together by suddenly flashing a lot of cash.

Now, Skylar prepared herself to face Virina. Steeling herself for whatever might come, she got out of her Jeep while mentally rehearsing her greeting. Mark had warned her that his mother was not easy to please and was rarely satisfied with anything anyone did for her. His suggestion was to ignore any remarks that his mother might make that could be considered insulting and remain pleasantly detached from her drama.

Hello, Miss Dagrun. Welcome to Aspen. Sorry we weren't able to arrange for a limo to pick you up, but everything was absolutely booked. Black Winter Sports Reunion and all. The mountain is packed with visitors. The words bounced around in Skylar's head, drumming into her brain.

However, before Skylar had advanced two feet toward her passenger, she heard Virina tell the man who was with her, "I'm not riding in that dirty thing!"

Sucking in a sharp gulp of cold air, Skylar crunched her way across the fresh snow, wishing she had taken the time to run through the car wash on her way to the airport—mud was splattered over the front and sides of her Jeep. But, running late, she had had to make a choice: arrive on time or arrive in a clean, shiny car. Obviously she'd called it wrong.

Dismissing Virina's remark, Skylar extended her hand to Mark's mother, who pointedly ignored it. "Hello, I'm Skylar Webster, the concierge at Scenic Ridge. You must be Miss Dagrun."

"I am," Virina grudgingly stated, arms folded at her waist. "Where's my limo? I specifically asked Mark to arrange it."

"Yes, I know, and he turned your request over to me." A long beat. "Every limousine in Aspen is booked. We're very busy right now. However," she nodded at Henri and pressed on, "if you'll put Miss Dagrun's bags in my car and her skis on the rack, we can be on our way." Then she glanced pleadingly at the handsome man standing beside Virina, as if asking for his assistance, too.

"Sounds good," Richard spoke up reaching over to shake Skylar's hand. "I'm Richard Nobel, here to cover the reunion for *Sports Challenge* magazine."

A surge of relief flooded through Skylar. At least the man was pleasant and hopefully he would be able to calm Mark's mother down. She shook his hand, giving it a warm squeeze. "Oh, yes. You're staying at Scenic Ridge, too, aren't you?"

"Right," Richard said, shouldering his single duffel bag.

"But I thought you were coming in on a later flight," Skylar remarked as they started toward the Jeep.

"I was, but Miss Dagrun offered me a seat on her jet, so we could fly in together. How could I refuse?" He chuckled and glanced at Virina, who rolled her eyes and gave her platinum hair a quick shake.

"And aren't you glad you didn't have to deal with the craziness of a commercial flight?" Virina offered, her tone a tad less frigid. "This airport is a madhouse."

"I've been here when it's worse," Skylar added, while keeping her focus on Richard. "Is your cameraman with you?" she asked.

"No. He's coming in on the later flight, along with the bulk of the press. I'm sure the airport will be jammed tonight and all day tomorrow, too," Richard finished.

"For sure," Skylar agreed. "The reunion activities start tonight and every hotel is packed."

"I understand you're throwing quite a bash tonight at Scenic Ridge, aren't you?" Richard added.

"Yeah. The Slide and Glide Gala. It's turned out to be the hottest ticket in town."

Virina stepped up and linked her arm through Richard's. "Be sure to save a dance for me," she whispered into Richard's ear.

Skylar widened her eyes, unsure of what was going on. "So, you two are friends?" she ventured, trying to put it all together.

"No. We met by accident at a restaurant in New York," Virina rushed to say. "When Richard told me what kind of work he did and that he was coming to Aspen for the Black Winter Sports Reunion, I was thrilled. I invited him to fly in with me. I don't enjoy flying alone, you see, it's so much more fun with company."

"That was nice of you," Skylar admitted, doubting Virina's version of the story. There was something about the way the woman spoke that definitely had a false ring to it. "Well, it'll be great to have both of you at Scenic Ridge. Shall we get going?" Skylar asked.

Without waiting for a reply, she walked around to the back of the Jeep, opened the hatch, and waited until Henri had loaded the luggage and fastened Virina's skis to the top of the car. When Henri headed back inside the terminal, Richard opened the passenger side door for Virina and stood to the side. She made an icy grimace, reluctantly climbed inside and then sat down, remaining rigidly positioned on the edge of her seat as if the cushions were as dirty as the outside of the car.

Once they were underway, Skylar relaxed and let her thoughts wander to Mark, who was never far from her mind. Since their encounter in her suite last week, they had begun to spend most of their free time together while keeping their attraction under the radar. The last thing Skylar wanted was for her fast-growing interest in Mark to become a distraction—or the subject of kitchen gossip among the staff.

They had gone into Aspen for dinner, to Snowmass Village to shop, ice-skating at midnight on the rink at the square and had trekked once again up to Brookman Mill to sit and talk and linger and kiss.

Skylar knew she was falling hard for Mark and was doing little to keep it from happening. It filled her with joy to realize how quickly and how perfectly they actually clicked; that their conversations were so easy and engaging; that they each filled a need in the other's life that both had thought would be difficult to fulfill. However, Skylar knew she was not doing a very good job of hiding her feelings for Mark, and very soon, everyone at Scenic Ridge would know that they were a couple.

Mark stayed on Skylar's mind day and night. She waited by the phone when he said he would call and counted down the hours and the minutes until they were together again. The undercover aspect of their relationship created a heightened sense of anticipation that kept Skylar tightly strung, breathlessly anxious to be with Mark again.

Mark made no effort to hide the fact that he was falling in love with her and seemed blissfully happy about it. His pleasure radiated in bright, unmistakable rays that beamed from his face and tugged at her heart. She would never forget the intense way he had looked at her when he'd admitted to her that before her arrival at Scenic Ridge, he had felt lonely and lost amidst the constant crush of people who surrounded him. Now, he felt complete.

Mark's kisses were driving Skylar mad. God, how she wanted him, totally and completely, but she knew it would be a dangerous move to give in to her fantasy and go all the way too quickly. First of all, she wasn't going to be at Scenic Ridge forever: as soon as Deena found a replacement, Skylar was going to leave and go back to Florida—back to the warm, tropical climate she was used to, and maybe back to school. Secondly, her heart was barely healed from her last romantic disaster and she didn't want a repeat of that kind of pain anytime soon.

For now, Skylar knew that Mark's kisses and caresses were all that she could accept from him and luckily, Mark was patiently adhering to the boundaries she'd placed on their fast-developing relationship. He was caring, tender, sincerely interested in what mattered to her, and she respected his restraint.

When she came to a four-way stop, Skylar cleared her mind, braked and then chanced a glance into the rearview mirror, immediately catching Virina's attention.

"If you're the concierge," Virina began, in a clipped voice, "what are you doing out here driving people around? Who's tending to the guests back at the lodge?"

Skylar gave Virina a weak half-smile. "Kathy, the food service director, is filling in for me. She's been at Scenic Ridge forever. She can handle anything that might come up."

"The food service director? Doesn't sound very efficient," Virina remarked, not trying to mask her displeasure. "I thought hotel staff like yourself had to be on site at all times…available to the guests. What kind of a place is Scenic Ridge?"

"First, it's a ski school, designed more for students than tourists, though we get a fair number of vacationers. It's set up to be a safe, comfortable place to learn how to ski and we get a lot of people who have never seen snow before, let alone been on the mountainside."

"So Mark has told me." Virina sniffed loudly. "I do applaud his desire to work with underprivileged children and with those who are adventuresome enough to expose themselves to a new sport. I guess it bolsters their self-confidence and all of that, but I doubt Mark will want to teach at your ski school very long. He's so talented, you know. He really ought to be at a much larger facility. Some place that will challenge him, allow him to continue to grow. Do you know what I mean?"

Unfortunately, I do, Skylar wanted to say, but instead, she simply murmured an unintelligible response. "Scenic Ridge might be smaller than other well-known ski schools like Buttermilk and Snowmass, but the staff is just like family and Mark fits right in. We all help each other out and try to keep things fairly uncomplicated. In fact, the owner, Deena Simpson, is my sister."

"Oh, really?" Virina managed vaguely, now leaning forward. "I see. So, it's a small bed and breakfast, family kind of place?"

Squinting into the mirror, Skylar chose her words carefully. "No, it's more like a miniature Swiss chalet kind of place that is surprisingly elegant and extremely comfortable. You're gonna love it, I promise."

Sinking back, Virina let her face go slack, and then asked with a smirk, "How long have you been the concierge there?"

"A little over a month," Skylar answered with pride. "My first job as a concierge and so far, I'm really enjoying it."

"So? You're new at this?" Virina coughed lightly.

"Very new."

"What were you doing before you came to Aspen?"

Skylar opened her mouth to respond, and then shut it, reconsidering her answer. How much did she really want to tell Mark's mother? Virina Dagrun struck Skylar as the kind of person who would not hesitate to do a bit of background digging once she realized that her son was interested in the concierge. Why give the woman any ammunition? "I'm from a small town in Florida. I was unemployed when my sister offered me the job up here," Skylar answered truthfully, struggling to hide her smile.

"My, my," Virina murmured. "You must have really needed a job in a bad way to leave sunny Florida and come to work in such a remote, cold place."

"I needed a change," Skylar responded, watching Virina in the mirror. "And so far, it's been a good one."

With a shrug, Virina let the conversation drop and snuggled deeper into her blue fox fur while Skylar pulled onto Interstate 82 and focused on the road.

After a few minutes of silence, Virina spoke up again. "I want to stop by the St. Regis Hotel. Just for a second, if you don't mind. I want to see if a friend of mine has checked in."

Skylar nodded as she executed a curve in the road. "Sure, it's on our way."

The parking lot of the St. Regis Hotel resembled a luxury car showroom. It was packed with Jaguars, Escalades, Hummers, shiny Ford pickup trucks and several Mercedes Benz SUVs. Skylar sat behind the wheel of her Jeep, making small talk with Richard Nobel as they waited for Virina to return.

As soon as Skylar had pulled up at the entrance to the ritzy hotel, Virina had sprung from the Jeep without even waiting for the doorman to help her out. With a toss of her head, she had told Skylar to wait right there while she ran inside, and then she had disappeared through the tall wooden doors. Unfortunately, security had forced Skylar to move to an adjoining parking lot to wait for her passenger, and that had been nearly half an hour ago.

"So, you've worked for *Sports Challenge* magazine long?" Skylar asked, making small talk with Richard to pass the time.

"Not exactly. I'm a freelancer. I work for myself and whoever finances my projects." He chuckled and sat back in his seat. "The way it usually works is, I come up with the story idea, then I find money people willing to finance my film. Once it's done I sell it to a distributor connected with major media outlets. In this case, I contacted *Sports Challenge* about covering the Black Winter Sports Reunion with a focus on the growing number of minorities that are hitting the slopes. They grabbed it and here I am. They plan to do a feature story with photographs as well as a short video for streaming on their website."

"Cool," Skylar commented. "So, you'll be on celebrity-watch big-time, I suppose?"

"You bet."

"You might get lucky at the Slide and Glide Gala tonight. There're supposed to be some very important types dropping by and you'll have lots of opportunities for interviews and photos."

"Oh, yeah. I understand Mariah Carey is slated to pop over and I'm keeping my eye out for Will and Jada, too."

"Ought to be a pretty wild party, and a pretty wild week for that matter," Skylar commented, thinking about all of the work waiting for her back at her office, wishing Virina would hurry up. "I guess you'll be interviewing Mark Jorgen, the head of our ski school? Folks around here consider him a celebrity."

"For sure," Richard hurried to reply. "As a matter of fact, but he doesn't know about this, so keep it to yourself, I'm in discussions right now about a biographical documentary on Mark Jorgen's life and career. I've got investors lined up already and my hope is to convince him to participate. Could be a very inspirational piece."

Skylar nodded her agreement. "Oh, I don't see why he wouldn't do it. I'm not surprised that investors have already jumped on that. Mark is doing so much for the sport, introducing it to young people who might never have had a chance to ski. We're lucky to have him at Scenic Ridge."

"I heard you say that your sister owns the ski school?" Richard clarified.

"Right. She and her husband, Jerome, started the school twenty years ago. It was a real struggle for them to make a profit at first, but as time passed, the ski school became more popular, and it's grown every year since then."

"That's a story right there," Richard said. "A black-owned ski school in the heart of Colorado's most exclusive ski area, and their lead instructor is an African-American Olympic gold medalist. That'd be a great angle for the piece. Think your sister would agree to be included in my project?"

"Think? I know she would," Skylar eagerly replied. "It'd be great publicity for Scenic Ridge. Why wouldn't she go for that?"

"Good. We'll talk it over while I'm here."

After another twenty minutes had passed, Skylar was anxious to get going. The Slide and Glide event was tonight and she had so much to do. She was sure Deena and the entire staff were scrambling to get everything set and she knew she had to hurry back and help.

"Richard," Skylar began. "Will you please go inside and find out what's keeping Virina? We really need to get going."

"Sure. Be right back," he said, pulling on his sunglasses as he stepped out of the Jeep.

Inside the castle-like structure, he stationed himself beside a massive Eagle sculpture and scanned the lobby, a warm and inviting area filled with gleaming black marble accents and throngs of animated tourists. Virina was nowhere to be seen. Convinced she was not there, he made his way to the St. Regis's chic dining room, Olives, and told the hostess that he was looking for a friend. She allowed him to step inside to check, and he spotted Virina right away. She was seated at a corner table, picking at a salad and sipping wine while chatting animatedly with a raven-haired woman dressed head to toe in bright blue suede.

Not entirely surprised by his discovery, and knowing better than to interrupt Virina and her friend, Richard slipped out of the restaurant and returned to the Jeep to tell Skylar what he had seen.

"She's eating lunch!" Skylar snapped. "While we sit out here and wait for her? Who the hell does she think she is?"

"Virina Dagrun. That's who she is, and she's going to make sure you and I understand exactly what that means," Richard glibly replied, before he burst out laughing. "Skylar, I think we're being tested."

Skylar clamped her jaw shut tight, slumped down in her seat and glared out the windshield at the elaborately carved front door of the turreted, red-brick hotel. "We'll see who passes this test," she grumbled under her breath, calculating her odds. She had Mark on her side, and that counted for a lot. A fact that Virina Dagrun knew nothing about.

Forty-five minutes later, when Virina reappeared at the hotel entrance, Skylar pulled the Jeep around and sat stoically silent behind the wheel, determined not to blow up.

What use was there in starting an argument now? All Skylar wanted to do was get on the road and get home.

However, as soon as Virina climbed inside, she told Skylar, "Now, I've got to go by *Gorsuch,* and then over to Aspen Grove. The salesgirl at one of the stores there is holding a necklace for me. You don't mind, do you?" When Skylar didn't respond, Virina didn't hesitate to add, "Blame Mark, not me, my dear. If he had arranged for my limo on Saturday evening, when I asked him to, he probably could have secured one. Then I wouldn't be bothering you."

"Oh, it's no problem, Miss Dagrun," Skylar replied in a sugary sweet voice, fed up with the woman's obvious manipulation, but not about to take her bait. Virina Dagrun was spoiled, self-absorbed and demanding, but not as clever as she thought she was. No way was Skylar going to let Virina's antics get to her. "As I recall, Saturday evening was a very busy time," she began. "Let's see, Mark and I went to dinner at Snowmass Village and then for drinks at the Fireside Inn. It was so late when we got back to Scenic Ridge he must have completely forgotten about calling the limo service."

Skylar had to bite her tongue to keep from laughing out loud when a flash of surprise lit Virina's ice blue eyes and cast a shadow of annoyance over her pale features.

Chapter 17

"No, Mark, I didn't fly in alone. And Muffin Lark did not come with me, as she had promised. She's gone to St. Tropez for her third divorce. Don't you remember? I told you she was going off to heal her heart and she'd stay there until after Valentine's Day." A soft Frank Sinatra tune came from the CD player and filled the bedroom where Virina was humming along with the crooner as she sorted, inspected and hung up her clothes.

"No, I don't remember and I don't care where Muffin went to get her divorce," Mark commented in a flat tone, already bored with his mother's detailed update on the crowd he used to follow. All of that seemed so far away and long ago, holding absolutely no interest for him now. He continually wondered how he could have been friends with people who were so self-absorbed and shallow.

"Anyway," Virina continued. "I was accompanied on

my jet by Richard Nobel, a filmmaker from New York," she told Mark while unpacking her many suitcases. Scarves, cosmetics, jewelry and magazines were scattered all over the bed, the soft chenille love seat, the bedside tables and the Indian rug that covered the floor of the Vista View Suite, a private cabin not far from Mark's. Shopping bags and packages from trendy stores in Aspen, the result of her impromptu excursion in town, were scattered about, making it nearly impossible to maneuver through the crowded bedroom.

"*Your* jet? I think you mean Wilhelm Willard's jet," Mark corrected, unfazed by his mother's vain attempt to heighten her jet-set status. He leaned against the doorjamb of the bedroom and watched his mother, who had changed into a pale blue, French terry sweatsuit with matching slippers as she bustled about the room. She looked fabulous. It amazed him that she never seemed to age, possessed incredible energy and continued to dress as if she were still a runway model.

At least she's in a good mood. Mark was relieved that his mother had not launched into a tirade about the missing limo, a subject he was not about to bring up. She hadn't even said a word about Skylar, either, and he thought that was strange. Let it go, he told himself, because a discussion about Skylar was the last thing he wanted to have.

Skylar must have suffered greatly while driving Virina all around Aspen. Mark sighed. He had only himself to blame for that mix-up. He had planned to arrange everything far in advance so that Virina's arrival would be perfect, but then he and Skylar had decided to go over to Snowmass for the evening and all thoughts of Virina had vanished. First thing tomorrow, he'd call around and secure a car and a driver for her. No way was Skylar going to play chauffeur again.

"Whatever," Virina snapped back, clearly upset by Mark's observation. "The plane is at my disposal for the season, so it's mine as far as anyone knows. All right?"

"All right, but I won't lie for you, Mother," Mark replied in a level tone.

"I didn't ask you to lie, you simply don't need to divulge any information about the plane or my financial status for that matter, okay? Wilhelm and I parted amicably enough for me to be able to call on him from time to time, if I should need…help. So I don't want any nasty gossip going around that might mess that up. Image is *everything,* Mark. *Everything.* People only believe what they see and only know what you tell them. You ought to remember that, son. The truth is meant to be bent, shaped and molded into what you *want* it to be. That's the only way to make it in this crazy world." She tossed an Hermès scarf across the foot of the bed, and then sat down, fingering the soft patterned silk.

"All right," Mark agreed. "You don't have to blow everything I say out of proportion. I'm just telling you that the way you look at your situation and the way I see it are very different. But it's your life, so tell people whatever you want. I don't care."

Brushing a hand through her hair, Virina slumped back on a pile of pillows, the scarf clutched in a fist. "Sorry I snapped, Mark. Really. But things are a little tight for me right now. I'm under so much stress." She kept her eyes lowered on the scarf as she spoke.

"You're stressed? Why? What's really going on?" Mark wanted to know.

Now, Virina looked up, jaw raised defiantly. “You can’t tell a soul, promise?”

“Sure.”

“Deleur Cosmetics is not renewing my contract. It ends next month.”

“Oh?” Mark responded, genuinely concerned. He had been relieved when his mother signed on with the French cosmetic giant because it had given her an independent income and something to do other than meddle in his life. As the face of Deleur, she had been able to remain in the public eye, connected to the fashion-conscious world that was so important to her, and she no longer had to depend on a husband to support her. What would happen once her income stopped and there was no new man in her life? Mark shuddered to think about that scenario and how it might affect him. “What did the people at Deleur tell you?” he ventured.

“I spoke to my agent by phone last week, and of course, she didn’t actually say why I was being released, but we both know it’s because they want a younger face, even though Deleur’s demographics indicate that their target audience is women between thirty and sixty. I fit right in. I gave the public exactly what it wanted. Just this morning, at the airport, a woman asked me for my autograph and told me how much she loves the night cream. Why can’t Deleur see that I’m perfect for the job? I don’t plan to go away without a fight, so don’t go telling anyone that I am about to be out of a job.”

“Fine, but I can’t imagine why they *want* to let you go,” Mark murmured, slightly alarmed by the ring of defeat in his mother’s voice, something he rarely heard. He knew she could be difficult, snobbish and downright manipulative, but weren't such characteristics fairly normal among the models, designers, photographers and other creative types who populated the fashion industry?

Long ago, Mark had learned to tolerate Virina's regal airs and her heightened sense of self-importance, and as much as he hated to admit it, at one time he had been just as royally obnoxious. For the duration of his career, she had been his mentor, his ski instructor, his business manager and his cheerleader while traveling the world and coaching him. He had allowed her to shape his opinions, pass judgment on his decisions and permeate his life in a way he hadn't fully understood until he moved halfway across the world and out of her sphere of influence. At last, he was free of the hold that his mother had established when he was young and vulnerable. Now, he planned to keep it that way, no matter how much it might hurt her.

"So, as you can see," Virina continued, her voice cracking miserably. "My finances are not so stable and I don't have a husband to take care of me. I have no one to count on except you, Mark. No one. My future is in your hands, you understand what that means?"

A flicker of guilt passed through Mark to hear those dramatic words. He knew that she was leading up to her favorite line. *I did everything possible to make you what you are and now you owe it to me to do as I say.* He'd heard it all before, and there had been a time when it had made him feel guilty enough to give in to his mother's demands. But not now.

Silence hung awkwardly in the room for a long moment before Virina continued. "And you can stop frowning at me, Mark! You're going to have to make some very serious decisions soon about your future. You're thirty-eight years old. Not so young anymore. Not so flush with cash, either. You need to be settling down with the right kind of wife, living the life I worked so hard for you to have. If you marry wealth, you'll marry well. Choosing a wife is a very important matter."

For you, Mark thought, strengthening his resolve before plunging into the discussion he knew he didn't want to have. "I understand what you're saying, Mother, but money does not ensure happiness. Look around you. All of your wealthy friends don't seem to be so happy, but if it's important for you, go for it. You're a vibrant, beautiful woman with class and style. Who knows what, or who, might come your way? You'll marry another rich man again, I'm sure. But as for *my* romantic life, let's just say that I have it under control and it really doesn't concern you. All right?"

Mark wished he could tell his mother that he had already met the woman he wanted to spend his life with, but knew it would be dangerous to bring Skylar into the picture too soon. He needed time. He wanted the two women to get to know each other, and for Virina to realize on her own that Skylar was a wholesome, stable, honest woman. Even though she wasn't wealthy, she was the perfect mate for him.

He still wondered why Virina had not mentioned Skylar. Other than a grumbling complaint about having been picked up by the concierge in a mud-splattered Jeep, she had not said anything negative about her afternoon with Skylar, and Mark was unsure if that was good or bad. He knew Virina well. It would be just like her to hold back with her opinion of Skylar until she could use her observations to her advantage. Well, he could play her game, too. He could wait for Virina to make the first move.

"Don't take such things as marrying *up,* lightly. Your love life does concern me!" Virina shot to her feet and began pacing the room. "How can you expect me to dismiss such an important topic when things are so…so fluid in my life right now? This is a very distressing time. You might try to understand! You're all I have, Mark. Your future *does* affect me," she said.

"Okay, okay," Mark gave in, not about to get into a full blown argument. "I do understand how you feel, and I promise to inform you of any major romantic decisions I might make when the time is right, and not before. That's all I can offer, so let's drop the subject."

He had not seen his mother in over a year, and less than thirty minutes after their reunion here they were sniping at each other already. He didn't want to fight, he wanted her to enjoy her time at Scenic Ridge, and he preferred not to be drawn into her drama. Letting Virina have her way was usually much easier than trying to get her to see things from his perspective. If it made her happy to let people think that she owned a private plane and was still the face of Deleur Cosmetics, so what? And if she wanted to hold out hope that he might marry a rich woman in order to take care of her, let her keep on dreaming.

Eager to end the discussion, Mark left the bedroom and went out into the great room of his mother's sun-filled cabin.

Dropping the scarf onto a pile of lingerie, Virina left her unpacking and followed her son to the fireplace, where he stood with his back to the fire.

Mark took a deep breath. "Now, what about this man you flew in with? How long have you been dating him? Is it serious?"

Virina threw back her head and gave up a hard laugh. "Oh, I wish. But really, Mark, it's not like that at all. I barely know him. He's an independent filmmaker and he wants to do a documentary on you. Isn't that fantastic? A film, and probably a book deal, too. This project could totally revitalize your status as one of the most important figures in the world of winter sports. Put you back in circulation with the right people, too."

"A documentary? Really? No one contacted me about it," Mark replied, ignoring her obvious remark about mixing with the right people. He had been there, done that, and wanted no part of that fast-paced rat race again.

"That's because I've taken care of everything. Richard and I met over dinner in New York, and I assured him that you'd be very interested in doing this project. I'm going to produce it."

"You, a producer? What do you know about making a movie?"

"Nothing. I'm going to raise the money to produce it. What's the difference? I'll have input and control of how it's shaped. That's very important, Mark. I want this film to reflect exactly who you are and how important your accomplishments have been. If I'm producing, I can guarantee that you'll be treated right. Creative types can get carried away sometimes and I'm not about to leave this to chance."

"Can you raise the kind of money something like this would cost?"

"Oh, of course. A few phone calls and the money will be in the bank. Isn't it wonderful? Richard plans to begin shooting footage right away so he can create a rough cut for me to show the investors."

"You told this filmmaker that I'm in on his project and

I know nothing about it?" Mark repeated, incredulous that Virina would take such liberties with his name. "You seem to forget that you no longer speak for me. I manage my career, remember?"

"Oh, don't be so touchy," Virina snapped. "I met with Richard to get an overview of his idea, and once I heard it, I knew it sounded perfect for you. Saved you the trouble of wasting your time with him, in case he wasn't serious. He'll be at the gala tonight. Talk to him, okay?"

As Mark listened to his mother ramble on about how the documentary would help raise his profile in the world of sports and entertainment, and how much money he could make, his heart sank in dismay. A warning voice in his head clicked on.

She's back, and she thinks she's back in control. So, what are you going to do about it?

Chapter 18

Every public area of the lodge, including the spacious lobby was filled to capacity, and even the heated outdoor tents were bursting with festive, chattering partygoers. A baggy-pants DJ in a black knit ski cap and black shades was busy spinning one special request after another, playing tunes that ranged from old school Aretha to hip Snoop Dogg to sexy Mariah Carey, who was expected to arrive at any moment. Waiters balancing trays of king crab, shish kebabs, caviar puffs and smoked oysters threaded their way through the stylishly dressed guests who mixed and mingled in the huge great room where a tall ice sculpture rose inside an elaborate martini fountain.

Skylar picked up a stack of brochures that detailed the extensive shopping opportunities in the area, stepped out of her office and went directly into the mix. A group of sisters from Atlanta who were dressed in eye-catching après-ski outfits, which Skylar calculated must have set each one back several thousand dollars, hurried over. Leather, cashmere, fur and suede abounded and Skylar could tell that these women were into some serious retail therapy.

"Here're the brochures," she said, handing each one a pamphlet.

"I can't wait to hit the shops in Aspen Grove tomorrow," the girl wearing a fringed, red suede jacket over black leather pants gushed. She held the pamphlet up to one side of her mouth and whispered loudly to Skylar, in a most conspiratorial tone, "Actually, I don't give a damn about skiing. I just came to the reunion for the shopping and the parties."

"And the guys," her friend chimed in.

"You've got that right," the third girl added.

"If you really want to experience shopping in Aspen, go to *Gorsuch,* ladies," Skylar advised. "Can't come to Aspen and not make that stop. But, don't be shocked by the prices," she cautioned. "Buy something fantastic for yourself that will remind you of this trip. Think of it as a memory investment. You won't be sorry when you get home."

"I won't be sorry, but I might be broke," the one in tan cashmere quipped. "My American Express is already on meltdown and I just got here three hours ago."

The sister in red fringe bumped her hip against her friend's, laughed and gave her a fast high five. She jerked her head toward the crush of partiers in the great room and said, "Honey, with all these fine brothers around, you better ditch your wallet and hide those low-limit credit cards of yours. You don't need to be paying for nothin' else while you're here."

They all hooted in agreement, waved their fingers at Skylar and walked off, giggling as they disappeared into the crowd.

Skylar smiled as she watched them leave, recalling how she and Tanya and Loretta used to party together—before her accident and her sudden wealth. It still hurt her to realize how quickly her girlfriends had changed and what she had thought was true friendship had evaporated. It brought to mind the comment that Mark had made about having a lot of money: it often caused more unhappiness than most people believed possible.

Skylar rubbed the back of her neck and stretched her back, beginning to feel the effects of her long day. After playing chauffeur to Virina all morning, she had returned in time to help pull the final details of the Slide and Glide together, get dressed and jump into the mix. Now, she smiled at Deena, who flitted past with one of the major donors at her side, and gave her sister a big thumbs up. Everything was going off as planned.

"How's it going?" a voice from behind Skylar asked.

Skylar whirled around to find Mark standing right behind her. He looked so fine that she involuntarily gasped and took her time taking him in. He was wearing a brown, houndstooth blazer over a chocolate turtleneck and brown cords with a wide cowhide belt hung low around his waist. His thumbs were tucked into the belt's shiny horseshoe buckle and he was standing as if he had been watching her for some time.

"I was wondering if you were coming inside," she said, shifting her eyes from his belt to his face.

"Just finished getting the valet parking straight. The boys can take over now, so I can get back to my office and take care of a few things. We've got so many people booked for ski lessons tomorrow, I can't even begin to think about how crowded the slopes are going to be." He sidled up to Skylar, slipped an arm around her waist and gave her a quick squeeze. "You look great," he whispered in her ear.

"Thanks," Skylar said, pleased with herself for buying the reverse-cut velvet jacket and pants set at Chico's while she'd been waiting around for Virina to decide which turquoise necklace to buy. It was the first really nice outfit Skylar had bought since coming to Aspen, and while it wasn't outrageously expensive, it did send a classy sophisticated message without raising any questions about how she could afford it. She wanted to look nice, but not flamboyant, to let Mark know that she did have a sense of style and good taste. After all, a concierge's salary only went so far.

"Glad you like it. My first Aspen splurge," Skylar commented, suddenly wishing they weren't trying so hard to restrict their public displays of affection. In the midst of so many fun-loving, happy people who were laughing, dancing and having a great time, it would have been nice to spend the evening on Mark's arm as his official date. Already, she noticed the curious sisters raking Mark from head to foot—salivating sisters with designs on him, ready to pounce. Skylar was steeling herself for the commotion he would surely cause as soon as he entered the main party room.

It was not easy, but Skylar was determined to keep her growing interest in Mark in low profile. Her reason was that if their relationship lasted for a few more weeks, then everyone would know about it soon enough, but if it crashed and burned tomorrow...well, it was just as well that she'd kept things quiet. Less explaining to do. Less pain. Fewer people to give her advice because, other than

Deena, no one else knew about her off-site dates with Mark. He had assured her that he was keeping mum, too, though his assistant, John, had begun to ask a lot of questions about how Mark was spending his free time now.

"Seen my mom?" he asked, glancing around.

"Right over there," Skylar said. She nodded at Virina who was holding the attention of a lanky man in a green and white plaid sweater while chatting animatedly with him. "She seems to be enjoying herself."

"She usually does in a crowd."

"Did she tell you about Richard Nobel and his documentary?" Skylar asked.

"A little, but I really want to talk to him myself. Is he here yet?"

"Yes, he and his cameraman are outside in the tented area interviewing some of the guests and getting photos. You know he's covering the reunion for *Sports Challenge* magazine?"

"Right, my mother told me all about him."

"And what else did she tell you?" Skylar prompted, certain that Virina had complained to Mark about being picked up in a dirty Jeep by the concierge and not by a limo driver.

"Oh, nothing much."

Though Skylar doubted that, she didn't press the issue. "I have to confess," she started. "I did allude to the fact that you and I were more than just coworkers when I was talking to your mother." Skylar watched Mark carefully for his reaction.

Mark's brows lifted in surprise. "Really? Well, she didn't say anything to me about it."

"Good," Skylar breathed. "I didn't want to cause trouble, but she was pushing my buttons and actin' all superior. I had to bring her down a notch."

Mark laughed aloud, clearly impressed. "Good for you! Now, you see what I have to deal with? She did fuss at me for not arranging her transportation as I'd promised, but I truly forgot about it." He leaned closer to Skylar and grinned down at her. "I had other things on my mind that night."

Skylar shook her head back and forth, wagging a finger at Mark. "Well, you sure left me hanging. I caught the brunt of your mom's attitude, which was bristly, to say the least. You owe me big-time for picking her up and running her all over town. I didn't get back here until nearly four! Really, she's something else."

Mark brushed a finger across Skylar's chin, galvanizing her with a smoldering expression. "I know, and you're right. Dealing with my mother can be exhausting. I do owe you, so, how would you like for me to pay my debt?"

His teasing excited Skylar, making her swallow hard to clear her mind of exactly what she'd love for him to do. "I'll think of something, don't worry."

"I'll hold you to that," he whispered, taking her by the arm. He eased Skylar away from the crowded lobby, to the open door of her office, only footsteps away from the party. Inside, he shoved the door partially closed with one hand as he pulled Skylar to him with the other.

He kissed Skylar lazily on the lips; long, lingering kisses that branded her flesh like fire on ice. This time, when his hands slipped under her jacket and caressed her bare skin, she did not resist his touch. Bending into his embrace, she locked her lips over his and gave in to the thrill of letting him arouse her, unable to help herself.

When the kiss ended, Mark rested his lips above her ear, continuing to hold her close as she placed her head on his chest, eyes closed, savoring his presence.

"Please, don't pay any attention to my mother's drama," he murmured. "I'm just sorry she felt entitled to abuse your kindness. She had no right to tie you up like that."

Skylar snuggled closer to Mark, unconcerned about Virina Dagrun. "Maybe it was just as well," she murmured. "Gave me a chance to spend some time with her, even though she wasn't very happy."

"Well, eventually you two will get along fine, but believe me it might take some time."

"Do you want us to get along?" Skylar whispered, almost afraid to ask the question. He was moving so fast, acting so sure of what he wanted, assuming she was keeping pace with the future he obviously saw for them.

"Yes, of course," Mark assured her, easing his hold on her to lean back and watch for her reaction.

"Is it very important to you?" Skylar pressed, her heart racing so fast, it was getting difficult to breathe.

"Extremely," he admitted.

"Then don't worry about me, Mark," Skylar replied softly. "I can handle whatever your mother throws at me."

Mark took Skylar by the shoulders and studied her with care. "You know what? I think you can." He kissed her again, more playfully this time, as if a huge decision had been made.

Skylar ducked under his arm and out of reach, realizing how close they were edging toward a new level of commitment. We have a long way to go before getting into discussions about potential mother-in-law issues, she decided.

As strongly as she felt about Mark, could she really take on Virina? The pace of their fast-developing relationship was dizzying, and yet, Skylar knew she was doing little to slow it down. She had been involved with Lewis for a long time, but still really hadn't known him at all. And while she'd known Mark for only a month, she felt as if they were meant to spend a lifetime together.

It was all so confusing, yet so exciting, too. Was she being naive to believe they had a future? What would Mark do when he found out that she was a rich woman, pretending to be a working girl? How could she tell him that she might not be able to give him the children that he'd told her he wanted so badly? And when the time came for total commitment, as Skylar sensed it would very soon, would she be ready to give herself without hesitation to a man she had known for such a short time?

Pushing her worries aside, she exhaled in a rush. "I'd better get back to the party, Mark. I'm working, you know?"

"Right and I need to find this filmmaker, Richard Nobel, and see what's on his mind."

"So, you go out first. I'll follow in a few minutes." She gave Mark a gentle shove. "Go. Talk to Richard. He's probably looking for you."

Mark started to leave, but then stopped and gave Skylar a sensuous nuzzle on the neck. "Don't you dare run off with anyone while I'm gone," he whispered in a low voice.

"Run off with whom?" she quipped.

"One of those hungry-looking guys out there," he replied, jerking his head toward the lobby. "I saw them standing around, ogling the girls. It's party time, they're on the hunt, and you're definitely the prettiest girl here."

"You have nothing to worry about," Skylar sassily reassured Mark, giving his arm a playful jab. "I'm not *even* interested in hearing their tired old pickup lines."

After Mark left, Skylar counted to ten and then stepped

out of her office. Immediately, she saw Virina standing across the lobby and at an angle that would have provided her an unobstructed view into Skylar's office.

I hope she got an eyeful. Skylar adjusted her jacket, not at all surprised that Virina would spy on her and Mark.

A grim-faced Virina palmed her hands into hard fists, incensed by what she had just seen. Mark had actually kissed that woman. Caressed her. Acted as if he really cared about her! A bristling sensation shot through Virina and fueled her outrage that her son had sunk so low. Mark and the concierge! An impoverished nobody from the Florida swamps! That was not going to happen. Oh, no. Not as long as she had anything to say about it. A hotel concierge was not the kind of woman her son ought to be involved with, not when there were so many wealthy, attractive, cultured women in Aspen who would jump at the chance to spend time with him.

Virina knew she would have to plot out a strategy to make Mark understand that he could do better. When they had spoken earlier, she had been smart to deliberately omit what Skylar had told her in the car about going on a date with him. *I will have to wait for Mark to tell me he's serious about the girl,* Virina calculated. *And by that time, I'll have found the ammunition I'll need to show him exactly why he'd be making a huge mistake to remain involved with her.*

Mark found Richard Nobel standing at a chocolate fountain deep in conversation with a buxom young lady wearing a fluffy mink vest and the tightest jeans Mark had ever seen. He wondered how she could breathe, let alone sit down. When the girl moved on to fresher ground, Mark approached Richard.

"Richard Nobel?" Mark inquired stepping closer.

Richard jerked around and grinned. "Mark Jorgen! I recognize you." He extended his hand and took Mark's.

After the usual pleasantries, Mark got right to the point, eager to hear what the filmmaker had in mind. "I understand from my mother that you're interested in doing a documentary film on me."

"Right," Richard agreed. "I want to do a series on African-American sports heroes, and my first will be on black champion skiers. As you must know too well, there aren't many of you guys around."

"I hear you. So what did you have in mind?"

"As you know, the brothers and sisters are getting out on the slopes in larger numbers, black ski clubs are gaining in popularity and the members are raising lots of money for good causes. I envision a fairly complex piece on you. Your career, how you got started skiing, what it was like to compete and live in a world where very few people of color were around. I see this as educational and entertaining. Something to motivate young people to take up skiing." Richard went on to more fully explain his film to Mark, adding that he had already secured financial backing.

"So, I heard. My mother is producing?" Mark clarified.

"Right, and I can't thank her enough for agreeing to back this project."

"Hmm, it is flattering, I suppose," Mark commented, going on to ask, "Are you going to feature the ski school here at Scenic Ridge, too?"

"Well, you know, I had thought about that. Skylar, the

young lady who picked us up at the airport, agreed that it might be a good angle to include. Expand interest in the piece."

Mark quickly nodded. "Exactly. If it weren't for this school, a lot of the skiers who are in town for the Black Winter Sports Reunion wouldn't be attending. Many of them learned to ski right here, and more than likely, Jerome Simpson waived their fees. I don't think it would be fair to exclude the story of how and why Deena and Jerome devoted their lives to creating Scenic Ridge. To be honest, Richard, I don't think what I have accomplished in my lifetime is any more important than what Deena and Jerome have built right here, and I don't care much about being profiled unless the documentary also contains a heavy focus on Scenic Ridge."

"Good point," Richard agreed. "And once the documentary airs, it would give the school a boost in publicity and hopefully, a real financial push, too."

"That'd be great," Mark said. "The ski school is busy now, and we're keeping up, but we could do a lot more if Deena could afford to increase the teaching staff and improve some of the trails."

"Sounds good to me. Let's move forward then," Richard added enthusiastically. "I'm excited. You know, it just might make a lot of money for you, and your mother's investors."

The animation on Richard's face as he detailed the financial windfall that could result, irritated Mark, who realized that Richard was beginning to sound very much like his mother. However, since the documentary would benefit Scenic Ridge, as well as himself, he was willing to go along with whatever Richard wanted.

"Well," Mark told Richard, "Mother had better get busy

tapping her friends and asking them to start writing checks. I think your project sounds great. I'd love to be a part of it."

"Fantastic. I have a preliminary contract we can start with. Maybe go over the details tomorrow?"

"Sure," Mark replied.

"And my cameraman is here, so I'm ready to get some spontaneous footage," Richard said. "I'd like to get some shots of you in action on the slopes while you're giving lessons tomorrow, and even some while you're relaxing off the powder, as I'm sure you do. A real overview of what life at Scenic Ridge is like for a former Olympian, you know?"

"No problem. We can jump right in tomorrow," Mark agreed. "Meet me at the ski school at ten, okay?"

"See you there," Richard said, shaking Mark's hand.

Just as Richard was about to walk away, Deena arrived, holding a green apple martini in one hand and a skewer of shrimp in the other. "So you two finally caught up with each other I see," she commented before taking a sip from her martini. She focused on Mark. "I told Richard that you'd be in and out tonight, as you were overseeing the valet parking, so I'm glad you guys were able to connect."

"Right," Richard replied. "We had a good conversation and I've convinced Mark to be the subject of my autobiographical documentary."

"Wonderful," Deena remarked, nodding at Mark. "You've led such an interesting and inspiring life. Few men, especially black men, have achieved half as much as you have. Your life story ought to be shared."

"But Richard hasn't told you everything," Mark interjected, focusing on the filmmaker. "You want to tell her?"

"Of course," Richard said. "Mark has agreed to devote a good portion of his story to Scenic Ridge. I want to include the history of this place, how your husband's family acquired the land, why you and your husband started the school, the challenges you've faced, not only in operating the ski school, but in attracting African-Americans and other minorities to the slopes. And of course, I want to highlight the personal side of living in a ski lodge. It would be a rare peek into a very different lifestyle, especially for African-Americans."

"Oh yeah, it's different, all right." Deena chuckled. "The stories I could tell you! There've been lean years and times when we weren't sure we were going to be able to keep the school open, but we're doing so much better this season." She paused to look at Mark. "And I know that having Mark Jorgen on staff has added tremendously to our profile. If this keeps up, next season will be even better. Maybe I'll be able to hire additional instructors and open that trail on the mountainside beyond Brookman Mill. Jerome has wanted to do that for years."

"Well, you're lucky to have Mark on staff," Richard said. "Once the documentary airs, the other ski schools in the area had better watch out. Scenic Ridge will really be on the map!"

Chapter 19

It was nearly one o'clock in the morning when the DJ spun his last tune and the party was officially over, but that did little to cool down the festive atmosphere. Laughter filled the great room and everyone was buzzing about Mariah Carey's brief, but dramatic visit. She'd popped in, dressed entirely in white fur, signed a few autographs, spoken briefly with the media and posed for photos, including one with Deena and her staff. Then she was gone, leaving a trail of expensive perfume and a crush of breathless fans behind.

"I'm going up," Deena told Skylar, sticking her head into Skylar's office. She was holding a cup of coffee in one hand and a small plate piled with decorative sweets in the other. "I've been dying for a cup of coffee all evening and I want to eat my dessert in peace. You coming?"

Skylar snapped off her desk lamp and followed Deena

into the lobby, where she paused next to the registration desk. "No, not right now. I need to check one thing, then I'm turning in. It's been a long day, hasn't it?"

"Really, but a good one. The party was fabulous and I think we got quite a bit of media coverage, too. But tomorrow," she grimaced, "back to the regular grind."

"I hear you," Skylar agreed. "I'm whipped."

"I know you are. What do you have to check on so late?" Deena wanted to know, already edging toward the elevator.

"Buttermilk trail maps. I think we're out. At least I don't have any more in my office."

"Oh, check with Mark. He's got tons. I think they're in the file cabinet next to the computer in the ski school office."

"Great. I'll take care of it."

"Don't stay up too late, okay? Tomorrow's gonna be a bear."

"I won't be long," Skylar tossed back, her mind abuzz with the rush of the party, the crowds and the jam-packed day. There would be no time to rest until the reunion was over, and while it was going to be a hectic time, it was also very exciting. She had met so many interesting people from all over the country and now understood that for black skiers, the camaraderie and sense of connection that came with belonging to a ski club was just as important as hitting the slopes together. The clothes had been fabulous—just like a fashion show. The food and music had kept everyone swinging and in a real party mood, which would most likely continue throughout the reunion. It had been a long time since Skylar had enjoyed herself so much, even while working!

"Well, my coffee's getting cold. Gotta run," Deena

called out, hurrying to catch the elevator as soon as the doors slid open.

Leaving the lobby, Skylar slipped on her jacket and headed toward the eastern wing of the lodge, where the ski school was connected to the main building via a short breezeway. The blast of cold air that hit her when she stepped outside felt surprisingly good, and she sucked in a long deep invigorating breath.

The school was dark, as she had guessed it would be. She took out her key and was about to shove it into the lock when the door opened in her face and Mark stepped out.

"Oh, my God. You scared me!" She jumped back. "I didn't think anyone was in there."

Mark took her by the arm. "Sorry I frightened you. I was just about to come looking for you. I was hoping you hadn't turned in."

Skylar put her keys back into her pocket and rubbed her hands together. "Well, I wasn't exactly looking for you," she admitted. "I need some more trail maps and Deena said you had some."

"I do." He made no move to go back inside. "I can bring them to you first thing in the morning. No need to go in there." He looked at her as if expecting her to protest, and when she didn't he went on. "Want to have a drink? Are you hungry? Tired?"

Skylar laughed aloud and nodded. "Yes to everything. What I'd love is a glass of champagne, some of those fancy cheese puffs and a foot soak."

"Then let's go," he decided, taking her by the hand. "I can take care of all your needs. No sense in standing around out here in the cold."

He led her over to his Range Rover, which was parked

in the lot in front of the school, and opened the passenger-side door. Without commenting, Skylar climbed in. He circled the car, slid in beside her and started the engine.

Skylar held her breath when he swung onto the service road leading to the Snow King Suite, anticipating what lay ahead. In the midst of the frenzied party, she had not been able to shake the impact of their earlier encounter in her office. Something about their moment alone had struck her as a prelude to a much more serious reunion, and she had actually been hoping to see Mark before the evening ended. Maybe it had been his admission that he wanted Skylar and his mother to get along. Maybe it was Skylar's own unrelenting need to feel loved again. Maybe it was simply a reaction to a very magical evening, but whatever was fueling this sensation, Skylar knew she was going to play it to the end.

She sat very still and didn't relax the muscles in her stomach until Mark came to a stop outside his cabin, where lights were burning softly in the windows. She hurried from the car, crossing the hard-packed snow quickly, and then waited while Mark fumbled nervously with his keys.

Inside, he had barely closed the door before he reached out and took Skylar in his arms, pressing his body into hers. She whimpered helplessly to feel his fingers on the zipper of her jacket, then on her breasts, kneading and stroking and driving her wild. When his hardness brushed against her leg, the firm length of it excited her, initiating a promise that made her go weak.

His lips sought hers in a flurry of throwing off jackets and gloves and scarves, all while moving toward the bedroom, where they tumbled down on the soft, fleece quilt of his king-size bed, unable to let each other go.

"The champagne?" she managed weakly, though not

remotely interested in doing anything other than holding onto Mark.

"Later," he murmured, and he then pulled back and looked at her, one eye squinted half-closed. "Unless you seriously want me to…"

"No," Skylar interrupted, laughing in a husky voice, raw with need. "That can wait. I don't want anything but you. Right here. Right now. Don't you dare move."

The urgency in his kiss told Skylar that he was not going anywhere anytime soon. And as he molded his lips more tightly to hers, she responded with an eagerness that matched his, only faintly aware of how fast she was slipping toward loving him completely.

His kisses were brutally passionate, yet tenderly reassuring, awakening Skylar's dormant desire to be loved. Singed by his fiery lips, she felt branded, as if he had already claimed her. Breathing hard, she lifted her chest and gathered him even closer, sealing the space between them.

Easily, they shed their clothing in bursts of yanking and tugging and peeling off layers until nothing separated the silky warm flesh of their bodies. In the soft bedroom light, Skylar marveled, again, at how erotically golden Mark was, and the sight of his perfectly toned physique initiated a catch in her throat that tugged at her core and made her eyes flutter closed.

He eased his naked body over hers. She looked up to meet his gaze, caught in the spiral of passion that was rapidly pulling her down.

"You're so beautiful," he murmured, stroking one taut brown nipple that was begging to be touched. "You're perfect, and you're all I want, Skylar. I hope you know that by now."

She moaned her reply when he buried his face between her breasts and rested there for a moment before taking one hard nipple and then the other in his mouth to tease and suckle until she gasped in pleasure. Releasing her with a shudder, he traced his tongue downward, over her flat stomach, to the curly dark hair that nestled between her legs. And while his fingers brushed her inner thighs, he tasted every inch of her, bringing her throbbing need to a point of near explosion.

Skylar threaded her fingers in his hair and luxuriated in his delicious taunting, content to accept his unselfish, erotic gesture. She cried out softly, unable to hold back from letting him know that he was giving her exactly what she needed and she was loving every moment of his passionate attention.

Gently, she urged him upward, and then followed his lead as they switched places, moving her to straddle on top of his hard, firm torso. She locked her thighs firmly around his hips, braced her knees at his sides and threw back her head. A ripple of relief, threaded with anticipation, came over her when she realized that Mark was reaching under his pillow and then opening a packet of protection.

With that in place, she parted her legs, inviting him in, and with her eyes closed, her breasts thrust forward, she allowed herself to be swept along as he thrust into her, in long sensuous strokes, fitting his body to hers.

"Love me, Mark. Please, love me," she whispered over and over as she rode the waves of pleasure that rose and crashed throughout her body.

"That's all I plan to do from now on," he assured her, stoking the fire that was rapidly building between them.

When she thought nothing could keep her from exploding in a light-filled wave of pleasure, Mark moaned and eased her down beside him, not breaking their connection. He tasted her neck and caressed her back as they gently shifted positions, with him settled firmly over her.

Skylar pressed her head into the pillow, cupped his buttocks with both hands and forced him deeper, eager to prolong the dizzying ride that they were taking together. In a cadenced sway of hips and legs they found their rhythm and entered into a journey that took both of them over the crest of their electrifying need, where they crashed in unison with cries of joy.

"I never want this to end, Skylar. Never. I love you very much...and I need you," he whispered with conviction, as if their union had given him a burst of strength, not taken his breath away.

"And you're all I want, too," Skylar murmured, tracing her fingers along his spine. A sense of peace suddenly came over her, a feeling of satisfaction that she had not felt in a long time. Loving Mark *was* the right thing to do, and she would never regret her decision.

Chapter 20

Sunlight glinted off the banks of snow, creating fiery pinpoints of light that made Virina think about the diamond choker that her ex-husband had given her for Christmas one year. It had been an intricate heirloom necklace, designed by a famous Russian jeweler especially for Wilhelm's grandmother. Too bad he'd asked for its return as part of their divorce settlement. Virina had been forced to hand the fabulous piece of jewelry over, but now, she wished that she had fought to keep it. It made such a statement of old money and class and whenever she'd worn it, it had caused quite a stir.

The trail leading from Vista View to the Snow King Suite was deserted, as Virina had hoped it would be when she set out on her early morning walk. Exercise and fresh air were very important to her and she rarely deviated from her routine of power walking for thirty minutes every morning, no matter where she might be or how late she might have been up the night before.

Filling her lungs, she plodded along, her insulated boots making a soft brushing sound with each step she took. She adjusted her blue tinted sunglasses and looked around, realizing why Mark had fallen in love with Scenic Ridge. It was an unspoiled jewel of a place, all right, but far too isolated and provincial for her taste. She had to admit that the party last night had been a nice affair, and for a good cause, too. But other than brief stops by Mariah Carey and a few B-list celebs, whom she did not recognize, no one of any real social status had attended. And after witnessing Mark's unpleasant behavior with the concierge, Virina had had enough. By ten o'clock she was back in her cabin and in bed reading the latest issue of *Vogue* magazine.

When the Snow King Suite came into view, Virina increased her pace. She had a list of things she needed to discuss with Mark and wanted his undivided attention before he got busy with his students.

First, she wanted to know how his meeting with Richard Nobel had gone and if he was as excited about the film as she was. Surely, Mark could see how lucrative such a documentary could be and how much he could profit from it, financially, professionally and socially. She had to get busy raising the funds right away, and that was going to require a quick trip to Los Angeles to visit with those she planned to tap for cash. It might take a few days to get everyone on board, but she knew she could do it if Mark was serious about moving forward.

Secondly, she wanted to know exactly what his intentions were as far as Skylar Webster was concerned. A casual date with a coworker was harmless, but Virina feared that her son was much more serious about Skylar than she had dared to imagine. What she had witnessed last night remained etched into her brain, making her slightly nauseous to think that Mark might actually settle for such a woman. That little affair had to be stopped right away, before it went too far.

When Virina reached the front porch, she climbed the three steps, stamped snow off her boots and knocked hard on the door. She could hear music coming from Mark's CD player, a good sign. He was not still asleep.

Mark opened the door, and was not surprised that his mother walked right in, before even saying hello.

"I'm glad you're up," she told him, moving deeper into the room. She pushed back the hood of her baby blue parka, shook out her hair and began to pull off her gloves. "There are a few things we need to discuss."

"I just got out of the shower," Mark muttered, tying his belt and turning up the collar of his thick white robe. He had a towel thrown around his neck and his hair was still dripping water. Clearly, this was not the time for a visit from Mom. "I don't have time to talk now, Mother. I've got to get dressed and over to my office. Our schedule is crazy today and classes have already started."

"All right, all right. I won't keep you long, but I wanted to talk to you about…" She paused, her blue eyes sweeping the room, as if to make sure they were alone. When her gaze settled on Skylar's burgundy, reverse-cut velvet jacket, the one she had been wearing at the party, Virina stalked over to the sofa and picked it up. "What is this?" she asked, eyes wide and unblinking.

Mark simply stared at her, sending the message that he

wasn't about to discuss Skylar or her jacket. He knew Virina was aware of the fact that he and Skylar had gone out on a date and he'd wondered why his mother hadn't brought the subject up when she first arrived at Scenic Ridge. Well, now she had, and he wasn't biting. An argument about his love life was not how he wanted to start his day.

"Answer me, Mark!" Virina snapped, giving the jacket a hard shake. She held it out and away from her body as if the piece of clothing were contaminated. "Please don't tell me *she* spent the night here with you."

The dramatic screech of Virina's voice made Mark flinch, and he prayed that Skylar was still asleep and not able to hear what was going on. Groaning, he reached out, took Skylar's jacket from his mother and hung it over his arm. "I'm not going to tell you anything. Who spends the night here is none of your business." Squaring his shoulders, he calmly waited, letting his words sink in.

"Don't be so damn smug about this. You're making a big mistake, Mark. What do you know about this girl? Who is she, really? What does she want?"

Realizing that shutting his mother up without getting into a full discussion was going to be impossible, Mark clinched his fists and plunged in. "I know enough about Skylar to feel fairly sure that our relationship has a future."

"A future! Oh, please!" Virina shot back. "She probably thinks you're rolling in cash and wants to get her hands on your money." Virina chuckled sarcastically.

"That's not true. She knows the truth…that I'm not rich. That I spent as fast as I earned when I was skiing professionally and that I earn enough now to live comfortably."

"Comfortably? Maybe in a place like this, but certainly not in the style you've been accustomed to," Virina bluntly observed. "And that's why you'd better think twice about settling for a woman with no financial resources. She was on unemployment before her sister gave her a job! You weren't raised to mix with people like that, nor to live an ordinary life, and if you try to change, you'll get bored, frustrated and angry. Then what will happen to this so-called 'relationship,' huh? It'll crash and burn and you'll be hurt."

Mark blew air through his lips and shook his head. "God, you really have an imagination, don't you?" He edged closer to Virina, anger darkening his deep green eyes. "I think you'd better leave. I refuse to get into a discussion about finances or my personal affairs. If that's all you came over here to talk about, you can go." He folded his arms across his chest and clamped his lips together, ending the conversation.

"All right. If you're determined to work at Scenic Ridge and teach skiing to underprivileged youth, I won't complain. Your mission is commendable. However, you don't have to live here. You ought to move out of this isolation and take a suite at the St. Regis Hotel, where more sophisticated people stay. You could easily commute back and forth."

"I'm happy where I am."

"No, you're not. You're confused. But I'll let it go, for now. However, you'd better be careful with that girl. Something about her makes me nervous. A tad too sure of herself if you ask me."

"I didn't ask you, remember?" Mark threw back, his frustration with his mother beginning to rise. All of his life she had done this to him: made him feel as if his decisions had no merit, reminding him that she had all the control. A familiar sense of dread crept over Mark as he studied the determined set of Virina's jaw and the flash of irritation in her ice blue eyes. He couldn't give in to her, and he certainly wasn't going to allow her to push him into saying something that wasn't true. He loved Skylar and he was certain she loved him, too. If there was any hope for them, he'd have to fight to keep Virina from spoiling everything.

"Okay, okay. Don't get snippy," Virina said, backing down. "But before I leave I need to ask you one more thing."

"What?"

"Are you going to do the documentary with Richard Nobel?"

"Yes. I am," Mark answered tersely, carefully omitting the fact that he and Richard had decided to feature Scenic Ridge. "I told Richard that he can start getting some footage of me on the slopes today and we're going to meet later for a long interview. I even pulled out some of my old scrapbooks for him to use for background research."

"Good. That's all I wanted to hear," Virina said as she walked to the door. "I have some videos I can give him, too and don't forget to show him all of your medals and trophies, which I assume you still have?"

"Of course. Some are in storage, but the important ones, I have with me."

"Fine. Now, one more thing. I won't be around tomorrow. I'm flying to Los Angeles."

"Los Angeles?" Mark queried, surprised. "Why? You just got here yesterday."

"I know, but I've got to start raising money. It's business that needs to be taken care of right away. I have the jet, remember? So, it's no big deal. And I'll be back before you know it." Tossing him a dazzling, runway-model smile, she pulled the door open and then turned around. "Don't do anything crazy while I'm gone."

"Good-bye, Mother," Mark managed tightly, shutting the door behind her.

During her walk back to her cabin, Virina's mind clicked through the list of people in Los Angeles she planned to tap for the money she needed to finance her son's film. Now that Mark was on board, it would be up to her to make it happen, and she was excited about the future once more. Once she got settled in L. A. she was going to tackle one more thing. She would find out just who Skylar Webster was and why an unemployed girl from Florida would settle for a concierge job in the Colorado mountains. Something about that little scenario simply didn't ring true and she was going to get to the truth.

Towel-drying his hair, Mark crossed the great room and headed toward the back of the cabin, wishing Virina luck. He knew her well enough to know that she was not going to take no for an answer once she started with her pitch for money. He shrugged, actually glad she was raising funding for the film. "At least," he muttered, shrugging, "she'll be out of my way for a while and I won't have to listen to her nagging complaints."

Entering his bedroom, he found Skylar beginning to stir. He had managed to slip out of bed while she slept and into the shower, with a plan to fix her breakfast before she awakened, but Virina's unexpected visit had ruined that.

Skylar sat up in the middle of the bed, yawned, and rubbed her eyes. "Hey," she said softly as she wrapped a red quilt around her naked shoulders. Her hair was tousled from sleep, but her eyes were wide and staring straight at Mark. "I wasn't eavesdropping," she started, "but did I hear voices? Was that your mother?" She tilted her head to one side, waiting for his reply.

"Yes, it was." Mark tossed his towel onto a side chair and flopped, belly down, onto the bed, his face only inches from Skylar's. Leaning up, he kissed her lightly on the cheek. "But, she's gone. For now, at least."

"Gee, what'd she want so early?"

"She's leaving. She has to get busy playing producer, raising money for the film that Richard Nobel is going to do on my life."

"Oh, right," Skylar said. "That's great. So, your mom is really going to be the producer? Has she done this kind of thing before?"

"No, but she's got connections with rich folks in Los Angeles who will probably come through. Gonna be gone a few days." No way could he tell Skylar that his mother was also on a mission to break them up, even though there was nothing she could ever say or do to make him give up Skylar. Virina was just going to have to accept the fact that Skylar was the only woman he wanted. And accept Skylar for who she was. After all, she might be Virina's daughter-in-law one day.

"Too bad she's leaving though. She just arrived," Skylar commented.

"I know, but that's the way she is. Flitting here and there, always on the go. We used to live like gypsies when I was younger and competing. We moved from hotel to hotel, city to city, country to country. Never stayed in one place very long."

"That must have been hard on you," Skylar offered, slipping down to snuggle next to Mark.

"It was, at times," he confessed, pulling her to him. He rested his chin on her shoulder and went on. "Back then, I went along with whatever the plan was. She never consulted me about what came next."

"How did that make you feel?"

"Disconnected, mainly. I was alone, remember. No father, no brothers or sisters." He cleared his throat with a nervous cough. "That's why I want to have a big family of my own, one day. Lots of kids who will always have each other, no matter how old they get or where they live. I want to be a grandfather, too, and I plan to spoil my grandchildren terribly. I never had that kind of connection with either my mother or my father's family, and it's something I've always thought about."

"Having children is *very* important to you, isn't it?" Skylar asked.

"Very," Mark agreed. "I'm sure that's why I'm thirty-eight years old and not married. I've been waiting for just the right woman to be the mother of my children, and my wife, of course." He scooted forward and kissed her tenderly on the neck. "I didn't realize how chaotic and lonely my life had been until I quit the ski circuit and met you. Coming to Scenic Ridge was fated."

"It was a very wise decision," Skylar commented, tracing a finger along the side of Mark's face. "And if I hadn't let Deena persuade me to come to work at Scenic Ridge, I never would have met you."

"I know. And now that we've found each other, you can bet that I'm not letting you go. Skylar, you *are* the woman I've been searching for. You're amazing, you know? You work so hard, you never complain, you're gorgeous, adventuresome and so easy to talk to. I know we can make it, don't you?"

Skylar simply nodded. "We have come a long way in the few weeks we've been together."

"And I can't wait to see where we'll go next." He leaned back and placed both hands on either side of Skylar's face, holding it still as he took her in, feeling uncontrolled waves of arousal beginning to creep over him. "Don't forget. Tonight, we're going into Aspen for the ski club karaoke at Que's. Nine o'clock, right?"

"Right," she agreed, "I'll be ready."

"Good." Mark shifted to one side, holding her even closer. She was warm and soft and smelled of an intoxicating mix of her femininity and his lust. He could feel his breathing quicken as he thought back over the thrill he'd experienced while making love to her last night.

They had come together a second time during the night, with a searing need that had exploded in a frenzy of kissing and touching and bodies slick with desire. As he'd tasted, teased and stroked her—from her full luscious lips to the supple skin of her stomach and thighs—she had yielded to him, pushing him to heights of arousal that he had only imagined existed. Even now, he could feel the strong throbbing in his groin and the red-hot pulse of his blood as it raced through his body with electrified speed.

She trusted him. She was finally allowing him to melt the ice around her heart, and this progress brought Mark a deep sense of satisfaction, as if he'd finished first in a very important race.

The natural way in which they had so easily consummated their attraction had not surprised him: somehow he had known they would fit perfectly together, and he could hardly wait to feel her naked skin flush against his once more.

A fiery jolt of need shot through him. Edging closer, he smothered her mouth with his. "God, how I want you," he groaned, sweeping his hands down between her legs.

"No time for that," Skylar giggled as she placed her hand on top of his, halfheartedly trying to remove it. "Aren't you already late for work?"

"Not that late," he protested, entwining his fingers with hers.

"But then you'd have to shower again," she teased.

"So, I'll shower again. And with you, this time," he decided, easing ever closer.

"I guess I can handle that," she murmured, smiling as she slid beneath him, spreading her legs in promise.

The warm water that slid over Skylar's naked body melted her resistance to Mark's sensuous touch as he slid his soapy hands over her back and shoulders. She tilted her head back and accepted a moist kiss on her neck, closing her eyes in pleasure. His firm body pushed up hard against her buttocks. His fingers roamed around her torso to the front, finding her slick wet breasts, where they lingered and teased, turning her nipples into hard brown nuggets. Groaning, she reached behind her and settled a cupped hand over Mark's groin, and was not surprised to find him as stiff and ready for action as he had been only moments ago.

With a quick twist, she turned to face him and then guided him from beneath the rain of warm water over to the cool tile wall. She pressed her back against the wall and pulled him to her, moaning as his mouth slanted over hers. She shifted her hips and fit her body to his, in an easy move that fused them together, nose to nose, their lips barely touching. His nearness made Skylar gasp in delight and go weak, eager to surrender completely again.

"You can't imagine how it makes me feel to be with you. I'm a lucky guy, Skylar," Mark whispered, his breath warming her face. "With you at my side, we can have a great life. Children, a home, a real future."

A hot ache tore through her body and filled her up, temporarily blocking out the nagging worry that she didn't want to face: How could she tell Mark the truth? That she had held back an important part of her past from him. That she might never be able to give him the family that he dreamed of. That she wasn't the honest, hardworking woman he thought her to be.

"I'm the lucky one," she managed in a voice filled with longing. "And you really caught me off guard, you know? I wasn't looking for anything like this when I left Tampa and came here. All I wanted to do was lose myself in my job and forget about my problems. But then you came along and changed everything."

"We were meant to be together, Skylar."

"You think so?"

"I know it, and I feel that way every time I look at you, touch you, kiss you." He traced his tongue across her wet shoulder in a lazy, silky way. "Who would have dreamed that I'd ever find a beautiful, uncomplicated woman like you in a remote ski school in the Colorado mountains?" He chuckled and shook his head. "Loving you is so easy." He swept his tongue over her warm smooth skin once more, licking away a few drops of water.

Suddenly, Skylar chilled and shifted away from Mark's touch. He had just called her "uncomplicated"? What could be further from the truth?

Untangling her body from Mark's, she went to stand beneath the shower of water once more, her hands at her sides, her mind churning as the water sluiced over her body and brought her back to reality.

What was she thinking? She was a multi-millionaire and just might have more hard cash in the bank than he did. Uncomplicated? She was far more complicated than he could ever imagine

Skylar fell quiet and thoughtful as she considered her reaction. The pace at which their relationship was moving had finally caught up with her and she knew it was time to slow things down or come clean. But how could she tell him now? When they both were about to rush off to work? No, that would not be right.

Maybe this was a big mistake. Maybe she'd better rethink this, she thought. After all, she couldn't keep her secret from him forever, but until the time was right, she'd be wise to cool this situation down a few degrees.

"You'd better get going," she laughingly told him, ducking out from under the water. Quickly, she stepped out of the shower and grabbed a big, white towel, which she wrapped around her body. "Go!" she jokingly ordered. "Get out of here so I can get dressed and to work. We're both already late."

Frowning, Mark stepped out of the shower. "What's wrong?" he asked, pushing the door shut while watching her carefully. "Did I say something that upset you?"

"No. Of course not. Nothing's wrong, it's just getting late, Mark, and I do have a busy day."

"All right, all right. But tonight, we continue where we left off. Okay?" He gave her a wink and a quick peck on the back before disappearing into the bedroom.

With a worried sigh, Skylar began to dry off, calculating her next move.

Chapter 21

When Deena stepped into the sun drenched café on the first floor of the main lodge, her attention was immediately drawn to Virina, who was dressed in a velvety peach velour running suit and sitting alone at one of the small round tables, drinking a cup of espresso. For a split second, their eyes locked, and when Virina lifted an arm and waved Deena over, she quickly complied, always eager for an opportunity to speak with one of her guests.

"Good morning, Miss Dagrun," Deena greeted. "How's everything going? Are you comfortable in the Vista View Suite?"

Nodding, Virina set down her coffee cup and beamed up at Deena. "Perfect," she replied, raising one pale brow. "The suite is most comfortable. And I must tell you that the party last night was simply wonderful, and for such a good cause, too. I'm enjoying myself immensely."

"I'm glad to hear that," Deena said. "If there's anything you need, don't hesitate to let me or a member of my staff know. We're pretty easy-going around here, and we want everyone to feel at home. Like family, you know?"

"Yes, I can see that things are much more casual and relaxed here than at other resorts. Your staff has been most accommodating," Virina said, and then she motioned toward the empty chair across from her. "Do you have a minute to talk? I'd like to know a little more about your ski school and resort. It's a lovely piece of property. You should be so proud."

"Oh, I am," Deena said as she pulled out the chair and sat down. "We're doing well this season, and a lot of our success is due to having Mark on staff. We've needed a boost like the one he's giving us. You have an extremely talented son, Miss Dagrun."

"Thank you, I think so, too." She paused, a finger at her chin, as if carefully considering her next remark. "He seems to be happy here, and I'm pleased about that, but I must admit I'm somewhat surprised that he chose Scenic Ridge to settle down and teach."

"Surprised? About what?" Deena asked.

Virina leaned forward and lowered her voice an octave. "Well, he's always been drawn to the more glamorous places, like Innsbruck and St. Moritz, you know? He's such a social person. Loves the parties, the attention, the constant travel, and though he may not admit it, he even enjoys the flow of celebrities in and out of his life. Scenic Ridge is so different from what he's used to. Rather isolated and disconnected from the Aspen social scene. Not the kind of setting he's frequented in the past. But don't get me wrong," she hurried to add. "I applaud Mark's devotion to teaching and I'm certain he does an excellent job."

"He does," Deena replied with firm assurance. "We've never had a complaint, so far."

Virina focused her ice blue eyes on her tiny espresso cup and twirled it around in its saucer a few times. "So, has your sister adjusted to mountain life? I understand she's from Florida. Miami, perhaps?"

"No, Tampa," Deena quickly corrected, knowing where this discussion was headed. She sure didn't want to get into an in-depth discussion about Skylar, especially since Virina must know by now that Skylar and her son were more than casual coworkers.

Deena had headed to Skylar's room earlier to see if she wanted to join her for breakfast, arriving just as the housekeeping maid had shown up. When the maid opened Skylar's door, Deena had peeked over her shoulder and seen that the bed was still made from the night before and Skylar was nowhere around. Apparently, she had not come home last night, and Deena had a good idea where, and with whom, Skylar might have slept.

"Oh, yes, Tampa," Virina repeated. "And she likes being a concierge?"

"She does. Quite a change from being a paralegal."

Virina's eyes widened. "Oh? Did she work for a large law firm?"

"No, she worked for the county. Assisting court appointed lawyers. She was skeptical about taking on the concierge position, but she jumped right in and is doing a heck of a job." Deena chuckled, shaking her head. "She had a few rough days when she first arrived, but she's adjusted just fine."

"Good for her. What made Skylar decide to leave Florida?"

"Oh, she was in a kind of slump. Out of work and needed a change, so I convinced her to come up here to work. The best decision for both of us, as my husband had to leave for a while to take care of some family matters."

"How nice of you two sisters to help each other out," Virina commented. She finished off her coffee and pushed the cup to the center of the table. "I've truly enjoyed chatting with you, but I've got to get going. Gotta pack. A thousand things to do before I leave." She stood up and shouldered her peach, gold-studded, leather purse.

"You're leaving so soon?" Deena asked, standing, too. She shoved her chair up to the table and held on to its back.

"Only for a short trip to Los Angeles. Business that cannot wait. You know, I'm going to produce the film on Mark's life. I've got to get busy pulling my investors together. However, I'm not moving out of my suite. Just leave my things as they are and bill me for the days I'm gone. It's a lovely cabin and I don't want to lose it."

"No problem," Deena said, watching as Virina walked away.

She's digging into Skylar big-time, Deena thought, hoping she hadn't given away too much. *All I promised Skylar was that I wouldn't tell anyone that she's rich, and so far I've held to that,* Deena rationalized. *But it won't take Virina Dagrun long to find out the truth, and I can't wait to see the expression on her snooty face when she finds out that her son is involved with an extremely wealthy woman.*

Skylar was standing in the lobby talking to a bearded man who was listening intently to her directions to Ruby Park, when she glanced up and saw Virina come out of the café and hurry into the gift shop. For some reason, Skylar tensed. Why did just the sight of that woman make her nervous? What had she really come to Mark's cabin for this morning? Surely, not to tell him she was leaving town for a few days. The woman was the most snobbish, self-absorbed person Skylar had ever met, and it was a wonder that Mark had turned out to be as normal as he was.

A real piece of work, Skylar thought, as she folded the map and handed it to the man. "Just walk one block from Aspen Square to the Aspen Transportation Center at Ruby Park. You can get on a free shuttle that will take you to Highlands, Snowmass or Buttermilk. The buses run all day, so don't worry about rushing to catch a particular one. If you can, try to hit all four of the mountains while you're here and have a good time!" she told him, still distracted by Virina's appearance.

Skylar went into her office and snapped on her computer monitor. Sliding into her chair, she stared blankly at the screen, seeing nothing, but feeling everything. A quiver of longing ran through her and made her shudder as memories of her night with Mark came rushing back.

I wonder where he is now. What he's doing. Is he thinking about me? About last night? She had never felt so completely alive and romantically satisfied in her life, and the depth of her contentedness was alarmingly raw.

Mark knows exactly what I need and he gives it to me, as I do for him. We're perfect together, she realized, still in awe over the level of their intimacy and the compatibility of their bodies. *Mark has managed to blot out all memories of Lewis,* she realized, sensing that she was finally healed of her past disappointments and ready to enter a new phase of commitment. *Mark is tender, strong, intelligent and sexy. He loves me just as I am.*

Skylar frowned as that thought sank in. *Just as I am?* That was so far from true, and the longer she held on to her secrets, the more difficult it was going to be to level with Mark.

"But I'm the woman he wants," Skylar murmured to herself. "When he learns that I'm rich, it won't be such a big deal. He'll probably laugh about it and agree with my decision to keep my financial status a secret from the staff."

My having money might not be a deal breaker in this relationship, but the fact that I could be barren surely is, she silently groaned, dreading the day when she'd have to have that conversation with him.

It was hard for Mark to concentrate on his instructions amidst the riotous laughter that was coming from the overweight, former pro football player and three of his equally bulked-up buddies. The guys were struggling to master the powder. Between cracking jokes and a lot of vigorous back-slapping, they were having a good time. And Mark was glad of that, because he sure couldn't tell them the truth—skiing might not be the sport for them and it might be wise to spend the rest of their reunion time indoors socializing with pretty girls by the fire. Steeling himself for another rough try, Mark repositioned his comic quartet and urged them to try a new maneuver.

"This is how you control your speed. It's called a 'gliding wedge,'" Mark began.

"Uh, oh," the leader of the pack quickly reacted, shaking his head. "I can tell right now, that this one is going to be a real ball breaker."

His companions screamed their laughter.

"Stay with me now," Mark urged. "It's not as difficult as it looks. You're gonna make a V-shaped position by sliding both ski tails an equal distance apart while keeping your ski tips together. This will create resistance and slow you down as you come down the hill. Gradually make the wedge wider as you ski straight down the hill until you come to a stop. Okay, let's try it."

The men set off, grunting and shouting as they headed down Bunny Hill. Mark simply held his breath and prayed.

While they were practicing, Mark watched, thinking that Richard could use this kind of footage to demonstrate that skiing could be a lot of fun even if you were over forty and somewhat balance challenged. For their second try, Mark stepped away to let his assistant, John, work with them, while he observed. Standing there, his mind wandered back to the day when he first introduced Skylar to the slopes.

She had been an excellent student, and they had had so much fun that day. He couldn't wait to get her out on the mountains again. But when? He worried. She was so busy working all the time and, in his opinion, too dedicated to her job. Mark understood that she probably needed the money and was thankful to have the position, but she couldn't work all the time.

This morning, she had been quite firm about getting rid of him so she could get to her office, and the way she had broken off their romantic interlude in the shower still disturbed him. After giving herself so completely to him last night, what had happened? Had Skylar overheard what his mother had said about her? Was she worried that he was going to do as his mother wanted and dump her?

Mark gritted his teeth, calculating possible reasons for

Skylar's change in attitude. He'd definitely felt the brunt of her chilly dismissal when she stepped out of the shower, even though she had tried to laugh it off. They'd have to talk it out tonight. Clear the air of whatever was bothering Skylar. The last thing he wanted was any friction between them.

After several successful Bunny Hill runs, the rotund group set off toward the lift with John right behind them while Mark jumped on a lift to head back down. With his last session of the morning over, Mark headed into his office to warm up and give Skylar a quick call. He needed to hear her voice, feel reassured that everything was okay between them. She had always had a mysterious air about her, but lately, it seemed as if she was worried, or holding something in that was bothering her. He wished she would trust him with whatever was on her mind.

"Just thinking of you," he told her in a sexy voice as soon as she answered her phone. "Busy?"

"Very," Skylar quipped right away. "In fact, I can't talk right now, Mark. I have an emergency request from a woman who needs a replacement for a broken hearing aid, and I've got to get right on it."

"Okay, okay. I won't hold you up. Want to meet for lunch? I can break at noon and won't have another class until two-thirty."

"Lunch?" Skylar paused. "Um. No. Sorry. I can't, too much to do."

"Yeah," Mark replied, trying to sound much less irritated than he actually was. "We still on for karaoke tonight?" he ventured.

"I dunno. Better not count on it," Skylar said in a brisk tone. "Deena asked me to help out at a corporate banquet tonight and I told her I would. Call me later, okay?"

“Sure, I’ll check back when I finish for the day.” Clicking off, Mark scratched his head. Something was wrong and he had no idea what it could be. Only Skylar knew and obviously, she was not ready to tell him.

Chapter 22

Back in New York, Richard viewed the rough cut of the film that he had shot at Scenic Ridge, and knew he had something special. Using the ski school as a forum to showcase Mark Jorgen's Olympic career, as well as the work he was currently doing, had turned out to be a unique angle that would encourage minorities to take up skiing while creating a buzz around the project.

The executives at Black Entertainment Showcase loved what he showed them and immediately gave Richard the green light to go ahead and complete the project. As soon as he got out of the meeting he called Virina in Los Angeles.

"Good news, Richard," Virina said when she heard that the rough cut of the film was exactly what BES wanted.

"Yeah, and I've got to get the ball rolling. How's the money looking?"

"No problem. I've got investors lined up just waiting to write checks, so go ahead and proceed with the project."

Richard hesitated for a moment, and then asked, "Are you sure? Because I'll be making financial commitments that I'll have to personally cover if the money folks don't come through."

"I told you. It's all set. I have commitments from my people for more than enough money to cover the final project. However, if you need cash right away, I can transfer some money tomorrow. How much do you need?"

"Hold off for now," Richard advised. "Let me finalize negotiations I've got going on for legal fees and studio time. Once those costs are firm, I can adjust our original budget and get back to you."

"Fine. Call me in a few days," Virina told him, clicking off.

Relieved that Virina was coming through with the funding, Richard got busy. In record time, he put together a full film crew, hired a director, a logistics person, make-up, wardrobe and graphic talent and put down deposits for studio time that he would need to edit the piece after filming was completed. He contacted a good friend of his who was a lawyer and got him to draw up the necessary releases and contracts with a promise to pay him as soon as the funding came through. Then he booked air fare and rooms for everyone going to Scenic Ridge.

Within a week, Richard and his crew were back in Colorado, and for the next ten days the men and women working with him shadowed Mark everywhere he went. They shot him teaching beginners, coaching the new wave of budding professionals, giving lectures on how to safely hit the slopes and even at home in the Snow King Suite after a full day on the powder. When it became clear to Richard that Mark and Skylar were more than coworkers, he managed to get some shots of them having drinks together in the main lodge.

Richard studied a great number of photos, mementos and scrapbooks that carefully detailed Mark's stunning career, including his Olympic trials and eventual win. Using a digital voice recorder, he interviewed Mark and captured stories about his youth, which provided insight on what it had been like to be among the few black competitors in a mostly white sport. It was evident that Mark had moved in a world populated with world class athletes and socially important people and that his life experiences had been very different from those of an average black male living in America.

When Richard wasn't with Mark, he was talking with Deena or shooting footage of the lodge and its surroundings, as well as documenting the inner workings of the ski school and the resort. He got plenty of footage of Skylar, too, as she interacted with guests who were more than happy to be included in the film.

The ski school instructors, the resort staff and even guests at the lodge were not shy about approaching Richard to express their interest in and support of his project. Many of them asked if they could be interviewed, eager to add their voices to the film and give their approval of the important contributions to winter sports that the Simpsons and Mark Jorgen were making, especially for minorities.

By the end of the second week in Colorado, Richard had accumulated enough raw film and taped interviews to fly back to New York, sort it all out and decide what else he needed. As soon as he put together a rough cut of the film, he sent it to Virina in L.A., eager for her reaction.

In Los Angeles, Virina hung up the phone, picked up her Tiffany pen and made an *X* over the name of the person she had been talking to, Abdul Jaran. Another rejection. And she had only asked him for twenty thousand dollars. Crossing him off her list meant that she had exhausted all of her potential investors without raising one cent of the financial commitment she had made to Richard Nobel. Why had her friends suddenly become so damn cautious about their investments? They were holding on to their money as if it were glued to their hands. She had been shocked at how snippy some of them had been with her, too. What was going on?

Did they think of her as an outsider now that she was no longer married to Count Wilhelm? Or maybe they were snubbing her because Mark's star status had faded and he no longer traveled in their circles, preferring to bury himself in a second class resort? Had news leaked about her imminent departure from Deleur Cosmetics? She simply had no answers. But one thing she did know: the cool reception she had received from people she had thought were her friends was frightening, and she had to do something about it or risk being permanently shut out of the world to which she absolutely *had* to remain connected.

Calling potential investors, leaving messages for them, and then tracking them down had taken much more time than she had thought, but she'd done it, and now she had to face the truth. She had failed in her mission and Mark's documentary would not be made, at least not with funds she raised.

Nervously, she glanced over the list of names again, depressed by the way she had been treated. Why hadn't she managed to persuade them to commit to Richard's project? Even when she had informed them that Black Entertainment Showcase was on board as the distributor, they still had not budged. Couldn't they understand that a permanent record of her son's life and his achievements was only the first step? That a book deal, a DVD and his media appearances would surely rake in the cash and give them a healthy return on their money?

At one time, when Virina had been married to a wealthy Palm Springs Realtor, she had earned the reputation as the most effective, sought-after charity fundraiser in the state. Back then, she had honed her skills to a fine art and brought in record-breaking sums for a roll call of nonprofit organizations. Now, she couldn't raise a dime to benefit her son, as well as ensure her own future.

Contemplating her dilemma, Virina set down her notepad, opened a bottle of Evian and took a quick sip. If there was one thing she hated, it was failing, and even worse was for anyone to know that she had failed. Now, she'd have to find a creative way to break the news to Richard without letting on that she had miscalculated her leverage with people she'd thought were her friends.

When the doorbell rang, she hurried to answer, pushing depressing thoughts from her mind. It was Federal Express and the package she signed for was from Richard. She ripped it open and was both delighted and uneasy to see that it was the DVD first cut of the film that he had promised to send her. How much had this cost and how many people did he owe money to? she worried. But most importantly, what reason could she give him for not coming through with the funds to complete the project?

She took the DVD into the living room and slipped it into the DVD player, anxious to see what Richard had done. It started out with an overview of Mark's childhood and his early years, using photos that she and Mark had provided. Her eyes grew misty as she watched a montage of early pictures of herself, Mark and his father, James.

God, James was so handsome, Virina mused, now able to see how much Mark resembled his father. Seeing the three of them together brought a rush of memories back. Her early days of modeling. The fun she'd had while living in New York. Resettling in Norway as a single mother after James walked out on her. It all seemed so long ago, and yet Virina still missed the hell out of James and wished they could have made it together.

Other photos followed. Mark when he first arrived in Norway, wearing a baggy knit sweater and his first pair of skis. Virina on the mountain with Mark, giving him pointers on how to do parallel turns on his first slope.

The memories tumbled around, crowding into her mind, making Virina both proud and sad. She and Mark had been so close back then, almost like brother and sister. He had trusted her completely, followed her advice. But now he seemed so distant and angry all the time. What had she done to deserve this kind of treatment? All she had ever wanted to do was look out for him, prepare him for a better life than she had had as a child. Why didn't he understand that she had never wanted him to know what it was like to go to bed hungry, to wear thin-soled shoes and second-hand clothing and to feel cold all the time?

Virina's parents had been Norwegian farming peasants,

as her grandparents had been before them. Stoically accepting their station in life, her family had been content to live in their small wood-and-sod house, to own two changes of clothing, to earn their living with an ancient plow and a pair of mules. But Virina had never stopped yearning for more. She spent all her spare time skiing, to stay out in the open and out of her tiny crowded house. When it became clear that she was a talented skier, she had begged her father to let her go to Oslo to train for the Olympics. He had refused: he needed her on the farm. Angry and resentful, she put away her dream, but as soon as she turned eighteen, she fled the farm, worked odd jobs in Oslo and eventually made her way to the United States. To her good fortune, James Jorgen had come along and made her journey worthwhile, and she'd always be grateful to him for that, even though he'd dumped her for that bitchy Ethiopian and abandoned his only son.

The film rolled quickly through Mark's high school years, documenting his rigorous training schedule and his many competitions, including his Olympic win in 1992 at the Albertville Olympic Games in France. What a great time they'd had! Norwegian skiers won every cross-country skiing race at the competition that year, and Mark had been right up there with Björn Daehlie and Vegard Ulvang, each of whom won gold medals, too.

The next section of the film started with Mark talking about his decision to leave the competitive world of skiing at the age of thirty-six to explore teaching.

When a shot of the exterior of Scenic Ridge came up, Virina paused, waiting for more references to Mark and his work at the school. However, the story took a turn away from Mark when Deena Simpson's face appeared and she began talking about how and why she and her husband had started the ski school. An in-depth piece followed, showcasing Jerome Simpson, whose family had acquired the backwoods property in the Roaring Fork Valley for very little money seventy-five years ago. Next came details about the construction of the resort. Then interviews with various staff members, including Skylar Webster. Testimonials from former students. Endorsements by black ski clubs. Another shot of Skylar, this time with Mark, relaxing in front of a fire while chatting with a group of students.

Virina gasped. What was this about? The documentary was more of a promotional piece for Scenic Ridge, than a feature story on her son's life. It was a good thing that her investor-friends hadn't come through. This was not what she had pitched to them at all!

While staring at the images on her television screen, an idea began to form in her mind. A slow smile curved her lips. Richard had just provided the answer to her dilemma and she was going to use it.

Quickly, she snatched up the phone and began punching the keypad while mentally rehearsing how she was going to blast Richard with outrage and turn her failure to her advantage.

"I want to know why this material is focused so heavily on the ski school at Scenic Ridge!" she shouted into the phone as soon as Richard answered.

"I thought we agreed that I would include Mark's current status as an instructor at the ski school. We talked about it when we were at dinner in New York. Remember?"

"No, I don't remember any such conversation. I agreed on shots of Mark at work! Not the Simpson family's life story."

"But their story adds so much to the project and it's right in line with the vision I have for the film."

"I don't care. It's not what I envisioned and it's certainly not what I told the investors they'd be buying. I never agreed to any shots of, or references to Deena Simpson, or her sister, Skylar Webster, either. That damn little hotel concierge might think she's got a place in my son's life but she damn well doesn't have a place in my son's life story. This was not to be a promotional piece for her sister's business venture."

"Then I guess we really aren't on the same page, Miss Dagrun. Mark made it clear to me before I began that he'd only participate if the ski school was featured, too."

"He never said that to me!" Virina snapped.

"Then I guess you two didn't communicate very well," Richard said, trying to smooth things out. "I thought you understood the direction of the piece."

"Well, you can forget about getting a dime from me. I'm through with you and now I've got to go back to my investors and tell them the project is off. How do you think that will make me look? You've caused me a great deal of embarrassment, Richard, and I don't take things like that lightly." She slammed down the receiver, completely satisfied that she had solved her problem. As for Richard, let him find someone else to raise money to promote Scenic Ridge, she sure as hell wasn't going to.

"What in the world is wrong with Mark?" she muttered crossly as she shoved her notebook into her desk drawer. "Why is he so dead-set on promoting that school anyway? What has gotten into him?"

After a few churning moments of rage, she settled on an answer to her question: Skylar Webster. That's what happened to Mark and Virina knew what she had to do.

Picking up the phone again, she connected with information and got the number for the county courthouse in Tampa, Florida. That would be the place to start. If Skylar had been a paralegal there, then surely there was some record of her connection to the court system. It might take some doing, but Virina would not give up until she learned everything possible about Skylar, and she was certain some of it would not be good.

And when I get my ammunition, Mark will realize that I am right to steer him away from that woman and that place, she vowed. Grabbing her pen to jot down the phone number for the Hillsborough County Courthouse.

Within seconds, Virina got through to the county Human Resources department and politely asked for an employment reference for Skylar Webster.

"Oh, yes, Skylar," the woman replied. "All I'm permitted to tell you is that when she terminated her employment with the county after her accident she had an excellent work record."

"She was in an accident?"

"Oh, yes," the woman concurred, going on to describe the elevator accident in great detail. "You know, the accident is public record, so I'm not violating any rules by telling you what happened. Such a shame. Good thing Skylar came out of it okay. Everyone at the courthouse loved working with her."

"So, she's fully recovered?" Virina probed, hoping to lead the woman deeper into the conversation. "Her injuries won't interfere with her ability to work as a salesgirl at my cosmetics company, will they? Are there any restrictions or workman's compensation issues that I need to be aware of?"

"Oh, let's see," the woman replied.

Virina could hear the lady shuffling through some papers.

"No. Everything is settled. Dr. Pope approved her return to work." A beat. "But why is Skylar applying for a job with your company anyway?"

"Because she needs the money, I guess," Virina replied.

"I doubt that. Would you be looking for a job if an elevator company awarded you four million dollars?"

"Four million dollars?" Virina repeated, clutching the handset of her phone, her throat beginning to dry. "Are you sure?"

"Sure? Of course, it was in the papers. Everyone knows about her settlement."

Everyone except Mark, Virina thought, realizing that she had found the ammunition she needed.

Richard Nobel stared at his phone, which was still humming with a deadly buzz. Virina Dagrun had just sabotaged his project! He jammed the handset back into its cradle and placed his fingertips to his lips, worried. Anxiously, he scanned the pile of bills on his desk, the folders filled with contracts committing him to thousands of dollars.

I've got no investors, and I'm already in the hole for a hell of a lot of money in preproduction costs. Richard got up and paced the floor of his studio, thinking. *The film is half finished. I've already spent too much time and money to toss it in the trash. What in hell am I going to do?*

Richard knew he had enough material to create two different pieces if he had to: One on Mark Jorgen to satisfy Virina's investors, and another on Scenic Ridge that could stand on its own. But that was not what he wanted to do and not what BES expected him to deliver. If he didn't straighten this mess out quickly, he'd lose all credibility with the network and he was not about to let that happen. He had to either find other investors or change the focus of the film. At this late date, neither option seemed promising.

Chapter 23

Snowflakes drifted down, adding to the accumulation that already covered the brick walkway that led from the main lodge to the ice skating rink. Skylar lifted her face toward the star-filled sky and stuck out her tongue, smiling to feel the tiny bits of ice melting in her mouth. Winter weather was still so new to her, but she enjoyed it and had come to love the peaceful quiet that fell over everything when snow blanketed the land. The moon was full, adding to the luminous sheen of white that surrounded her, creating a feeling of being lost in a wintry fairyland.

Stopping at a wooden bench facing the rink, she sat down, tucked her hands into the pockets of her parka and leaned forward, focusing on a middle-aged couple in the center of the rink who were trying hard to remain upright.

From the way they were interacting, Skylar guessed that they were married—and definitely still in love. They were laughing and holding hands, oblivious to the other skaters, who whirled past without giving them any notice. When the woman crashed to the ice and landed on her backside, her companion quickly leaned down to help her up and then kissed her gently on the lips. The romantic gesture made Skylar's heart lurch in longing. She missed Mark so much and wanted nothing more than to be sitting with him right then, her arm linked through his, her head resting on his shoulder.

For the past two weeks, she had made it a point not to be alone with Mark and knew he was upset with the way she'd been acting. Even during filming when Richard's crew had been in town, she had made sure that her contact with Mark had been limited to times when other staff or students had been around. By cooling down the relationship, she had hurt him very much, but not as much as she feared she would once she told him the truth.

Though she had been busy with guests' demands during the Black Winter Sports Reunion, and then involved with Richard during his filming, all of that was over now, and she could no longer use work as an excuse not to spend time with Mark.

The last time she saw him was in the main dining room yesterday afternoon, and he had actually turned his back on her and struck up a conversation with a buxom sister from Georgia who was not shy about showing off every one of her curves in her skin-tight, red ski suit. The sight had made Skylar slightly nauseous.

But she had no one to blame for her misery but herself, and it would be up to her to make things right. Mark had stopped inviting her to dinner and no longer called every night to hear her voice before he went to bed. They had drifted so far apart that the possibility of losing him completely was great, making Skylar shift nervously on the bench.

She loved Mark, and knew he wasn't going to hang around forever, waiting for her to tell him what was wrong. Why should he stick by her, only to be brushed off again and again? He deserved better, and she had to tell him everything or pull out of the relationship all together.

"Tomorrow," she decided, prepared to take her chances. "Whatever happens, I'll deal with it, but at least I'll know where I stand."

When Mark answered the knock on the door of his cabin, he was shocked to see Virina standing on the porch, dressed in a camel suede poncho and a fluffy coyote fur hat. He had barely recovered enough from her surprise visit to say hello, when she blurted out the reason she had come.

"We need to talk," she stated in that flat, demanding tone that Mark had heard too often during his youth. It meant that she was upset with him, was determined to have her way, and was not going to listen to a thing he had to say. There had been a time when that crisp edge to her voice would have made him very nervous, but no more. All he could think of was that it was late, he was tired, and not in the mood for one of her ranting, raving outbursts over something petty that didn't concern him.

"Well, welcome back," Mark said, ignoring her rude declaration. "When did you get here?"

"Two hours ago."

"Come on in. What's up?"

Virina stepped inside, quickly shed her outer clothing

and then glanced around, as if to make sure they were alone. "Is anyone here with you?"

"No, why?"

"As I said, we need to talk." She sighed and went over to the bar. "Fix me a *Linie Aquavit,* will you, Mark? My nerves are absolutely shot. The flight in from Los Angeles was horrid! Turbulence all the way, and Henri forgot to stock the plane's bar before we left. I swear I'm going to fire that man."

Mark grunted his reaction as he went to the bar and fixed his mother's drink. "You can't fire Henri. He doesn't work for you, he works for Wilhelm, doesn't he?"

Virina simply glared at Mark, accepting the glass he offered to her. "I can get Wilhelm to fire him if I complain enough. That man is worthless. Absolutely worthless." She swallowed a hefty gulp of the schnapps and then licked her pink-tinted lips. "It's so hard to get good help, people who want to do their jobs. I just don't understand it."

"So, did you come all the way back to tell me you're firing Henri, or is there something more important on your mind?" Mark asked, moving to sit on the sofa. Virina sat down on the love seat opposite him and crossed her legs.

"Oh, I came with plenty to say, but I'm afraid you're not going to like most of it."

"Go on," he urged.

"It's about Richard's documentary. I was extremely upset when I saw that he had turned it into a promotional piece for this place. It was supposed to be about you, Mark. Not about Jerome Simpson and his family. You are an Olympic gold medal winner who happens to head their ski school. That's it. I can't raise money for a film if it's not exclusively your story. It's one thing to mention where you work and refer to Scenic Ridge in passing, but all that back story on Jerome Simpson's family. And why the hell was Skylar even interviewed?"

"She is Deena's sister and she's a member of the staff, too," Mark managed to get in.

"Whatever," Virina grumpily acknowledged. "As I told Richard, all that stuff on the Simpson family has turned my investors off. They all backed out because they felt it smacked of too much promotion."

"What kind of people were they? If the history and importance of Scenic Ridge as a minority-owned ski resort isn't of interest to them, then it's their loss. I'm not really interested in participating unless Scenic Ridge is in it," Mark told her.

Virina squinted her cold blue eyes at him. "That's what Richard told me, and frankly, that's why he lost funding. People want to invest in you, Mark…not the Simpsons. Don't be naive. You know how it goes."

"Oh, yeah. I know all about sponsors and their demands, that's one of the reasons I'm out of the competitive arena and content to teach. Now, I can wear whatever kind of ski wear I like, use the brand of equipment that I prefer and live my life exactly as I please. It feels good not to have to ask permission from anyone before I make a move. And that's how it should be, you know?"

"In a perfect world, maybe," Virina tightly conceded. "But you're not living in a perfect world. I had to chase the money and then call off the project because of your demands. That was very humiliating for me, Mark."

"Sure, sure," Mark responded with very little compassion. "Well, you know where I stand. If you're out of the picture, then fine. Richard can get his own money people, who will agree with our vision. Otherwise, I guess he'll have to find some other athlete to profile. I don't really want to discuss this again. The documentary can stay on the shelf as far as I'm concerned."

"That's a stupid call, Mark, but it's yours to make."

"Right, so drop it, okay? I'll get in touch with Richard and see what we can figure out."

"Fine with me. I only agreed to produce it to help you. Now. There is another matter that we need to discuss." She took a moment to pull herself together and settle herself more firmly on the love seat, as if preparing for the next round.

"What?" Mark prompted.

"This obsessive allegiance you seem to have with Scenic Ridge is all because of that girl, Skylar, isn't it, Mark? I don't think she ought to..."

"Stop right there, Mother," he interrupted. "I told you not to bring her up."

"Why? Do you love her? Plan to marry her? Have a family with her?"

"Yes, as a matter of fact I do love her, and yes, I'd like a future with her. I'm grown. I can choose for myself and I *know* she's the one for me."

Though he was trying hard to sound convincing, he secretly wondered if there was any future for him and Skylar. For the past two weeks, she had been distant and edgy, not really eager to see him. Hopefully, it was just because she'd been overworked during the reunion, and then caught up in the chaos of having a film crew on the premises. But now all of that was over. Surely, things would get back to normal with them. He hoped so, because his feelings for her had not changed.

"Do you know why Skylar came to Scenic Ridge? Why she left Florida?" Virina was asking.

Mark gave himself a mental shake and refocused on his mother. "Yes, she needed a job and wanted a change."

"A job? Why would a woman who is wealthy need to take a job as a concierge?"

Mark narrowed his gaze. "What're you talking about? She's not wealthy. She's just a working girl who had a tough break back in Tampa."

"Her elevator accident?"

"Right. I know all about it. Anyway, how did you find out about that?" Mark wanted to know.

"I have my sources," Virina coyly answered. "Did she tell you that Dorchester Elevator awarded her four million dollars?"

Mark pulled back, lifting his chin. "I don't believe you."

"Ask her!"

Now, he shot forward, his elbows on his thighs, his face level with Virina's. "I will!" His eyes bored into his mothers. "You're lying! Skylar told me that she received a small amount of money and that the elevator company covered her medical expenses, but that's all. You're just twisting everything to make it sound so damn dramatic."

"There's more I could tell you, Mark, but I can see that you wouldn't believe me. Go to her and ask her what else she's been hiding, what she hasn't had the decency to reveal to the man who says he wants to marry her. I've checked out Skylar Webster thoroughly and she is not the kind of woman you want for a wife, or I need for a daughter-in-law. She's a deceitful, untrustworthy liar and a penny pincher, too!" Virina paused to sit back and fluff out her hair. "What self-respecting woman hides her wealth and lives like a pauper? Not one in her right mind, as far as I'm concerned. What's the use of having money if you deny yourself the more pleasurable things in life?"

Rising from the sofa, Mark went to the hearth and stared into the blazing fire, his mind frozen in shock. Was this why Skylar was pulling away from him? Did she know her lies were about to catch up with her? But why had she lied in the first place? The fact that she had been awarded such a large sum of money was a shock, but not a big deal. In fact, he was happy for her. But what else was she hiding? What could be so bad that revealing it would destroy what they had found together?

Grabbing his jacket off the hook by the door, he pulled it on and then turned back to his mother. "I plan to get to the bottom of this, and you'd better not be lying."

Virina simply shrugged her shoulders and widened her eyes, but did not respond.

Chapter 24

"Oh, Mark!" Skylar said, startled to see him approaching from the opposite side of the ice rink. She shifted over, making room for him to sit beside her on the bench, positioning herself so that she could see his face. Skylar could tell that he was winded, as if he'd been running. His parka was unzipped and he wasn't wearing a hat or gloves. "Is something wrong?" she asked, thinking there might be an emergency at the ski school or the lodge.

"No, but I've been looking for you. We need to talk."

"I know, and I'm glad you came," she told him, a surge of nervous relief filling her chest as she realized it was time to have the conversation she had dreaded for so long. "I've been sitting here, thinking about you…about us. I've missed being with you, Mark."

"Really? You gave me the impression that you wanted to be left alone. That's why I haven't bothered you."

Skylar lowered her eyes, hurt by the hard edge to Mark's words, but knowing he spoke the truth. "You're right. I did want to be alone for a while. I had a few things I needed to sort out."

"Were you successful?" he quipped, a bit sarcastically as he sat down beside her.

"I...don't know." She hesitated, sensing a definite tone of hostility in his voice.

"Want to talk about it?" he prompted.

Again, she paused, but then nodded. "Yes, I do."

Mark crossed his arms, slipped low on his spine and stuck out his booted feet, as if settling in to listen. "Shoot. I'm all ears."

Skylar reached for his hand, wanting to hold on to it while she talked, but he pulled it away and stuck it in his pocket. Alarmed by his reaction, she summoned the strength to plunge ahead with her confession.

"Mark, I need to tell you something about me that you don't know."

"Just one thing?"

"Well...two very important things," she began, inhaling slowly. "Remember the accident I told you about?"

"Dorchester Elevator, wasn't it?"

Skylar flinched. She had never told him the name of the company that had awarded her the settlement and wondered how he had found out. Had he been checking on her? Had Deena slipped and told him? And if so, how long had he known the truth? "Why, yes. Dorchester. How did you know?"

"That's not important. Go on, please."

Realizing that he was not going to reveal his source and that he wanted to hear it from her, she continued, eyes lowered, afraid to watch his expression. "Dorchester did more than just cover my medical expenses. They settled out of court with me for a very large sum of money."

"About four million dollars?" Mark added.

With a jerk, Skylar looked up at Mark, eyes narrowed, her heart pounding very fast. He had a smug look on his face, as if he were enjoying watching her squirm and his expression told her all she needed to know. He had known all along. He knew she had been playing a game with him. But why hadn't he said anything before now? "So, you know all about my settlement?"

He nodded, eyes locked with hers. "Enough, but not everything, I'm sure."

"And?" she ventured, fearful of his reaction.

"It makes me want to know what else you're hiding." He flexed his jaw, making the muscles in his neck move back and forth while he stared stonily ahead.

"All right. Here it is. I was seriously hurt when the elevator crashed. I wound up with a shattered right elbow and a fractured pelvis. My bones healed, but my body didn't."

He glanced over at her, now paying attention. "What does that mean?"

"It means that my chances of carrying a child to term are very slim, nearly impossible. You see, a piece of bone punctured my womb. It was a serious tear. The doctors stitched me up, but they aren't sure how the injury will affect a pregnancy in the future. Every specialist I consulted told me the same thing."

"What?"

"Better not count on ever having a successful pregnancy."

A long pause. "I see." A bitter sigh slipped from between his slightly parted lips. "No children for you, huh?"

"Probably not," Skylar continued. "Mark, I wanted to tell you, but after you began talking about how much you want children and how important a family is to you, I knew I couldn't just blurt this out. I didn't plan on falling in love with you, Mark. When I met you, I was hurting, and you made the pain of my past disappear. I forgot about Lewis, the accident, his betrayal. Finally, I was happy again. I didn't think about the consequences of holding on to my secrets. I wanted to tell you, but I didn't know how, so I stepped back to take time to decide what to do. During this time apart, I've realized how much you mean to me. I've missed you so much, and I know it's selfish of me to believe that we could ever…"

"Yes, it is selfish of you," Mark interrupted, his voice brittle with anger.

Timidly, Skylar reached out and touched the sleeve of Mark's jacket, trying to get his attention. "Mark. Please, don't hate me."

Standing, he shook her off and threw back his head, shaking snowflakes from his hair. "Hate you? No, I can't say that, but I'm very disappointed that you felt you couldn't trust me with the truth. I had to hear it from my mother, and you'd better believe she loved rubbing it in my face. And you know what? I have to admit that I'm glad she butted into my business this time. I needed to hear the truth and she delivered. Why couldn't you at least have been honest with me?"

Skylar had no reply. What could she say that she hadn't already told him? There was nothing left to do to regain his trust. She'd hurt him too badly to hope for a second chance.

Mark hunched his shoulders and looked down at his boots, a miserable scowl on his face. "How could you let me talk to you about marriage, children and a future, knowing you were playing games with me? What a pathetically childish thing to do." He laughed now, a bitter chuckle of defeat. "And I thought you needed your job and enjoyed it. I envied the way you threw yourself into your work. And to think that I used to ask you to do special things for me just so I could give you a big tip." He lowered his voice and shook his head. "I wanted to help you, Skylar. I thought you needed the extra money. I guess you were laughing at me behind my back, huh?"

Skylar stood abruptly and moved closer to Mark. "No, that's not true. Mark, I never laughed at you. I made a huge mistake when I asked Deena to keep my settlement a secret. I wasn't thinking about anyone but myself at that time. I wanted to fit in when I got here and I wanted my coworkers to think of me as a regular member of the staff. It was bad enough that I was the sister of the owner, and then to add the fact that I didn't really need the job…well, it would have been a lot for the staff to accept. If everyone had known about my money, it would have become a distraction. But then I met you. My lie was already in place and, unfortunately, I just let it slide. I was going to tell you the truth tomorrow. I knew I had to. Can't we try to…" She let her words drift off into the snow-filled air, fearing it was useless to try and salvage anything from the mess she had made of their love.

"No, I don't think we can try again. I feel as if I've been duped. I thought you were an honest person, grateful to your sister for giving you a job. And I thought we had something special going on. But now I see that my mother was right all along. You're not who I thought you were." He pulled in a big gulp of air. "I'm sorry it's turned out like this, Skylar. Really sorry."

"Me, too," Skylar whispered, watching his face, which had become hard and unreadable. "See you around?" she ventured, still hopeful.

Mark shrugged and walked away.

The tears that fell from Skylar's eyes mingled with the snowflakes that settled on her cheeks. She sat on the hard wooden bench for a long time after Mark disappeared, not moving, not feeling the cold or the wind or the rapidly falling snow. All she could feel was the pain that was ripping her heart in two.

Chapter 25

From the fourth floor balcony window of her apartment, Deena watched as Mark and his mother drove away from Scenic Ridge. The early morning sunlight glinted off the roof of Mark's Range Rover, sparking back at Deena until the vehicle passed beyond the stand of pines that marked the end of the two lane road. A great sense of loss washed through her, leaving a bitter taste in her mouth. Brushing aside a few stray hairs that had slipped from her ponytail, she let out a sigh that emptied her lungs.

She hated to see him go. He was such an excellent ski instructor and she had come to think of him as a member of her family, as she did with all of the staff at the resort. Sure, his Olympic championship status had been a bonus, but he had been more than simply a celebrity draw. He was a professional who took his work seriously, while passing on his passion for the sport. What was she going to do without him?

Turning from the window, Deena returned to the kitchen to pour herself a third cup of coffee, hoping it might give her a much needed boost of energy. A weakness that seemed to start in her feet and make its way through her entire body filled her with fatigue. She had gotten up at six o'clock that morning to finish some paperwork and had been deep into reviewing invoices related to the Slide and Glide Gala when Mark telephoned and asked if he could come up to see her.

When he arrived at her apartment, she could tell from the expression on his face that whatever he wanted to discuss with her was not going to be good news. She had not been wrong. He had nervously informed her that he had decided it would be best for him to leave Scenic Ridge due to personal reasons that he did not want to go into at that time. When Deena asked if there was anything she could do to help him with his problem he'd told her, "No. I don't think anyone can solve this but me, and it's going to take some time. Time away from Scenic Ridge."

And Skylar, too, Deena had thought, certain that his decision had something to do with her sister. For the past few weeks, Skylar had refused to discuss her budding relationship with Mark by turning the conversation to other subjects whenever Deena had brought it up. That was until last night, when everything fell apart.

Mark had told Deena that he and Virina were moving to the St. Regis hotel in Aspen, where he was going to work as a private ski instructor for the wealthy guests staying at the luxury hotel. The position paid extremely well, he had said, and now that the Black Winter Sports Reunion was over, and things had slowed down enough at Scenic Ridge for John to handle the classes, it was time to go. Again,

Deena had tried to persuade him to stay, but he had held firm with his decision to quit.

Though hurt by the news, Mark's abrupt decision had not caught Deena completely by surprise. He had been subdued and distant for quite some time and Deena knew that he and Skylar were going through a pretty rough time.

Last night, Skylar had filled Deena in on what happened at the ice rink, between sobs and tears of regret. Skylar had been devastated, and blamed herself for messing up her relationship with Mark, confessing everything to Deena, who had not known about her sister's inability to carry a child to term. The money was not the issue: Mark's longing for a family and Skylar's medical condition would be difficult obstacles to overcome.

While digesting Mark's news about leaving, Deena had thought that things couldn't have gotten worse, but they did when he brought up the subject of Richard Nobel's film.

"My mother's investors decided not to commit to the project because it focuses too much on the ski school," Mark had told her.

"Really? That's terrible," Deena had replied.

"Well, it leaves Richard in debt with a half-finished film," Mark had commented, going on to admit to feeling partly responsible for not cautioning Richard about his impulsive mother, who had a tendency to exaggerate everything. "I never dreamed she'd fall through on her commitment—not after bragging about her easy access to people with money. I don't know what happened, but as far as I'm concerned the documentary is dead, and it's just as well. The whole thing has become a distraction." Then he had given Deena an awkward hug and left.

This never should have happened, Deena thought, her

eyes riveted on the bright, red coffee cup in her hand. *I'm partly to blame. I never should have agreed to keep Skylar's secret. And I never should have encouraged Richard to include so much about Jerome and our family in the documentary. How did everything get so mixed up, so quickly?* She worried, wondering how Skylar was doing this morning.

The painfully hollow sensation that had gripped Skylar last night remained with her in the morning, even more intense and insistent. Her limbs were numb, her stomach was growling and her head was spinning with bits and pieces of Mark's final words. Skylar turned onto her side, pulled the quilt up to her chin, and stared at the alarm clock on her dresser. Seven-twenty-five. On a normal day, she would have been up, dressed and gulping down a quick bowl of oatmeal before rushing into her office to start her day. But today was not normal. It was the worst day of her life, even worse than when she found out that Lewis was cheating on her. Back then, her anger at Lewis had overshadowed her sense of loss, but now, nothing stood between the raw ache in her heart and her longing to make things right with Mark.

I should have known better than to think that I could hold on to him very long. He comes from a different world, where I don't fit in, and his mother has been working overtime to make sure I never will. Mark was just a winter fling. A sexy guy who came along to help me move on with my life. We never had a future. Not really. I took a risk with him and I lost. And all the money in the world can't fix what's wrong with me or make it possible to have a life with Mark. Enough of this pretense and stress. It's not worth it. Deena better get herself a new concierge right away because I'm going back to Tampa.

A knock on her door interrupted Skylar's pity-party. Groaning, she slid out of bed, pulled on her robe and went to peek through the peephole. "Deena," she said, not particularly happy to see her sister. She wasn't up for a pep talk or sisterly advice about how to salvage her love life. All she wanted to do was get back in bed and hide under the covers until the trauma of losing Mark went away. However, Skylar knew that was going to take a long, long time and she couldn't hide forever. Pasting a fake smile on her face, she opened the door.

"Just getting up?" Deena started, coming right in.

"Nope, not really. In fact, I was trying to go back to sleep."

"No time for that," Deena said in a disgustingly perky voice. "I've got news."

Skylar stuck her feet into her Big Bird slippers and headed into her kitchenette. "Yeah? So, talk while I make coffee. Want some?"

"No thanks," Deena said, following Skylar over to the counter that separated the kitchen from the living area. "I've already gone over my quota. Got an early start."

Skylar poured water into her coffeemaker and snapped it on. "So, what's going on?" she casually asked Deena, hoping she had come to tell her that one of the guests needed some extra-special attention, and not to rehash what Skylar had revealed last night. Her failed love affair with Mark was old news now and she couldn't go there again.

"Mark is gone."

Skylar glanced over at Deena and blinked several times. "Gone? Where?"

"To work at the St. Regis. He quit! He and Virina moved out this morning. Vacated their cabins and drove away."

"You're kidding!"

"I wish. John will have to handle things at the school until I can hire some help."

Leaving the coffee to brew, Skylar went to sit on a bar stool next to Deena's. "He really left?" she breathed the words. "That doesn't sound like him. He's so…so responsible. I can't believe he'd do that to you. When did he tell you?"

"He came to see me this morning. Said his mother had arranged everything at the St. Regis. Seems she knows the manager and she got Mark a job giving private lessons to their guests. I got the impression that he wasn't that thrilled by what Virina had done, but he sure as hell didn't turn down the job."

"Did you try to get him to stay?"

"Of course, I tried to talk him out of going, but I guess Mom won out."

"Deena. I'm sorry. He quit because of what happened between us, didn't he? Oh, God, what a mess. He must really hate me to give up teaching here. He loved this place, loved his job."

"Well, he didn't say why he was leaving and he didn't say that he hates you, but I could tell that he's sad…disappointed. I've never seen him so low. Very somber. I guess he thought he had no choice but to go, so he wouldn't have to worry about running into you. I'm sure it would've been awkward if he'd stayed. For both of you."

"He shouldn't have to leave. I'm the one who should go. Deena, get a hold of Mark at the St. Regis and tell him to come back. Tell him that I'm returning to Tampa and I won't be here, so he won't have to worry about avoiding me."

"I doubt he'd return, not after leaving the way he did, and besides *you* definitely can't leave now."

"Oh, yes I can, and I will. You can get a new concierge easier than you can get another Olympic gold medal winner to run your ski school!" Sliding off the stool, Skylar poured coffee into a cup and took a short gulp. "Be real, Deena. You need Mark Jorgen on staff more than you need me. Things have slowed down. Kathy can handle guest relations until you hire someone else. There's no reason for me to stick around."

"Yes, there is. Here's the clincher to my day. I thought Mark's resignation was about the worst thing that could happen and then, Jerome called. His father died during the night."

"Oh, no."

"Yeah," Deena softly replied. "I think I've been expecting this, but still, it's hard to take. Anyway, Jerome is going to stay in Oregon to take care of the funeral arrangements and settle the estate."

"Right. Of course, he has to." Skylar assessed Deena through half-closed eyes, trying to read her sister's emotions. She could see that Deena was trying hard not to cry, but even though she was a strong, resourceful woman, at a time like this she needed to let go. "I'm so sorry." Skylar reached out and gave Deena a firm hug, and then stood back and said, "I know Jerome is devastated."

"He's holding up pretty well, but I can tell he's feeling low."

"I'm sure he is. Then you need to get going," Skylar urged in a calm, respectful tone. "He needs you with him, Deena."

"Yes, I'm going. And I might be gone a few weeks. Maybe a month. I'd like to leave this afternoon and I want you to be in charge while I'm gone."

"Me?" Skylar asked, astonished. "What makes you think I can run this place?"

"You can do anything you set your mind to, Skylar. I have complete faith in your ability to make sure the staff and the guests are happy and the place doesn't burn down while I'm gone. All of the employees like and respect you. You won't have any trouble."

Scowling at her sister, Skylar wished she could tell Deena to forget about *her* sticking around to oversee the resort. All of a sudden she wanted to get far away from Colorado, the mountains, the cold weather, the demanding guests—and memories of Mark. She was more than ready to return to warm, familiar Florida, but how could she do such a thing to her sister? This was a family emergency and Deena had to be with her husband.

"You're right, Deena. I can do anything I set my mind to," Skylar concurred with sudden conviction. *Even prove to Mark Jorgen—and his controlling mother—that I am not the selfish, dishonest woman they think I am.*

Chapter 26

The last person Mark expected to see in the lobby of the St. Regis was Goldie Lamar, but there she was, dressed in an ankle-length, black goose down coat and white furry boots. She waved excitedly and started toward him, a huge smile on her carefully made-up face.

"Why, Mark Jorgen!" She wrapped both arms around his shoulders and gave him a hard hug. "What a nice surprise. Are you staying here?" she asked, leaning back.

"Uh…I'm working here now. Giving private lessons," he told her, not yet used to talking about his new position. Goldie's perfume swept over him, and swept his mind back to the days when women like her were the only ones he'd wanted to be with. Rich, flighty, and far too gay. Now, he'd be spending every day giving lessons to women like her and the thought was not so appealing.

"Private lessons? Really? I didn't know."

"Started a few days ago."

"Well, my cousin, Angelica, and I just arrived this morning. She insisted on staying in Aspen, so we wound up here, otherwise I would have gone back to Scenic Ridge. I had such a good time when I was there. But now that you're here, I'll have to sign on for a few more lessons."

"Sure, Goldie. Call the concierge and arrange it."

"I will. Won't it be fun to pick up where we left off?"

Mark could only nod.

"First thing tomorrow morning, we'll hit the slopes." She giggled and lifted both hands to her bright red lips. "And this time I promise to do better."

I doubt that you'll ever do any better. Mark shoved that thought to the back of his mind, knowing he was going to have students far worse than Goldie to deal with from now on.

"Are you on your way out?" Goldie gushed, eyes wide with interest.

"No," Mark told her, "I'm meeting my mother in the lounge for a drink."

"Your mother? Virina Dagrun is here with you?"

"Yes," Mark replied. "She's taking some time off from her work with Deleur. You know, slowing down for a while."

"I can understand why. She seems so busy. Simply everywhere. I ran into her last week at *Perfect Faces* in Beverly Hills. Such a beautiful woman. May I join you? I'd love to chat for a while."

"I'm sure she'd love that, too," Mark assured Goldie, a touch of relief in his voice. For the past few days he had avoided spending time with Virina whenever possible and hadn't been looking forward to meeting her for a drink this afternoon, but hadn't had a good reason to refuse her invitation.

Now that she was living at the St. Regis, where her son was on staff, Mark could tell that Virina was elated to be back in her element and in full circulation again. She bragged on him with everyone she met, and her prideful demeanor was beginning to wear thin.

Coming to work at the St. Regis had been his mother's idea and she had called on her old friend, Franco, the manager, to make it happen. After deciding to put some space between himself and Skylar, Mark had been too distraught over Skylar's deception and too busy packing to argue with his mother, so he'd acquiesced to her wishes and here he was, though he felt as if he'd sold out to her demands by taking the job.

Mark glanced over at Goldie—the perfect match for Virina. As soon as the two women started talking clothes and cosmetics, he would be able to slip out unnoticed and return to his room.

His room. A lonely space on the seventeenth floor that was crammed with everything he had managed to bring with him from the Snow King Suite. John was sending what he'd left behind to a storage unit in town. Now, Mark lived in a room with a bed, a bathroom, a TV and a minibar, and besides giving ski lessons, he had nothing to do but sit around and think about how he had let Deena and her staff down, as well as the mess he'd made of things with Skylar.

Skylar. God, how he missed her, as well as his beautiful cabin in the woods and the wonderful people he'd worked with. Leaving had been his only option once he'd made up his mind to break it off with Skylar, but he wasn't happy. He would stick it out at the St. Regis until he found something better; however, there were few options for a ski instructor so late in the season. He was stuck, whether he liked it or not.

"What a coincidence, you working here," Goldie broke into his thoughts, sidling closer. "Why did you leave Scenic Ridge?"

"Oh, it was just time to try something new," Mark hedged, not wanting to go into details. He'd had two students this morning: a computer software mogul from San Jose and a dentist from Hong Kong, and he was already through for the day. His workday at the St. Regis was a picnic compared to the rigorous schedule he had kept at Scenic Ridge, but all that free time meant nothing to him. He was restless, anxious, bored and depressed. What he needed was something, or someone, to occupy his time.

Goldie linked her arm through Mark's in a possessive move and walked with him as they made their way toward the lounge off the lobby.

"Change is always a good thing," Goldie advised. "This place is fabulous. Much more sophisticated than the quaint little ski resort where you were living, and a lot more fun, too. Parties every night. You're going to love it. You made a wise choice."

"I hope so," Mark commented, though he wasn't feeling particularly enthusiastic about his decision. At least he was working, but would it keep him busy enough to dull the ache in his heart?

"As a matter of fact, I'm having a party tonight," Goldie was saying. "My suite. Eight o'clock. You and your mother must come up. Everyone who's anyone is going to be there."

Mark nodded and impulsively squeezed Goldie's hand.

"Then, you'll come?" she asked.

"I'll be there," Mark replied, thinking of how easy it would be to fall back into the fast-paced, party-hopping lifestyle that he had once enjoyed. Back then, his life had been so uncomplicated—filled with temporary, uncomplicated relationships that had never caused him any grief. Having a good time had been his priority. *So, why not return to what was easy and familiar?* he thought. At least there'd be no surprises.

"I know you made your reservation four months in advance, Mr. Overton, but your wife canceled it last week. I hate to tell you this, but every room in the main lodge is reserved until the middle of next week." Skylar held her breath, waiting for the blast of outrage that she knew was about to come at her. Mr. and Mrs. Randolf Overton were not the kind of guests who were used to being denied whatever they wanted and Skylar certainly didn't want to turn them away, but there was nothing she could do. Mrs. Overton had impulsively cancelled their reservation after an argument with her husband, but once they reconciled, they had simply shown up at the resort, expecting to have their room.

"Then you'd better put someone out," Mr. Overton, a lean, big-boned man with a ruddy brown complexion, demanded. "Sara and I came all the way from Cincinnati for this weekend getaway, and now you're telling me we don't have a room! I don't want to hear it!"

"I wish you had called first, maybe I could have arranged something," Skylar began, feeling rotten about the problem. "If you'd like, I can call around and find you a room at another hotel in the area. We'll be happy to provide transportation…"

"No. This is where we've celebrated our anniversary for

the past five years and we don't plan to spend our sixth anyplace else. You'd better find us a room, young lady. Deena Simpson knows we always stay in the corner room on the second floor, facing the western side of the mountains. Where is Mrs. Simpson, anyway? This is not acceptable!"

"Mrs. Simpson is away on a personal matter." Skylar sighed aloud, understanding the man's disappointment and his anger, but it was not her fault that his wife had messed things up.

Damn. Skylar was beginning to think that she'd made a big mistake by agreeing to manage the resort while Deena was away. The past three days had been filled with hours of hassling with suppliers, calming testy employees and working with the local authorities to run a group of deer hunters off the property. She was exhausted. And now she had to deal with the Overtons!

Thinking fast, and not about to lose one of Scenic Ridge's long-term, valuable customers, she told the couple, "All I might have available is the Snow King Suite," she impulsively offered. "It's a fully furnished cabin, but at the highest end of our rates." Just saying the words, "Snow King Suite" made Skylar's stomach lurch, but she swallowed back the pain.

"Might have available? What does that mean?" Mr. Overton demanded.

"The former tenant just moved out a few days ago and I'll have to check to see if it's ready to be occupied."

"Well, go and check. That's exactly what I'd like for me and my wife. Something special. Cozy." He put his arm around Mrs. Overton, a black-haired beauty with a serene smile who was grinning smugly at Skylar, obviously used to getting her way.

Forcing a smile, Skylar nodded. "Why don't you two

go into the café and have lunch, on the house, of course, while I see what we can do?"

"Good idea," Mr. Overton replied, already turning away. "You'll know where to find us."

"Yes, I will," Skylar murmured to herself as she reached for the phone to call housekeeping.

When Martha, the head maid answered, she assured Skylar that she and John had sent all of Mark's things to storage and that the Snow King Suite had been thoroughly cleaned.

"Good," Skylar told Martha. "But I think I'd better take a look, just to be sure." After removing the keys to the suite from the drawer beneath the registration counter, Skylar put on her parka and left.

When she opened the door to what used to be Mark's home, she felt a shiver of regret grip her. The place looked the same, as far as the furnishings were concerned, but all touches of Mark's personality were gone. The inlaid wooden boxes on the coffee table, his medals and trophies which he had kept on the shelf next to the fireplace, the photos of him and his ski buddies that had been on display on the sideboard, his red parka, which always hung on the hook by the door. Even the cold dark hearth brought a chill to Skylar. Not once had she ever been inside the cabin when there had not been a blazing fire warming the room.

For some reason, her mind went to Lewis, and she realized how differently she felt about losing Mark. Lewis had been a prick, really, in his pin stripe, wide lapel suits, flashy jewelry and with his new Miss Diva on his arm. Not at all like Mark, who had been caring, conservative and loyal to her. She missed Mark more than she ever imagined possible. She longed for the fresh scent of his skin, the soft feel of his hair and waking up in his arms to gaze out at the snow-covered mountains in the distance.

Crossing the room, her footsteps echoed eerily on the wooden floor as she left the great room and headed toward the bedroom. At the door, she realized that she couldn't go in, so she stood in the entry and stared at the king-size four poster bed, freshly made and inviting. She was unable to keep her mind from whirling back to the kisses and caresses and the sensual embraces they had shared among the sheets. She could still feel Mark's warm flesh against hers, still taste his lips, his chest, his hard flat stomach. Her eyes traveled over the red star-patterned quilt, the fluffy soft pillows, the extra blanket that he always kept draped across the end rail.

We made love there and made promises to each other, too, but all I have now is a deep pain of longing that will not go away. What happened to those promises? Can we ever make it right? Would Mark listen to me if I tried?

Blinking back tears, Skylar forced herself to thoroughly inspect the rest of the cabin, to be sure it was ready for new guests. With each curtain she drew back and each drawer she pulled open, the wound of losing Mark was made fresh again.

Now, I've got to tell Mr. Overton that the suite will cost four times as much as the room his wife cancelled, and that means another nasty conversation, she calculated, dreading the encounter.

Pushing that thought aside, she moved toward the front door, preparing to leave, and then turned to give the place a final sweep. Standing at the door, she hesitated, a thought entering her mind. She'd let the Overtons have the Snow King Suite for free for the weekend, she decided. They'd had a fight, but they'd made up. They had managed to overcome whatever their problems had been and seemed as close as any couple could be. Obviously, they were still very much in love after six years of marriage. Why not let them have a special memory of their reconciliation? People in love deserved a break, she reasoned.

"Deena would have done the same thing, I'm sure," Skylar commented to herself, wishing that she and Mark could have solved their problems by simply going away for a romantic reunion.

With that settled, Skylar went to the phone and called Victor at the front desk to make the arrangements for the Overton's luggage to be brought to the cabin. As soon as she hung up the phone, it rang again and she picked it up, expecting it to be Victor.

"Hello. Victor?"

"No, it's Richard Nobel. I thought I was calling Mark Jorgen's suite."

"Oh, hello, Richard. This is Skylar Webster. You are calling his suite, but Mark isn't here anymore."

"Oh, really? Well, I'm surprised. Where is he?"

"You can reach him at the St. Regis Hotel. He's working there now."

"Hmm, sorry he left Scenic Ridge. What happened?"

"I really can't say. You'd better talk to him."

"I will. I'll give him a call over there."

"Richard, how's the documentary coming?"

"Oh, my...Mark didn't tell you?"

"Tell me what?" Skylar asked, moving to sit on the sofa, detecting a note of disappointment in Richard's voice.

"It's been canned," Richard said, going on to fill Skylar in.

Skylar was hurt and shocked to learn that Virina had

pulled her investors out after viewing the initial footage. The selfish snob! To think that she would ruin her son's chance to have a film made about his life just because she didn't want to share the spotlight with Scenic Ridge. What kind of a mother was she?

"Yeah, Virina left me hanging," Richard continued. "I'm stuck with a half-finished film and a bunch of folks who are threatening to sue me. It's a real nightmare, Skylar. I don't know what I'm going to do."

Slumping down on the sofa, Skylar listened as Richard continued to detail his problems, feeling sorry for him and sorry for Mark, too. He'd lost out on his chance to have his career documented for future generations of young ski enthusiasts. However, she was proud that Mark had stood up to his mother by insisting that Scenic Ridge be included in his story.

"So, the documentary can't get made unless you get financing?" she clarified.

"Yep, that's about it," he replied.

"How much money are you talking?"

"A lot," Richard replied. "More than you have, I'm sure," he jokingly added.

"Don't be too sure, Richard. I have something in mind that might work in your favor. I'd like to explore some possibilities. Can you come up to Scenic Ridge so we can talk?"

"Are you serious? You think you can find the money to finish the film?"

"Yes, I think so. And yes, I'm very serious, Richard. How soon can you get here?"

"I'll be there tomorrow."

"Good, e-mail your itinerary to me and I'll make sure

there's a rental car reserved for you at the airport. And don't contact Mark, not yet. "

"You know, Skylar, Mark's mother put too many restrictions on me and I'm glad she's out of the picture. If you find the money and I push real hard, we might be able to complete the film by the end of next month."

"Get ready to push," Skylar told Richard. "And push hard. I'm just glad I got to you before you spoke to Mark."

Chapter 27

When Goldie placed her final air-kiss on Bitsy Brown's cheek and closed the door behind the soft drink heiress, Mark realized that he was the last guest remaining in the suite. The party had been a nonstop swirl of overdressed women and well-heeled men who had come and gone throughout the evening, stopping only long enough to drop a famous name or two, take a few quick sips of champagne, and give everyone within listening distance a brief overview of their latest acquisition, trip abroad or social event.

Mark had found it all very boring, and had taken refuge at the bar with a bottle of Grey Goose Vodka and a bowl of Russian caviar while making only the most cursory attempts at interacting with the over-eager, socially connected women who were currently in town—alone and looking for companionship.

Virina had swept in with a race car driver from Miami

on her arm, making a splashy entrance that got everyone's attention. She had vigorously worked the room in a stunning, silver Versace dress, making sure everyone knew that her son was now a part of the St. Regis family and that she was back into social circulation before dashing off to another party in the Paepcke suite at the Little Nell.

Mark had been relieved to see her go, and just as relieved to learn that she apparently had a new man in her life: a rich man whose face regularly appeared on the covers of all the sports magazines. Maybe now his mother would keep her nose out of his affairs and concentrate on her own.

"Thank God. Alone at last," Goldie remarked with a roll of her eyes as she leaned onto the bar and slid both of her hands across the smooth, black granite. "I thought Bitsy would never shut up. I swear that woman talks like she's got a tape recorder stuck in her head, spewing out all that stuff about Muffin's divorce. How did she ever get access to all those details?"

Shaking his head, Mark tossed back another shot of vodka, feeling no pain. At last, he was numb, from his head to his feet, and the ache in his heart didn't burn so much. He didn't care if he ever felt anything again.

"Come on, let's sit on the sofa, by the fire. We haven't had any time to catch up," Goldie urged, taking Mark by the hand.

He didn't resist when she led him to the sofa and pulled him down next to her. In fact, the soft cushions felt a whole lot better than the hard bar stool he'd been sitting on all evening, and Mark quickly settled down, flinging back his head and closing his eyes. Damn, it felt good to simply let go. He liked the feeling of floating, drifting, spinning off into a netherworld where he didn't have to think about anything. If only he could stay in such a state forever and never come back to the reality of his situation. What was there to look forward to anyway? Only a hell of a hangover and an empty hotel room.

Just as he was about to sink into that soft dark place that would take him away from his worries, he felt Goldie's lips cover his. Her tongue darted quickly between his lips and she began to explore his mouth with tiny soft jabs, while her hands massaged his thighs. He could feel her firm small breasts rubbing against his chest and her knees were pressing into his side.

Her aggressive move caught Mark by surprise, and he jerked back at first but then relaxed. Whatever she was doing didn't alarm him enough to push her away. He wasn't crazy and he certainly wasn't offended by Goldie's decision to act on feelings he had always suspected had been simmering in her for quite a while.

Their kiss deepened. Her hands strayed from his legs to his sudden erection and remained there, gently stroking, pleasantly teasing him until he knew he was going to burst.

Mark's fingers, seeming to move on their own, found their way to the buttons of Goldie's sweater and it took only seconds for him to free one breast, then the other. With a groan, he buried his face in the folds of her sweater and squeezed his eyes shut.

Goldie pressed her hands against the back of Mark's head, pinning him to her in an urgent clasp. Mark captured one hard nipple between his lips, inhaling as he savored it, almost tasting the saccharine sweetness of Goldie's expensive perfume. *Electric Orchid.* How could he forget?

Unexpectedly, her scent jolted him back to the day when he had struggled with Goldie during her first ski lesson. She'd smashed her glasses against a tree. Then, their trip to *Gorsuch* the next day, where he'd first met Skylar while she was trying on goggles.

Skylar. Thinking about her initiated a sob that rose in Mark's throat and made him tense. He missed her with an intensity that was alarming, and he didn't want Goldie as a substitute for the woman he longed to be with tonight. Skylar. He might have walked out of her life, but he damn well couldn't get her out of his mind.

The admission snapped him back to reality. Lifting his head, he pushed away from Goldie and looked at her with bleary, sad eyes. "Sorry," he mumbled, realizing that he was going to have one hell of a headache tomorrow. "Can't do this. Gotta go." He stumbled to his feet, lurched to the door and without saying good-bye, he left.

Chapter 28

When Richard arrived at Scenic Ridge, Skylar put him in the Vista View suite, Virina's former cabin, and settled down with him to watch the first cut of the film. She absolutely loved what Richard had created. She loved the look of the piece, the music he had selected, the photos and early video of Mark's youthful beginnings, his rigorous training schedule, his career, his role as an instructor and his many achievements on the slopes.

She was just as impressed with Virina's skill at managing him, and got a better understanding of the depth of the bond between Mark and his mother. As a young woman, Virina had recognized her son's talent at an early age, and then had dedicated her time, her skill and a good portion of her life to making Mark an Olympian. And she had succeeded. Virina had every right to be proud of Mark and of herself, too, for playing such an important role in his eventual success.

The piece on Scenic Ridge was just as inspiring and informational, too. As Skylar listened to Deena talk about the difficulties she and Jerome had faced as they'd struggled to carve their dream out of an isolated mountaintop, her eyes filled with tears. She envied Deena, who had everything that Skylar longed for—a man who loved her, trusted her and had shared his dream with her—which had come true because they had worked together to make it happen.

"The film is very well done," Skylar commented when it ended. "There doesn't seem to be a lot left to do."

"Not much," Richard agreed. "Needs titles, some graphic work and better scoring in places. And with a final professional edit to bring it in line with the station's on-air segments, it would be ready to go."

"If everything went smoothly, when could it air?"

"Oh, a matter of weeks. Black Showcase is just waiting for me to deliver. The promotional package is ready to go, as long as Mark is still on board. He'll have to agree to get out on the road and push this to make it a success."

"I'm sure he will, once he sees this. So, I think you can get busy and make it happen," Skylar said, anxious to dig in.

"How? You know something you're not telling me? We need cash to get this done."

Reaching into her purse, Skylar removed her checkbook and waved it in Richard's face. "It's all right here. Every penny you're gonna need to create a top rate film. I'm producing now."

With a dubious squint, Richard tilted his head to one side. "You're producing? You've got to be kidding me. Okay, Skylar. Fill me in. What's this about?"

Richard was shocked when Skylar told him about her settlement and revealed that she was a very wealthy woman with money to invest. And he was pleased that she planned to put some of it in to his project. With no additional investors involved, he knew they would be able to move quickly.

"The fewer hands in the pot, the better," he later told Skylar, "and I will definitely list you in the credits as producer of the *Mark Jorgen Story*."

Over the next two days, Skylar and Richard spent many hours at Vista View hammering out details to finish the film. Once Skylar had contacted Mr. Ray at Tampa Commerce Bank and arranged for the transfer of the necessary funds, it was time for Richard to head back to New York to finalize the project.

"Will we need any additional releases from Mark?" Skylar wanted to know, aware that they couldn't pull this off without Mark's full cooperation.

"Not really," Richard replied, snapping shut his briefcase. "His original contract gives me the right to produce the piece, no matter who finances it." He draped a wool scarf around his neck and then slipped his arms into his coat. "However, I'm going to stop by the St. Regis and visit with Mark before I head to the airport. I need to make sure his commitment is firm and that he will still promote it once we get to that point. He's gotta be okay with the licensing deals I'm proposing, too."

"Then you've talked to him?" Skylar asked, following Richard out to his rental car. She was excited for Mark, but anxious, too. What if he refused to be involved in the film because she had put up the money? She could lose her investment. She had committed a very large chunk of her money to this. What if it didn't sell? What if no one found it as interesting as she did? What if she was making a bad investment?

Mr. Ray's words of caution came back to her: Your money will last if you invest wisely. Well, she believed in Mark, and loved him so much. What better investment could there be?

"Yes, I spoke to him this morning. He was extremely relieved, and pleased, that I'd found a new financial backer," Richard replied, shaking Skylar's hand.

"Did you tell him it was me?"

"No, not yet. But I will."

"I hope it won't be a deal breaker," Skylar told him, praying she was doing the right thing.

Chapter 29

Mark put the cap back on his gas tank, gave it a firm twist and then slipped the gas pump's nozzle back into place, eager to get going. It was a beautiful, sunny morning, and his first free day since he'd started working at the St. Regis almost a month ago. No ski lessons today, no sitting around his hotel room between students, and no more dodging Goldie Lamar, who had given up on him and taken off for Reno with her cousin. Even Virina was happily involved with the race car driver who was busily escorting her around town, so she no longer hovered over Mark, asking if he was okay.

Of course, I'm okay, he thought sarcastically. *I have a good job, I'm living in a beautiful hotel, surrounded by beautiful, fun-loving people. What more could I want?*

Skylar, that's what, he silently admitted, hating the surge of emptiness that hit him whenever he thought about her. All the late-night parties, hard drinking and pretty women in the world couldn't keep him from missing her.

When Mark awakened this morning, he had known what he wanted to do: go someplace far away from the smothering confines of the hotel, and away from the guests who were relentless in their requests to get free pointers from him on how to improve their technique on the powder. He was going to drive up to Glenwood Springs to spend a few hours at the hot springs pool, where he could be alone and think over his plan.

The ski season was winding down. The television premier of the *Mark Jorgen Story* was set to air on BES this Saturday night, and on Sunday he was leaving Aspen for New York to begin a round of media interviews. From there, who knew where things would go?

Mark had spoken to Richard last week to finalize this first leg of the promotional tour, and though he remained annoyed that Skylar had financed the film, he planned to use this opportunity to bolster the sport of skiing, change young people's lives and, hopefully, make enough money to establish his own ski school and pay Skylar back.

Finished pumping gas, he walked around to the front of his SUV and pulled back the windshield wipers, preparing to clean the windows. When he glanced over at the pump next to his, he saw a red Jeep pull up. His heart thudded under his jacket as he watched Skylar get out of her car, only a few feet away. He froze, one hand in midair as he stared at her, wondering if he dared approach her. The sun bounced off her shiny black locks and put a golden sheen on her smooth tan skin. She looked even more beautiful than he remembered and all he wanted to do was rush over, grab her and kiss those luscious lips.

When she reached for the gas pump, she looked up and saw him right away.

He nodded curtly, unable to speak.

She nodded back and lifted her jaw.

Mark returned to cleaning his windows, though he was paying absolutely no attention to what he was doing.

"You missed a spot," Skylar called over to him, craning her neck around the gas pump that separated them.

His head snapped around and he glared over at her, and then mumbled, "Yeah. Thanks," before swishing the plastic tool across the slippery glass.

"I'm looking forward to seeing Richard's film on TV Saturday," Skylar said, her voice cool and calm.

"Right," Mark tossed over his shoulder, trying to sound equally nonchalant, and then added, as if to clear the air of the unstated issue that hung between them, "I guess I ought to thank you for putting up the money." Now, he turned to face her.

"No, not if you don't want to," Skylar returned, continuing to fill her tank.

"Well, I'm pleased with the focus of the documentary and glad that Deena and Jerome's story was included."

"You ought to drop by and see them. They're back, you know."

"Won't have time. I'm leaving town on Sunday. Going to New York for media appearances."

"Really? Well, I hope the tour's a success." Skylar's tone was impersonal and dry.

"And I hope Scenic Ridge will benefit from the project," Mark said.

"Me, too. That's why I put up the money."

"Really? And not because you thought that financing

my life story would make up for the lies you told?" Mark's tone was as hard as the glint in his eyes as he waited for her reaction.

"Oh, you've got to go *there,* huh?" Skylar propped a fist at her hip. "How disgusting. That thought never crossed my mind," she sniped, scowling over at him.

"Don't worry. I plan to pay back every dime of your investment, Skylar, no matter how long it takes. I'll send you a check once a week."

"You can send it to me in Tampa, then," she told him, as lightly as if she were telling him the time.

"Oh? You're returning to Florida?"

"Yep, Deena has returned and I can't get out of here fast enough." Skylar jammed the gas nozzle into its holder and punched the button for a receipt, watching Mark while she waited for the piece of paper to slide out. "I've really missed Florida. I can't wait to get home."

"And back to your boyfriend, Lewis, I suppose?" Mark accused, suddenly wanting to lash out at Skylar and shatter that calm facade of hers, which he knew was as fake as her need to work as a concierge.

"Lewis? Hardly," Skylar quipped. "But even if that were true, what difference would it make to you?"

"None," Mark snapped, slamming the squeegee back into the pail of water. "You can do whatever you damn well please."

"I know, and I will." She snatched the receipt from the machine and then took a step toward Mark. "But for your information, I am not getting back with Lewis. I just want to get away from here. And from you!"

"From me? What did I ever do to you?" *Except love you,* he thought, a catch in his throat.

"What did you do? You manipulated me, bossed me around and treated me like a servant."

"You've got to be kidding. I told you why I started asking you to do so much for me. I wanted to help you out *and* get your attention."

"Oh? So, you're admitting that from day one you were already thinking about your own selfish needs, right? Everyone at Scenic Ridge, including myself, had been so fast to fulfill your demands. Keeping you happy was a priority and I think you enjoyed it."

"Don't be ridiculous. And don't call me selfish. How selfish was it of you to keep me in the dark about who you really were?"

With a jerk of her neck, Skylar rolled her eyes at Mark. "Give me a break, you spoiled, chauvinistic jock. I was helping my sister out. I tried to overlook your pushy ways, but I guess I was blindsided by your suave, Afro-European charm. Now, I clearly see what kind of a man you are, and I'm glad to be going home."

Mark opened his mouth to respond to her tirade, but she had already climbed inside her Jeep and started the engine. She sped off in a squeal of tires and a shower of frozen gravel, leaving him staring after her car until it turned a corner and entered a side street off the square.

How could she say such things to him? She was wrong. He had loved her, wanted a future with her, and had been ready to make a real commitment despite his mother's warnings. But Skylar had ruined everything by lying and hiding the truth from him.

Frustration spiraled into longing as their encounter hung in his mind. He ached to have her back in his life, back in his arms, back in his bed where they had come together in perfect union. He knew he would never reach such erotic heights with any other woman, and didn't want to try.

As much as Mark wanted to hate Skylar he knew he couldn't. His love for her burned as hard and deep as it had the first time they made love. It didn't really matter to him that she might not be able to have children. There were other ways to create a family, but finding a woman to love and trust was not that easy, and that was what mattered most.

Trust, he thought with a slump of his shoulders. *It's the bottom line in any relationship and we're both at fault for botching that up. By financing my film, Skylar came through for me when she could have easily turned away. I ought to be grateful for what she did, not angry. She loves me enough to invest in my future, to trust me with her money. So why am I too bullheaded to admit what a good woman she really is?*

Chapter 30

Virina moved the vase of pink and white orchids three times before deciding to place it on top of the baby grand piano, where guests could see it as soon as they walked in. Though it was only eleven o'clock in the morning, more than seven hours before her party, Virina was deep into organizing, decorating and finalizing the details for the gathering she was hosting in the ballroom of the St. Regis Hotel.

The *Mark Jorgen Story* was airing on BES tonight and she was in her element, planning a viewing party for Mark and all of their friends. He had been moping around long enough and it was time for him to put a smile on his face and enjoy his success. He was the star of a television documentary that had already received excellent advance reviews. He was going on an extensive media tour. Already, two major publishers had contacted him about publishing his biography, a book for young people.

The project was turning out even better than Virina had hoped, and she loved the attention her son was finally receiving, even though she would have preferred that the film focus solely on Mark.

"I guess I have Skylar to thank," Virina grudgingly confessed as she placed a stack of white, linen napkins in a silver tray. "Perhaps I misjudged her after all. Such a gutsy, independent woman could be exactly the kind of wife Mark needs, and I can definitely teach her how to enjoy that money of hers." Virina chuckled. "Life takes such strange turns when you least expect it. Who would have thought that the concierge was a millionaire in disguise? Or that I am going to have to convince Mark that she's the woman he needs?"

Going to the phone, she punched in the number to Scenic Ridge and asked for Skylar. When she came on the line, Virina drew in a deep breath and ploughed ahead, as if they were long-time friends.

"I'm throwing a viewing party for Mark at the St. Regis tonight, and since you *are* the producer you absolutely must attend." The line was silent for a long beat before Skylar spoke.

"I appreciate the invitation, Virina, but I had planned to watch it here with my sister and her husband. They just returned from Oregon, and we've got a lot of catching up to do."

"Well, you'll just have to bring them along," Virina offered, a bit too testily. How could anyone turn down an invitation to one of her parties at the St. Regis in Aspen? Was the girl that far removed from the social scene? Virina had come to the realization that Mark was truly in love with Skylar and the possibility was great that Skylar might wind up as Virina's daughter-in-law. *My God. I'll have to take this girl under my wing and teach her how things work in my world,* Virina thought, knowing she was up to the challenge.

She pressed ahead, determined to make tonight a happy one for Mark. He'd been so unhappy since leaving Scenic Ridge, and now *she* was going to make things right. A little nudge might be all he'd need to make up with Skylar and get on with his life—his new life as a media celebrity.

"I won't take no for an answer, Skylar. Richard Nobel is flying in. Food by Rachael Ray. Music and dancing afterward. Master P is on board as the DJ. The most important party of the month." Again, the line hummed empty. "You're coming, of course?"

Virina could hear the sigh that escaped Skylar's lips, and she tightened her grip on the handset.

"I'll try," Skylar finally answered. "But I know Deena and Jerome won't be coming. They just want to stick around home and get some rest."

"I understand completely. You can represent them. So, just come alone. Seven-thirty. Casual chic, of course."

Her office suddenly seemed too warm and Skylar was having trouble breathing. She got up from her desk, went to the window and pushed it open a crack. The fresh air that swept in cleared her head and made her feel a bit calmer.

Had Virina actually just invited her to a party for Mark? Was it for real, or some kind of a trick? Was Virina planning to embarrass Skylar? Make her feel out of place once she arrived?

It would be just like Virina to act as if I crashed the party to make Mark think I was that desperate to be near him. No way was she going to fall into that trap. She was perfectly content to view the film on T V with Deena, Jerome and the rest of the Scenic Ridge staff, many of whom were excited about seeing themselves in Mark's story.

Looking out the window, she focused on the skating rink in the distance, thinking about the argument she had had there with Mark when they ended their relationship. She had replayed it so many times in her head that their words were permanently etched into her brain. Yes, she had been wrong to hold back the truth, but it was too late to do anything about that now. By helping her sister, she'd been able to work at Scenic Ridge and meet Mark. She wouldn't change a thing about that experience, even though it had not turned out as she hoped. But now that the documentary was getting excellent advance reviews, Scenic Ridge would soon become known as *the* place for African-Americans to come to ski, and that was what Skylar had hoped would happen.

If only she and Mark could find a way back to each other. If Virina hadn't gotten to Mark first, Skylar was convinced that she could have softened the blow of her confession. Virina's interference had been the catalyst to their problems and Skylar was still angry that Virina had felt it her place to meddle in their affairs. Why had Virina deliberately worked Mark into a frenzy and forced him into a showdown with her? "Because she's a conniving bitch," Skylar whispered, wondering if she ought to show up at the party, confront Virina and set the record straight. *And I'd get to see Mark, again,* she admitted, calculating that she had more than enough time to drive into town to buy something spectacular to wear.

Chapter 31

After setting the DVR on the television in his room to record the premier of his life story, Mark checked his watch again. Seven o'clock. He knew his mother was expecting him to be downstairs by now, greeting her guests and accepting congratulations for his television debut. She had already called him three times, and he knew she was livid that he was dragging his feet, but his heart was not in it.

Why did Virina have to go and do this without telling him? He'd much rather be at Scenic Ridge, watching the program with Deena and Jerome and the staff. *And with Skylar at my side,* he admitted, overcome with a need to see her. He had not stopped thinking about her since running into her at the gas station earlier in the week, and his resistance was beginning to wear thin.

She loved him, he knew it! She missed him, too, as

much as he missed her. He had seen it in her eyes! All of this fuss that his mother and the media were making over Richard's film meant nothing if he couldn't share his joy with Skylar. She had financed it, produced it. She had believed in him and his vision for the piece when his mother hadn't. How could he go downstairs and act as if he was happy to be with those people when his heart was broken, his mind was on Skylar and all he wanted to do was get away?

"I'm not going," he decided, loosening his tie. He yanked off his dinner jacket and threw it into the open suitcase on his bed. He could leave Aspen tonight. Virina had arranged for him to fly to New York on Wilhelm's plane and the pilot was standing by, ready to leave when Mark gave him the word. *Why wait until morning?* Mark decided, tossing his toiletries into his bag. *I'm getting out of here right now?*

Virina kept one eye on the door as she air-kissed each guest that arrived for the viewing party, furious with Mark. Where was he? How could he not show up on time for his own party? It seemed as if he deliberately wanted to embarrass her. She'd called his room three times, and now it looked as if she'd have to go upstairs and personally bring him down. This was most embarrassing, and she had gone to a great deal of trouble and expense to put this affair together. He was not going to ruin it.

Turning her back to the full length mirror on her closet door, Skylar looked over her shoulder and checked herself out, liking what she saw—printed, Italian Ginevra shirt: $998; metal and beaded embroidered jeans: $1615; cowhide belt with Swarovski crystals: $428; pink, wool Austrian jacket: $1398; handmade, alligator boots: $3500. Now that everyone knew about her wealth, why not flaunt it? she'd decided during her whirlwind shopping spree in town. It had been so much fun. And the same salesgirl at *Gorsuch* who had waited on her the first day she arrived in Aspen had been so eager to help with her selections.

"I oughta turn some heads now," Skylar said with satisfaction, knowing she could hold her own among Virina's snobby friends, who would certainly be checking her out. Her jeans were so tight she could hardly sit down, but they cupped her butt in a sensual way that made her feel very sexy. "Let Mark get a good look at what he tossed away," she snickered, though nervous about her decision to go to Virina's party.

But how could she stay away? She was the producer. She also had to represent Scenic Ridge, a major piece of the project. Richard would be there, and she could hang out with him while doing her best to ignore Mark. *And he'd better not show up with a woman on each arm*, Skylar fumed, preparing herself for a very bumpy night.

A quick swipe of strawberry lip gloss and a fluff of her locks and she was ready to go. Reaching for her new shearling coat with fox fur trim, she tossed it over her shoulders and grabbed her car keys, ready to face Virina, Mark and his party-loving friends.

Mark came to an abrupt stop at the intersection of Highway 82 where the road leading to the airport turned off to the right and road straight ahead led on toward Scenic Ridge. He glanced into his rearview mirror. No traffic behind him. Nothing in front of him either. Nothing but the road that would lead him back to Skylar. Did he want to take it? Take a chance on her being able to forgive him for all the mean things he'd said? Or should he simply go on to the airport, get on the plane and fly out of her life all together?

"I've got to see her," he said to his reflection in the rearview mirror. "I can't leave without knowing where she stands."

Skylar roared down the narrow road that led into town, recalling the time when she would have inched cautiously along. But now she knew the road well and knew how to maneuver through the narrow passages and sharp turns without fearing for her life. Usher's newest single was playing on her CD player and she concentrated on the music to keep her mind off her destination. She'd deal with Virina and Mark soon enough. For now she didn't even want to think about either of them.

After rounding a curve, she entered the single lane portion of the road, automatically slowing down. However, she quickly realized that a car was approaching from the opposite direction and one of them would have to back up.

She slammed on the brakes.

The car in front of her pulled right up to hers, their bumpers nearly touching.

Skylar gasped. It was Mark and he was smiling at her through the windshield, as if pleased with what he'd found.

Mark got out of his Range Rover and walked toward Skylar, her headlights bathing him in a golden wash of light. When she rolled down the window, he leaned in, deliberately poking his face close to hers.

"Going into town?" he asked, a touch of a smirk on his lips.

"To your mother's party," Skylar managed, trying to sound annoyed. "Where you should be, so why don't you back up and turn around?"

"Can't do that," Mark said nonchalantly, arms resting in the open window.

"You've got to. There's no way I can pass unless you move."

Mark reached into Skylar's car and flicked open the door. "Slide over," he told her, getting in before she could comment.

Skylar threw him a freezing glance, but did as he told her and made room for him to sit behind the wheel. "What do you think you're doing?"

"Moving your car out of my way," he said matter-of-factly as he backed up. Looking over his shoulder, he continued to drive in reverse until he had parked Skylar's Jeep in a safe spot off the road. "Come on," he told her, getting out.

Skylar remained in the car, lips tight. "Quit ordering me around! I'm not going any place with you! And give me my car keys!"

"Can't do that," he grinned, pocketing her keys. "Unless you want to walk to the party, you'd better get in my car."

Teeth clenched in frustration, Skylar got out, slammed the door and followed Mark, taking very tiny steps in her too-tight jeans. With a great deal of effort, she managed to climb into his SUV, where she sat with her lip poked out and her arms clamped stubbornly across her chest.

"You look fabulous," Mark commented as he eased behind the wheel. "I almost didn't recognize you."

"Gee, thanks," she managed, watching him from the corner of her eye. "Thought I'd show your mother that I'm not the unsophisticated nobody she thinks I am."

With a whir, Mark started the engine and instead of turning around, as Skylar had thought he would do, he continued up the road toward Scenic Ridge.

"She doesn't think you're a nobody," Mark commented. "In fact, I think she likes you."

"Right. Only because she knows I have money," Skylar scoffed.

Mark shrugged. "That's just the way she sounds, but I'm telling you, she wouldn't have invited you to her party if she wasn't ready to make up. Trust me, I know her."

"Trust you?" Skylar commented, realizing that Mark was on the service road and he was going toward the Snow King Suite, not back to the hotel to attend his own party. "Why should I trust you?"

"Because I love you. I want a future with you and I'm asking for your forgiveness." He stopped the car in front of the cabin and turned in his seat to focus on her. "I made a huge mistake when I walked out on you. I didn't realize how precious our relationship was. What we had was beautiful and I miss the hell out of you, Skylar."

It took a long moment for Skylar to digest what he was telling her: That they had a chance at happiness together and he wanted to be with her. When he touched her cheek, she melted. "I've missed you, too, Mark."

"Still leaving Colorado?" he asked, his voice rough with uncertainty.

"I'm packed. I planned to leave on Monday."

"Don't. Do you really want to go back to Tampa?"

In her heart, she knew that she didn't want to go, but

had felt there was no other option. Now that she knew that he wanted her to stay, she was going to take a chance. "Mark, all I can tell you is that I don't ever want to be separated from you again."

"Then you have to stay."

She sought reassurance in his face, hoping she was doing the right thing. "I want to, but it's going to take time for us to find our way back to what we had."

"Then we'd better get started right away." He took her hand and covered it with his. "Come to New York with me tomorrow. I don't want to go alone. For that matter, I don't want to do anything unless you're with me. If there's going to be any joy for me in this film project, then I have to share it with you. After all, you made it possible." He leaned over and kissed her with a featherlight touch.

"New York? Tomorrow?" Skylar said, a sly smile curving her lips. "I'm already packed. Why not?"

"You know, you've changed my life, Skylar, and we'll face whatever obstacles come our way, together."

"Do you mean that?" She gripped his hand more tightly. "I want the same thing, Mark. Your love, a family, a future filled with exciting adventures. But are you sure you could accept it if our children had to be adopted?"

"Absolutely," Mark murmured, reaching for her.

She slipped into his arms and lifted her face to his. The kiss he placed on her was intense, passionate and ripe with promise: the kiss that Skylar had lain awake at night hoping to feel once more. When it ended, she shifted to rest her head on his chest for a moment and then opened the car door and hopped down. Her feet made a soft thud in the fresh layer of snow.

"Coming inside?" she invited, smiling seductively

while jangling the cabin keys in the air. "If we hurry, we can catch your life story on the television."

Mark got out, came around to where she stood and wrapped an arm around her waist. He pulled her hard to his side, embracing her with a tender fierceness as he leaned down to capture her eyes with his. "Don't worry, I'm taping it at the hotel. If we go inside now," he told her in a voice heavy with desire, "we can do something much more exciting than watch television."

"I'm all for that," Skylar agreed, falling into step beside Mark as they made new footprints in the snow that covered the walkway leading to the Snow King Suite.

* * * * *

Dating R&B megastar Reggie Martin was #1 on Lilah Banks's top-ten list of things to accomplish before turning thirty. But Reggie's older brother Tyler is making a wish list of his own—and seducing Lilah into falling in love with him is *his* #1.

"Robyn Amos has once again created a sensational couple that draws us into a whirlpool of sensuality, suspense and romance, while continuing to make her talent for writing bestselling novels seem effortless."
—*Romantic Times BOOKreviews* on *True Blue*

Coming the first week of January wherever books are sold.

www.kimanipress.com

KPRA0490108